DEMON GAMBIT

DEBBIE CASSIDY

Contents

Chapter One

I rushed through the maze-like corridors, away from a clandestine meeting I hadn't been invited to.

My pulse fluttered so fast in my throat it left me lightheaded and breathless. There was no denying what I'd heard. No wiping the memory of it from my mind.

If I only could.

If I could delete the overheard conversation from my memory banks...But now, the words were etched into my mind.

Sweet Veena, my gentle zuni sibling, was a murderer.

Veena was the spawn killer.

There was no misconstruing her conversation with the faceless male. Dammit, I should have tried to get a look at the speaker. I should have peeked around the corridor to see who she was conspiring with. But I'd frozen, a strange dread coursing through me, nothing to do with the revelation and everything to do with the voice that had been speaking to Veena.

I entered the resident floor and exhaled in relief.

Thank fuck no one was about.

I hurried across the marble floors lit by the starlight, past the gently billowing gauzy drapes, toward my chamber. An icy gust of air barely kissed my skin before the mystical heat that kept this floor warm surged up to brush it away. I ducked into my room and slammed the door, leaning up against it, heart pounding loud in my head, senses in such turmoil that it took a moment to register that I wasn't alone.

Artimus sat on the leather-bound armchair by the window, watching me with a curious expression.

Oh, God. He couldn't know. He couldn't know what I'd just found out, not until I'd had time to process it. I had no doubt what the consequences would be if he found out. I wasn't losing another sibling. Not if I didn't have to. I needed time to figure this out...figure out why...because this was Veena. There had to be more to this.

I took a moment to regulate my breathing, forcing my heartbeat to slow its galloping pace to a gentle trot. Only then did I push off the door and address him.

"Do you make a habit of entering women's rooms uninvited?" I crossed my arms and fixed him with a glare.

He slow-blinked, unfazed. "I wanted to make sure you were all right."

Was he fucking kidding me right now? The shock of Veena's betrayal was dampened by the memory of Charod's final moments and Mallini's breakdown.

A ball of indignant heat coalesced in my chest. "All right? I just watched my brother get torn to shreds by huge, fucked-up spider monsters, and my sister is in her room broken and soul crushed, and *you* allowed it to happen. So, no, I am not fucking all right, and *you* are the last person I want to see."

He steepled his fingers beneath his chin, his chest rising and falling in the kind of sigh that said he was wrangling his emotions, finding his words, whatever Nephalem with power and control did.

It made me nervous. I didn't like being nervous. "Just spit it out, okay? Whatever you came to say. Just spit it out."

He raised bright sapphire eyes to meet my gaze, and damn if that look didn't hit me straight in the solar plexus. "None of us want this. But if the contracts aren't followed, then the power held in Satan's seat will remain dormant. *No one* will get it, and chaos will rise. You have no idea how important it is that we fill that seat. The vacancy is a gaping hole in the fabric of order, a lure to every power-hungry devil and fallen. None of us want this, but we have no choice."

He lowered his hands, pressing his palms to his thighs and drawing my attention to the taut fabric stretched across the powerful muscles. I tore my gaze back up to his face in time to catch his eyes flinch, as if he'd checked my regard and wasn't sure what to make of it.

I blinked and looked away for a moment, gathering my own thoughts. "I get it. I understand. But I don't agree with any of it. It's barbaric and unnecessary and it has to be stopped."

"And you believe you can stop it?"

I raised my chin. "I'm sure as hell gonna try."

"Hell." He smirked. "Apt considering where you'll have to go in order to achieve your objective."

My stomach tightened. Hell was a name given to the demon realm by mortals, and it was exactly where I'd be going. I'd made my decision to petition whichever prince I needed to in order to get the death contracts destroyed.

He rose, slow and fluid, and bridged the distance between us. I'd been in his presence many times, but tonight was different. Tonight, I could *feel* his aura like a beast in the room with us, surrounding him, spreading outward to push against my skin, testing, probing. Maybe it was residual adrenaline from the trial or the cocktail of rage and injustice simmering in my veins that heightened my senses and warned me to flee or submit, but like hell would I do either of those things.

I locked my knees and narrowed my eyes. "Back

up." My tone was a husky growl. A warning to him not to test me.

His mouth parted slightly, and his nostrils flared as he inhaled. "It's a dangerous task, Nyx." My name on his lips was a verbal caress. "The princes have powerful allure, more than you could imagine. What you feel now, in my presence, is merely a fraction of what they could make you feel if they take offense to what you ask and decide to make an example of you."

He was so close now that his body heat wrestled with mine. I was forced to lift my chin higher to maintain eye contact, reminding me that he was much bigger in stature than me. He brought his hand up and ran a finger down my cheek, sending tingles skating across my skin. It took everything I had to keep my expression impassive and unaffected.

His gaze was intense and probing. "I don't want you to get hurt."

I snorted, injecting derision into the sound to mask the quiver in my belly. "I can take care of myself."

"Yes, you excelled today." His honeysuckle breath tickled my senses, making my head swim.

I leaned toward him unconsciously before checking myself and pulling back to put distance between us. I hated that his presence ate up so much space. Hated that I could be distracted from my ire.

"I don't give a fuck what you think about my performance in the trial. All I need to know is how soon I can get an audience with a prince. I'm Satan spawn, they won't hurt me on a whim. Besides, I know how to play nice when I have to."

He studied me for several beats as if mulling something over.

I rolled my eyes. "Hello?"

"There's to be a conclave in a few days followed by a grand ball where all three princes will be in attendance. The conclave is a closed meeting between the princes and their close advisors that happens once every century. It's hosted by a different prince each time. This time the conclave will be hosted by Prince Merihem of Libidine."

"The prince of lust?"

He gave me a small smile. "You remembered. Well done."

I was no praise whore, but damn if his words didn't give me a kick. "Okay, so we go to the petition hearing, right?"

"We?" He arched a brow.

I smiled coolly. There was no doubt in my mind that if I went, he would come with me. For some reason unknown to me, Artimus had attached himself to my fate. To my potential success in this fucked-up race, and only a fool would avoid taking advantage of that.

I was no fool. "You'll come with me, of course. As my secret mentor. Make sure my big mouth doesn't get me into too much trouble." I tipped my head to the side and gave him my most coquettish look. "Right?"

His eyes darkened. "As seneschal it is my duty to attend to represent Satan's seat. *You* will come with *me*." His attention dropped to my mouth. "You will adhere to my council, and you will do as I say."

For some reason his words evoked a thrill that shot through me and spread into a telling heat low in my abdomen. I mean, who didn't love a challenge?

I allowed the corner of my mouth to lift slightly. "Oh, Arty, do you even know me? Have you been paying attention to me at all?"

He smiled, lips parting to reveal the tips of his elongated canines. "Be thankful I'm not free to *know* you, Nyx. I doubt your sensibilities would survive my full, undivided attention."

My mouth went dry, and my pussy throbbed as if in anticipation of delicious invasion. The desire was followed quickly by a surge of annoyance. "I told you not to use your mojo on me."

His eyes darkened even more. "I didn't."

Oh, fuck.

We remained in a heady eye lock for long seconds, chests heaving as tension crackled between us.

His throat bobbed as he dropped his gaze. "Get some rest. I'll make the preparations for our journey." He headed for the door.

"What about the trials?"

"It's been agreed to postpone them until after the conclave."

My shoulders sagged in relief. "Thank you."

He paused, door partly open, then nodded curtly and stepped through. I crossed the room to the bed and dropped onto it.

Artimus's presence had been a welcome distraction, but now that he was gone, the problem I'd been distracted from surged to the forefront of my mind.

Veena was the spawn killer. What the hell was I going to do about it?

My gaze went to the ugly ornate mirror in the corner of my room.

Loke...What had he said?

If you ever need me, just touch the mirror and say my name.

I approached my reflection, noting the dirt on my cheeks and the wild glint in my eyes. My clothes were muddy too, dried stiffly in places after my impromptu swim in a rapid river and dive off a waterfall. I was a mess, but there was no time to tidy up now.

I needed Loke. I needed his cool, objective head and some of that throat-searing whiskey. I reached out and placed my palm to the glass, but before I could touch it, the surface began to ripple.

"Nyx, Nyx, are you there?" Loke's voice drifted through.

Great minds.

"I'm here." I stepped through.

CHAPTER TWO

I exited the portal and stepped straight into Loke. He hauled me against his bare chest and wrapped his arms around me.

Fuck, he was hugging me.

He pressed me to his body, large, powerful hands roving up and down my back as if testing for injury. A shiver ran through me and I nestled closer, reveling in the contact and his summer-day scent. My eyelids fluttered closed as I worked to imprint this moment into my memory.

I dug my fingers into the muscles of his back, anchoring myself, and relaxed, allowing the true horror of the past few hours to wash over me. I was safe here. I was safe with him. The shiver became a shudder as the image of Charod's face, etched with terror and hopelessness, filled my mind. Mallini's heart-wrenching screams echoed in my ears like a phantom torment. I exhaled sharply, then pressed my lips together, fighting the heat gathering at the corners of my eyes.

Fuck, I didn't want to cry.

"Nyx?" Loke's hand slipped into my hair, fingers massaging my scalp. "Look at me." I allowed him to tip my head back and looked into his dark eyes. "You made it. You're alive."

I swallowed past the tightness in my throat and forced my lips to smile. "Did you doubt it?"

"Never."

Liar. His reception and the relief in his eyes told me just how worried he'd been. "Charod is dead." My tone sounded thick and choked. I cleared my throat. "It was awful."

His jaw tightened. "I know. I'm sorry."

My scalp pricked. "You knew, didn't you? That one of us would die?"

"Yes."

I appreciated his honesty, understood that he couldn't have told me sooner. He'd explained the rules. The game. The fucking game. "I'm going to the conclave. I'm going to make sure no one else dies."

"I know." His brow furrowed. "Nyx, facing the princes may be more dangerous than the trials." His chest expanded on a breath, pushing against my breasts in sweet promise of something that would never come.

I both loved and hated how hyperaware I was of him when we were together.

I plastered a cocky smile on my lips. "What? Are you afraid for me?"

He exhaled, warm breath fanning across my cheeks as he brought his mouth tantalizingly close to mine. "Always, you crazy woman."

And this was it, the moment where I could bridge the gap between us and take what the source had denied me all those weeks ago.

Kissing Loke would be like taking a dive off a cliff toward jagged rocks with no tether. The flight would be exhilarating but the landing would tear me to shreds, leaving me broken and bleeding, because although he was here for me if I needed him, he wasn't here *for* me. My logical brain knew it was a bad idea, that giving in to my desires would leave me heartbroken, but the crap of the past few hours, the loss, the shock, had put my emotional brain in charge. In that moment, with his body pressed to mine and his mouth a mere hairbreadth from my lips, I was willing to take that dive.

His grip on me tightened for a moment and then he withdrew slightly, his gaze filled with a storm of emotion.

My throat pinched.

He touched his forehead to mine. "Nyx..."

Fuck, there was that fucking lump in my throat

again because this fucker was that guy. The one I'd have tried with. Tried for. Urgh.

We stepped away from each other and a heavy silence descended between us, filled with things that could be said but shouldn't.

I hadn't come here for this.

I'd come for advice. I had to focus on that. "I know who killed the other spawn."

His gaze sharpened. "How? Who is it?"

"I overheard the killer speaking to someone about it."

"Who is it, Nyx?"

"I can't tell you that."

"Can't or won't?"

"Won't."

His eyes flared in comprehension. "You want to protect the murderer?"

Fuck yes I wanted to protect her.

His frown deepened. "Nyx, this person is a criminal who *must* be brought to justice."

"It's more complicated than that. I think this person is being coerced and controlled. I know they don't want to hurt anyone."

His eyes narrowed. "Would you bet your life on it?"

Veena's sweet face came to mind. The way she'd clung to me so many times. She'd pleaded with the faceless figure who'd accosted her in the corridors to let her go. To let it be over. She didn't *want* to do this. She wanted out. Probably always had.

"Are you sure you're not interpreting what you heard in a way that fits your view of the killer?" he asked.

I'd considered this. "I'm a hunter, Loke. I catch bad guys for a living, and I can tell the difference between good and evil. I know what I heard. I'm not sure what to do about it, though, or how to help this person."

Loke wandered over to the drinks tray up against the wall. The clink of glass on glass filled the silence as he tugged the stopper from a crystal decanter. The sleeves of his open shirt were rolled up, leaving his forearms bare, and I was mesmerized by the play of muscle beneath his skin as he fixed the drinks. Male forearms were my kryptonite.

Moonlight played across his features as he approached, casting half his face into shadow and kissing the other half with silvery hues. I tracked the ink running over his pectoral, exposed where his shirt hung open, hand itching to reach out and trace the pattern, to linger on the smooth expanse of his taut skin. Instead, I allowed my fingers to curl around the glass he offered, gripping it tight.

He took a sip, his gaze fixed on me as he swallowed. I matched the move, reveling in the smooth burn as the whiskey slid down my throat.

"The drink is great." I held it up. "I needed it, but what I need more is advice."

"Tell the seneschal and get the murderer removed," he said bluntly.

Irritation flared in my chest. "Not an option."

"I didn't think so." He took another sip. "In that case, confront the murderer."

Veena would shit herself if I did that or...maybe she'd be relieved. To have it out in the open. To have me on her side.

But the others...

"If the murderer is under duress, they will kill again," Loke pointed out. "It's only a matter of time."

"And if I say nothing, then someone could get hurt and it would be my fault."

"You can't watch over all of them all the time," he said.

"And I can't keep tabs on the murderer all the time either." The solution was simple. "I need to find out what the puppet master has over the murderer and neutralize that threat."

His expression was somber and intense. "Be careful, Nyx. Don't do this alone." He looked torn, as if he wanted to say more. "I wish I could help you."

"You have. You are." Shit, my throat had gone all tight with emotion. "You're the only person in this place who doesn't have a hidden agenda. I can trust you to be honest and have my back."

He sighed. "Not enough, though, Nyx. It might not be enough."

"It'll have to be."

I downed my drink, allowing the burn to spread through me and fuel me with fire for what was to come, because once I left this room, it would be time to step back into reality and face the murderer who'd captured my heart without me even realizing.

Oh, Veena, what the hell are we going to do with you?

The decision wouldn't be mine alone, though, and that's where the problem might arise.

CHAPTER THREE

I'd expected Sev to be back in my room, but he hadn't returned, and Chase was also AWOL. Was he with Sev? I was torn, part of me wanting to go find him and smooth things over after our earlier argument, but the other part wanted to focus on the matter at hand.

Veena.

I'd learned a long time ago that making decisions based on emotions was never wise. Going after Sev was an emotional need; resolving the issue with Veena was a necessary evil.

Sev would have to wait.

If he wasn't back once I'd spoken to my siblings, I'd go looking for him, but right now, he wasn't the priority. Dealing with Veena was, and for that, I needed my siblings on board.

I already had a plan.

I headed out of my room and down the corridor to Tristeene's chamber and tapped lightly on her door. It was late, almost midnight, and part of me expected her not to answer, so when the door flew open, I stepped back in surprise.

She arched a brow. "Were you expecting someone else?"

"No, of course not. It's late, so I thought—"

"I'd be sleeping." She stepped out of the room, drawing her dark silk robe tighter around her. I caught movement in the room just before she closed the door.

"Company?"

She shrugged a slender shoulder. "A succubus has to feed."

Ah. Sex. Got it. "Any good?"

She wrinkled her nose. "I've had better." She gave me a shrewd look. "But you didn't come to check up on my bedtime exploits, did you?"

Perceptive and beautiful. "No. I wanted to talk to you—all of you—somewhere...private."

Her brows shot up. "Oh?"

"It's important."

Her expression sobered. "Is this about the contracts? Because I was going to come see you about that. We need to talk. The princes are—"

"I know. We can talk later. But there's something else we need to talk about and it can't wait."

She frowned. "O-kay..."

"Can you get Keelan and Gus and take them to your thinking spot? I'll grab Veena."

"Sure. Now?"

I looked at my watch. "Say we meet in half an hour?"

She gave me an intrigued look. "I best get dressed. The tower is cold."

I headed toward Veena's room.

"She's with Mallini," Tristeene called out.

My stomach dropped. "What?"

Tristeene frowned. "Veena wanted to stay with Mallini."

Panic squeezed my chest in a vise. "Alone?"

She shrugged. "Yes, alone."

I turned and ran for Mallini's room.

Veena sat in a chair by Mallini's bed, an embroidery circle in her hand. She looked up at me in surprise as I burst into the room. I scanned it quickly, senses taking everything in and looking for danger.

Soft lamplight fell across Mallini as she lay curled on her side, torso expanding and relaxing as she breathed slow and even. There was a strange smell in the air, a cross between jasmine and mint, not entirely unpleasant but not a combination I'd have put together.

"Nyx?" Veena looked at me warily.

Okay. Calm the fuck down, Nyx. "How is she doing?" I jerked my head toward Mallini.

"She seems calmer. The herbs Zinichi gave her are working, I guess." Veena's gaze softened as she looked toward Mallini. "I can't even imagine the pain she's going through. To lose your other half like that..."

There was genuine sorrow on her face. How could this sweet creature murder anyone? It didn't seem possible.

"Everything okay?" Tristeene said from the doorway behind me.

I shot her a smile. "Yeah, we're good. See you later?"

Her brow pinched, confusion skating across her features, but she didn't press me further. "All right." She retreated, closing the door behind her.

I approached the bed and leaned over Mallini. Her feathers were in disarray so I set about sweeping them back and smoothing them out. She sighed softly in her sleep, and I froze, not wanting to wake her.

"Don't worry," Veena said. "She won't wake for hours. Zinichi added a sleeping draught to the herbs. Sleep will allow her to heal."

"Nugen said her soul was torn... I don't understand."

Veena set down her embroidery. "Erinyes say that twins are two halves of a whole. Twins are one entity too big to inhabit a single body so they're split in two.

They are one soul in two bodies, so when Charod died..." Her mouth turned down. "Part of the soul died too."

Fucking hell.

"But Mallini is strong. She'll survive this," Veena said.

My gaze flew up to meet hers. "There was doubt on that?"

She looked at me wide-eyed. "Killing one twin risks killing the other or leaving them a shell of their former self."

So when Artimus and the Erinyes had chosen Charod to die, they'd been prepared to lose Mallini too? I had to stop this insanity. I couldn't lose another sibling.

I couldn't lose Veena.

Her dark, sad eyes, the downturn of her mouth, the stoop of her shoulders like a weight was sitting on them, and the way she'd kept her distance from us—all of it made sense now.

To carry such a burden...

No, I wouldn't lose her. "How long have you been sitting here?"

She blinked and looked up at me with a frown. "I'm not sure. Is it late?"

I smiled. "Very, but I doubt I'll sleep anytime soon." I caught my lip, allowing my eyes to light up as if the idea had just presented itself. "How about we take a little walk?"

Her face brightened. "You and me?"

"Yes, just the two of us."

She beamed. "Yes, please."

I hated myself for the subterfuge, but it had to be done. With no idea of what areas of the keep were under surveillance by her puppet master, the tower was the only spot I knew that might not be on his radar.

Still, the joy on her tiny face as she hurried over to me was enough to make me feel like a complete bitch.

She was a murderer. A killer.

This had to happen.

I grabbed a spare blanket off the bed and jerked my head toward the exit.

"Let's go."

Chapter Four

SEV

A long walk in the icy grounds has cooled my anger. Chase strolls beside me, my companion for the last two hours. I haven't spoken to him once and yet he's stayed.

We get to the steps of the keep, and I hesitate, not ready to return and see the disappointment in her eyes.

Her anger is nothing compared to that look of disappointment. Anger doesn't faze me. Pain and torture make me hard. But that look in her eyes...The look of betrayal.

I growl and lower myself onto the frozen steps.

Chase joins me, huge hazel eyes looking up at me questioningly.

"I am what I am."

He chuffs.

"She knows this. I told her. I was honest."

He chuffs again in agreement.

The pain I absorbed from the wounded Erinyes called Mallini did nothing to feed me. Taking it wasn't worth Nyx's ire, because although the hit had been strong at first, it dissipated quickly. My body was unable to hold it.

I have a suspicion as to why, and if I'm correct, then I'm fucked. There is only one way to know for sure.

The keep is filled with beings deep in slumber. I lean back, bracing my elbows on the steps, close my eyes, and fly. It's liberating to be free of this body for a moment. The runes in and around the stables prevent the nightmares from escaping the cage of their bodies. But here, I am free.

I rise into the night, an ethereal form, a slip of moonlight and shadow. Hunger twists inside me, the desire for pain a visceral clawing. I hover and reach out, searching, and I find it.

I RUN through corridors made of shimmering obsidian marble. It's nighttime but the sky is bright, not with moonlight but with fire. Explosions fill the air. The scent of blood coats my tongue. Terror is a vise around my heart.

Run.

I must run and hide.

But I can't leave without her.

I must find her. Save her.

I slip on something wet and fall to my knees, palms slapping the ground and sliding against moisture, thick and sticky.

I raise my palms...small palms. Small hands. The hands of a child coated in blood.

Mother?

The terror is in my throat now, beating like the wings of a moth as I rise and walk slowly through an arch and into a round chamber with a domed ceiling. There is a raised dais and an elaborate seat placed upon it. Not a throne but close.

But my attention goes to the figure sprawled in the seat. The abdomen of her cream gown is dark with blood and her head is turned to one side, dark hair covering her face. But I know who this is. I know because she has loved me all my life. Held me, sang to me, stroked my forehead until sleep claimed me.

Mother.

My heart shatters, tearing in two, and I fall to my knees, unable to breathe, tears streaming down my face.

Yes...this is pain. Glorious, delicious—

I'm shoved out of the child's head and a voice booms with rage. "Get out!"

. . .

I'm back on the stone steps, chest heaving with phantom exertion. "What the..." An entity must be insanely powerful to eject a nightmare. Whose head did I enter? The pain I've absorbed sits in my solar plexus, warm and filling. I sigh and close my eyes, reveling in the sensation of satiation. Seconds pass and then the full feeling seeps away, leaving me empty and craving once more.

"Fuck!" I stand abruptly and the world tips before righting itself.

I scramble up the steps with Chase close behind, heart thundering in my head because I know what's about to happen. I rush through the keep, entering the high-domed chamber that houses the portals.

I need to get back to Nyx's chambers, back to Nyx, before—

Darkness steals my vision and my feet falter.

Chase whines and nudges my thigh. I register the distant echo of bootfalls but my senses are consumed by hunger gnawing at my chest. A hunger that I now know will only be satisfied by her.

I fall into darkness, gut twisting in sorrow, because now she will never know.

Chapter Five

NYX

"Where are we going?" Veena asked as I slipped through the corridor of our old residences. There was no lock on the doors to our old floor. None needed now that we were all living in the quarters above, with Minorax guards to keep us safe.

"A special place." I smiled down at her and squeezed her hand.

"A secret place?" Her eyes grew wide.

I turned down the corridor that housed the tapestry covering the staircase to the tower.

"Something like that."

The tapestry appeared on our left, and I picked up the pace, hoping that Tristeene had managed to get the others into the tower already. I'd taken a detour to give her more time.

I pushed the thick material aside and Veena gasped. "A secret passage."

"Yep, come on." I ushered her in first, then followed her up the steps.

A breeze tickled the baby hairs at my temple, which meant the door above us was open. The others must be there already.

I was close behind Veena as she got to the door and reached a hand over her head to push it all the way open.

Tristeene was visible by one of the many arched windows. She'd dressed for the chill in a long-sleeved tunic, leggings, and boots, but her dark hair was unbound, falling in inky waves down her back. Keelan knelt by the huge hearth, adding kindling to a small fire. His vest, loose pants, and mussed hair told me he'd probably been sleeping. The flames roared to life, their light reflecting off the red-tinged skin of his bulging biceps, making them glow eerily.

Gus lounged on the padded chaise longue that Tristeene and I had sat on when she'd brought me up here a week ago. He hadn't bothered to dress, and was in a nightshirt and slippers, tiny wings fluttering behind him and communicating his confusion and agitation over being summoned here.

"Oh..." Veena looked up at me in confusion.

I closed the door. "Find a seat, Veena. I need to speak to you all."

Veena's gaze flicked to the door, then up to me. I smiled and nodded reassuringly, and she relaxed, moving across the room to join Gus on the chaise.

Keelan stoked the fire and it roared to life, crackling and popping. He stood slowly, hands on hips, a satisfied smile on his face.

"Thank you," Tristeene purred. "You are a treasure."

He snorted, exhaling mist from his nostrils, but there was no missing the gleam in his eyes that her praise evoked.

Everyone's attention shifted to me. "I'm sure you're wondering why I asked you all here tonight."

"I assume it's about the contracts," Keelan said gruffly. "Are you serious about going to the princes?"

"I am. I'll be leaving in a few days. There's a conclave and a petition hearing."

"Yes," Tristeene said. "The conclave. Of course, but Nyx, I've heard things about the princes, about their temper and appetites. I'm not sure being Satan spawn will provide you with much protection."

"I'll have Artimus for that."

Keelan snorted again. "An incubus Nephalem who fell out of favor with Satan is no protection against the princes."

"He's right," Gus said. "Artimus has power here but in the demon realm he'll be on the same social standing as a lord. Although, if he's been invited as a representative of the seat, then maybe he'll have some sway."

"It doesn't matter. I'm going either way. If I don't, then these trials will pick us off one by one, and once it's over, everyone except the chosen one will be killed."

"If we don't get picked off before," Gus muttered.

Beside him Veena tensed. No one else noticed, but then no one else was studying her as shrewdly as I was.

"You still think one of us is a murderer?" Tristeene asked him. "After everything we went through in the trials?"

Gus sighed and shook his head. "I can't believe that. We protected each other. Helped one another. The trial would have been the perfect opportunity for a killer to pick us off but that didn't happen."

Tristeene nodded in agreement.

"But there is a killer out there," Keelan said. "*Someone* killed our other siblings."

Veena sat head bowed, hair slipping forward to act as a shield. Her shoulders rounded and curved in, as if she was trying to make herself small and invisible.

Fuck, I hated to do this.

"You're wrong, Gus...Tristeene..."

Gus looked up in surprise.

Tristeene's dark brows pinched. "Excuse me?"

"The killer is here. In this room." I fixed my gaze on Veena. "Tell them, Veena. Tell them the truth."

THE ROOM FELL into pin-drop silence following my exclamation, and all eyes flew to Veena.

"Veena?" Tristeene opened and closed her mouth a couple of times, then snorted in disbelief. "That's impossible."

I could understand the horror on her face. Veena was the last person I'd have pegged as the killer. "I heard her talking to someone in the corridors earlier. He was telling her she had to continue with the murders, but she didn't want to. Did you, Veena?"

Tristeene's hand flew to cover her mouth. "But... you're a zuni..."

"Which is why we never truly suspected her," Gus said softly.

I wasn't sure what her being a zuni had to do with anything, but before I could ask, Keelan had unfurled his huge frame from his crouch by the hearth. "Answer her," he growled, lip curled, eyes darkening with betrayal.

Veena's shoulders began to shake, and for a moment I thought she was crying, but then the sound of laughter echoed around us, raspy, hoarse, and undeniably male.

Gus leapt off the chaise and away from her. "What the earth?"

"You fools." The inhuman voice came from Veena.

The same voice from the corridor.

My scalp pricked and every hair on my body rippled to attention. "Veena?" Even as I said it, I knew that the thing sitting before me was not my sister. I straightened my spine. "Who are you?"

Veena raised her head and I flinched at the sight of her face. Her eyes were bright yellow with only a pinprick of a pupil and her lips were twisted in a sneer. "You think she could do this alone? This pathetic, mewling creature."

Sobs echoed around us, heart-wrenching in their intensity. Veena's sobs.

"What are you?" Tristeene demanded. "What have you done to her?"

"She's possessed," Gus said. "Something is inside her."

"Way to state the obvious," Keelan said.

"How do we get rid of it?" Tristeene asked.

"You can't get rid of me," the thing inside her said. "I decide when to leave." The sobs increased in volume. "Shut up!"

"Please let me go." Veena's voice drifted around us like a ghostly echo.

"Well, I don't have a choice now, do I? You got yourself found out and you know what will happen now, don't you?"

"No...please..."

Veena threw back her head and roared, but the

bellow turned into a scream and the tiny zuni's eyes rolled back as she slumped to the floor.

The pricking under my skin ceased and the tension in the air ebbed.

Tristeene took a step toward her but faltered as Veena slowly sat up and raised her head.

"Veena?" I moved closer, peering at her pale face. She opened her eyes. Thank fuck they were no longer a freaky orange. "Veena?"

She focused on me, lips trembling. "It's gone. It's truly gone, and now they're all going to die."

Chapter Six

Veena toppled to one side, and we all rushed forward to grab her. Keelan got there first, scooping her up into his arms then sitting on the chaise with her cradled on his lap.

She looked so tiny and vulnerable in his arms. "I'm sorry," she sobbed. "So sorry." She screwed up her eyes and turned her face into his chest in shame.

Keelan's chest vibrated in a soft purring sound and his nostrils flared, expelling mist. I knew him well enough to recognize his reaction as protective and my heart squeezed.

Tristeene looked across at me, her gaze conflicted.

I crouched by Keelan and gently reached out to brush Veena's hair from her face. She made a soft sound of distress that made my jaw clench. "Sweetie, you need to talk to us. Tell us what happened."

She curled into Keelan even more and his purring grew louder as he held her tighter.

I sighed. "Veena, you have to speak to us."

"We want to help," Keelan said gruffly.

I met his dark eyes, seeing only compassion where I was so used to seeing rage or indifference. Yes, everything had changed between us. The trials had brought us together as a family, and yes, Veena had killed our other siblings, but in a twisted way that didn't count so much now. All that mattered was us.

This unit.

I had to protect them.

"What was that thing?" Gus asked softly.

"A monster," Veena said. "They put him inside me. They gave me to him."

"They?" Tristeene asked, claiming the seat beside Keelan. "Who are *they*?"

Veena blinked, lashes wet with tears. "So much happened. So much I wanted to tell you."

"You can tell us now," Gus said kindly. "We're here."

She nodded. "A few days after they found out I was Satan spawn, my family and I were invited to the clan leader's home for a meal. I was nervous. I didn't want to go. I didn't want any of it, but my mother was so proud, and the man I'd believed to be my father was adamant we attend. He'd known I wasn't his, but he'd loved me regardless, so I owed it to him." She broke off, sitting up in Keelan's lap to wipe at the tears on her face. "We were welcomed and fed and then our clan leader asked someone to take my parents on a tour of his home. Once they left, the robed figures arrived." She choked back a fresh sob. "They held me down and then he was there, hovering over me. All I remember is his burning eyes. Eyes like fire, and the smell, like ashes and sulfur. He told me he had my family, and they would die if I didn't submit to him." She swallowed and licked her lips. "I had no choice. I had to..." Her lips trembled. "I gave him permission to enter my body." She squeezed her eyes closed, shaking her head roughly as if trying to dispel the memory.

"It's okay," Keelan said. "Go on."

She breathed deeply and opened her eyes. "I passed out, and when I woke, I was no longer alone in my body. *He* was there with me. He told me I had to do what he said or they'd kill my family." Her voice cracked on a sob.

"He has your family?" Tristeene said. "The clan leader?"

She shook her head. "No. The clan leader doesn't have them."

"It told you that?"

"No. I just know. I could see its thoughts sometimes. I know my family is in the Court of Flame."

My heart skipped a beat. "Ignatius has them?"

She shook her head. "I don't believe the duke has anything to do with this. The monster didn't tell me, but while he was possessing me, I saw..." She frowned as if trying to find the right words. "I *understood* certain things. I knew he was angry. I knew he hated the nobility, in particular Ignatius, and I saw a symbol over and over in my mind when he slept."

A symbol could be a clue we could use.

I leaned closer. "Can you draw it?"

"Yes, but..." Her lip quivered again. "It's too late. He'll kill them now that his plan is ruined."

"And what was his plan, exactly?" Keelan asked.

"For me to win the seat." She dropped her gaze. "He made me kill them one by one. Planned it and used my body to execute the acts. Most of the time I was a watcher, but a few times he let me *feel* what I was doing." Silent tears slid down her cheeks. "It excited him, and afterwards he would...do things to me. Make me..." She pressed her lips together.

My chest heated, and my pulse thrummed with anger. She didn't have to go into detail for me to figure out what the bastard had done to her, and the tension in Keelan's jaw, the simmering rage in Gus's posture, and the look of horror on Tristeene's face told me that they understood it too.

"He made me use the mirrors to get around," she said finally. "He made me accept Umbrane as sponsor even though I didn't want to."

"I don't understand his motive," Gus said. "He can't want the throne because he wouldn't be able to sit on it, even clothed in your body. The seat would recognize a foreign entity."

Oh, shit. "That's why you didn't sit on the throne that day."

She nodded. "It made me stop."

But I had another question. "Why possess you at all? Surely taking your family from you and threatening you to do as he wanted should have been enough?" All eyes fell to me in horror. "What did I say?"

Tristeene sighed. "I forget how little you know about this world and its people. Zuni are peace-loving, humble creatures. Nurturers and carers. Even Lucifer didn't order them to fight in the Chaos War. He had them in healing roles. Many of them maintained households when the soldiers went to war."

"So... you never truly believed she could be the killer."

Tristeene shrugged. "No. But before you came, we were all pretty determined not to like one another." She smiled wryly. "Survival instinct."

So, this creature had taken her body to make sure she did the atrocious things it wanted of her. It had used her as a puppet, living amongst us and tormenting her. I needed to find this fucker and make him pay, and to do that we needed to understand its motive.

I sat back on my heels. "So if it can't rule through you, why go to all the trouble to take your body and murder the other spawn?" I chewed on my lip. "I mean, he'd have to vacate once you took the seat, then what?

You'd have had the power to root him out and make him pay."

"It makes no sense," Gus said. "We're missing something."

"Why make you pick Umbrane?" Keelan mused.

"For protection?" Tristeene said. "That thing wanted you to win, after all, but the full motive is unclear."

"Veena, your family isn't affiliated to the Court of Flame, are they?" Gus asked.

She shook her head slightly. "No, we're Morningstar affiliated. Our bloodline has enough fallen blood to reside here."

"The fallen certainly sowed their seed," Tristeene muttered.

"They had enough time to," Keelan added.

But my attention was on Gus. I could practically see the cogs in his brain working and mine worked alongside them, understanding his line of questioning.

He was wondering how a zuni not affiliated with the Court of Flame could be held prisoner in that territory. "The creature that possessed you must be a powerful member of the court, powerful enough to get invites for Veena's family."

"Exactly," Gus said, his stunning blue eyes lighting up.

Then we were going to need help. "Lucky for us we have the duke of the Court of Flame's ear." I looked to

Keelan. "Fancy a trip?" Ignatius was his sponsor as well as mine.

His eyes narrowed. "If it means we find and punish the scum who did this, then yes."

I allowed a wicked smile to curve my lips. "I think that can be arranged."

Veena made a soft exclamation that drew our attention. Her eyes were round and brimming with tears again. "You...you don't hate me? I killed our siblings. I *murdered* them. I should be punished."

"The *murderer* will be punished," Keelan said. "But that murderer is *not* you."

Her mouth twisted and then she broke down in a wail of a sob. Keelan hugged her to his chest and Tristeene leaned over him, wrapping her arms around the Minorax and Veena. I looked to Gus to see him blinking back tears and felt an answering sting in my eyes.

Fuck it.

We both leaned in and completed the group hug.

No one was going to mess with my family and walk away.

No one.

Chapter Seven

The entity that had possessed Veena was gone, but now we were on a clock to save her family. With an incomplete picture of the entity's true motive, it was impossible to tell what he would do with his captives.

The only solution was to find the fucker and make him talk. I had Veena's sketch of the symbol in my pocket. A tangible clue to search for.

Tristeene suggested a sleepover in Mallini's room to Veena. That way she could keep an eye on Mallini *and* Veena for the rest of the night.

It was five hours till dawn, and Keelan and I agreed to visit Ignatius at sunup.

I needed sleep and so did he. Just a few hours ago we'd been in a trial. Just a few hours ago we'd lost Charod and then found out about Veena's ordeal.

Yeah, I needed to shut down for a while and recharge.

"I wish I could come with you," Gus said. "I feel kind of redundant."

I pressed my palm to his shoulder. "You can help. Do some research and find out what types of demons affiliated with the Court of Flame might have the ability and the power to pull something like this off. Also find out if being possessed has any side effects." I looked back at Mallini's closed door. "That thing may be gone, but that doesn't mean it hasn't left damage."

Gus nodded quickly, eager to have a task. "I'll get on it now."

"No." I smiled. "Sleep first. I need you rested." I looked to Keelan. "You too. We have a long day ahead of us."

We split and headed for our respective chambers.

I entered my room and stared in confusion at the scene before me. Sev lying on the bed, his pallor dull and lifeless, and Ignatius sitting at his hip with his back to me.

Chase was on the other side of the bed, ears up, pointed at alert.

I crossed the room quickly. "What happened?"

Ignatius moved fast, standing to grab me by the shoulders and haul me close. His eyes blazed with inner fire and his hands branded me with heat that seeped through the fabric of my shirt.

"What happened?" He ground out the words. "What happened is that you neglected to feed him and now he's dying."

My breath came out in a rush. "What?"

"Why did you claim him? Why did you form the bond if you weren't going to honor it?" The raw rage simmering in his eyes made my stomach clench.

So far I'd only ever seen him cool and collected, a contradiction to his efreet nature, but now I saw the fire beneath the ice.

"Let me go." My eyes narrowed to slits. "Now."

He sucked in a breath, his grip tightening almost painfully before releasing me. "This is your fault."

Fucking hell, what had I done? I dropped onto the bed beside Sev. "Hey, Sev? Can you hear me?" I stroked his silver locks back from his forehead, my chest tightening at how cold his skin was. As cold as the grave.

"He can't hear you. His body has shut down in preparation for his demise. When was the last time you fed him?"

When was the last time? "When he was locked in the stables."

His brows shot up. "*Before* you claimed him with the blood debt?"

"Yes, why?"

He exhaled in exasperation. "I understand that you claimed the blood debt under duress, with very little information, but I would have *expected* you to determine the full nature of your obligation since then."

My cheeks stung with shame, and I pressed my lips together. "Look, I know I have to feed him, but I didn't realize he was starving." Or hadn't I? He'd said as much earlier after I'd raged at him for trying to feed off Mallini's pain. "He fed earlier, on Mallini's pain."

"Pain...Of course." Ignatius cursed softly. "He can't have fed on her pain. He can't feed on anyone but you. That is the full nature of a blood debt. It binds him to you and you alone. Your ability to withstand mortal air. Your body, and all it can provide."

Oh, God. "I didn't know."

"Obviously. Nightmares can siphon from the world around them. Enter dreams and feed on emotional energy, and in some cases blood. They're a versatile, hardy breed, but Umbrane has broken them." His mouth turned down. "I'd heard rumors about his experiments. I see now he's twisted the nightmares to crave pain above all else."

I took Sev's hand in mine and squeezed, forcing myself to breathe around the panic swelling in my chest. "There has to be something we can do. I can't lose him."

"He's too far gone to take your blood or to enter your mind to find the pain in your subconscious, but there is one way we might be able to draw him back. It won't be pleasant for you."

I looked up at him sharply. "I don't give a fuck how unpleasant it is. I'll do it."

Chase growled low in his throat as if warning, *ask what it is first, Nyx. Don't agree to things you don't understand.*

He had a point. "What is it I have to do?"

Ignatius gave me a humorless smile. "Experience excruciating pain."

CHASE LEAPT FORWARD, placing himself between me and Ignatius, body vibrating in a warning growl, teeth bared.

Ignatius didn't flinch, but his eyes narrowed slightly as he studied Chase, brows pinching as he muttered under his breath.

I stepped closer to Chase, my hand going to his scruff in an instinctively protective gesture. "What?"

He blinked and took a step away from us, lowering his gaze to meet my hound's. "It will be your mistress's decision," he said directly to Chase. "But it is the only way to save the nightmare. He can't take what he needs so we must saturate the atmosphere with it and hope he isn't too far gone to siphon it from the air."

He was speaking to Chase as if he was a person, just like Sev had, and that softened me toward the efreet.

Chase's growl petered out. He turned his head to look at Sev, then me, with a question in his eyes.

"I have to do this, Chase."

He chuffed softly, standing down so I could approach Ignatius.

I stepped up to the efreet. "How are we going to do this?"

He reached over his shoulder and dragged his tunic off his body in one fluid motion, leaving him standing half naked in front of me, golden torso glistening in the lamplight.

I'd been too far gone with pain to notice the details the last time he'd taken off his shirt in this room, but this time I made sure to drink it all in. The smooth planes of his pectorals, the small, tight nipples, and fuck, there was a piercing, gold to match his skin. I trailed my gaze down his abs to the Adonis belt carved perfectly for licking.

Thank fuck Sev didn't need sexual energy to feed off, because Ignatius's body would probably be the kind of ride a woman could get addicted to, and that was almost as bad as the dreaded L word.

I swallowed past the sudden tightness in my throat and fixed a wry smile on my face. "If you keep stripping in my room like this, people will begin to talk."

"Somehow I doubt you're the kind of female who cares much what *people* say."

I gave him my signature kitten grin. "You'd be

correct." And I was distracting myself from what was about to come.

Pain.

I was no stranger to it, of course. But only a sadist would welcome it.

I glanced at Sev. No offense.

"Take off your shirt," Ignatius instructed.

I wasn't wearing a bra but that didn't stop me from peeling off my shirt and dropping it on the bed behind me. My mouth tipped up at the corner as I noted the flare of flame in Ignatius's eyes. I wasn't the most well-endowed female in the boob department, but heck, he was a male and I was showing him my boobs.

Enough said.

He held out his arms. "Come."

"You're going to do that fire thing, aren't you?"

"Yes. And it will be agonizing," he said, matter of fact. "You'll try to escape. I won't allow it."

I stepped up to him, sighing involuntarily as he wrapped his arms around me, pressing me close so that our bodies kissed. His scent of freshly baked bread and honey filled my head, but my senses were more focused on the warm, taut, velvety texture of his skin against the softness of my breasts. I hugged his waist and pressed my cheek to his chest.

"Do it." I closed my eyes.

"Take a deep breath," he instructed. "Scream if you need to."

"I won't need to—"

Fire erupted in my veins, not the simmering buildup of last time but a naught-to-sixty hit.

I screamed loud enough to make a banshee proud.

47

Chapter Eight

I was being burned alive, the never-ending kind of burn that didn't chew away at your nerves, leaving you numb and cold. This burn continued, trapped in that phase where every nerve ending screamed in agony.

My shriek continued long after my lungs ran out of breath, becoming a silent, desperate plea, mouth open, head tipped back as I fought. Clawed. Raked at my captor's skin.

Peripherally I registered a throb in my chest, a flutter of life in my solar plexus.

A moan of pleasure.

Not mine. Not Ignatius's.

Sev. It had to be him.

The inferno in my veins ebbed and a whimper climbed up my throat, escaping as a sigh.

"Good, you did good." Ignatius's dulcet tone acted

like a soothing balm to my singed senses. "He's feeding. He's coming out of it."

I wanted to pull away, but my body was limp and spent. Held upright by his steely grip.

I opened my eyes slowly. "Ouch."

He stared at me, his mouth parting on a soft exclamation.

"What?" I blinked. "What is it?"

He frowned and shook his head. "Nothing. Your nightmare will live but he may need more sustenance." He released me and reached for his shirt, which was on the floor by our feet.

My gaze fell to his back, bloody and torn. Oh, fuck. "Oh, shit. I did that?" I reached for him, then thought better of it. Touching would only hurt him more. "I'm sorry. Let me clean you up."

"No need." He stepped away. "It will heal."

He headed for the door to the Court of Flame.

"Wait."

He paused.

"I need to talk to you about something else. It's important."

He turned his head, offering me his profile. "And I have important business to attend to. I've wasted enough time dealing with your issues. If you need me, you'll have to come find me later."

So he was back to icy efreet, was he? Fine. Whatever.

He opened the door and vanished in a flash of

light.

I'D LET Chase out of the room to stretch his legs in the hall because I had a feeling the next part of saving Sev might get a little intimate. He needed pain, and I'd delivered that, but he also needed blood.

He lay on the bed now, eyes at half-mast, chest heaving as he inhaled the residue of my pain that saturated the air. His skin was warm to the touch too. A good sign.

I stripped down to panties—blood was easier to wash off skin than clothes—and climbed onto the bed to straddle my nightmare.

"Sev?" I pinched his jaw. "Hey, you with me?"

His eyelids fluttered open and I caught a gleam of his silver irises. The knot in my chest eased. "There you are. You need blood, babe, okay? Show us your fangs."

His chest rumbled and his lips curved slightly.

The fucker was laughing at me. "You're in no position to find this amusing."

He sighed and inhaled, moaning softly.

Thank fuck he was lucid right now. "I make good pain, right?"

A groan and his groin bulged against mine. Okay, this was definitely working. I swept my hair over one shoulder to bare my neck and leaned in, turning his face to my exposed jugular. "Feed, babe. You need to feed." His lips brushed my skin, warm breath kissing the pulse at my throat. "That's right." Getting fanged was a thing in the Fringe. A fetish for some, but not for me. The idea of being someone's meal had never appealed, but this was Sev. He was mine to keep. Mine to provide for. I pressed against him, chest to chest, groin to groin. "Come on, big guy." His chest vibrated, and his hands came up to bracket my hips. "That's right." I felt the pressure of fangs against my throat.

Oh, shit. This was gonna—

I sucked in a sharp breath as he bit down, piercing me. Lightning-sharp pain radiated down my neck, and an icy fist gripped my nape, squeezing hard enough to force a cry from me.

He sucked once, hard, dragging fire through my veins. I squeezed my eyes closed and fisted the duvet either side of him. Fuck, that stung like a bitch. Why the hell did anyone allow this to...Oh...Oh, shit...

A ripple passed through me. The first prick of desire, blooming and expanding in my chest and pushing down to where my groin met his through the barely there fabric of my cotton panties.

I throbbed against him, releasing a soft moan as he sucked on me again, drawing my life blood into his mouth.

My pussy clenched, releasing slick wetness, perfect for the images rolling around in my mind right now.

He gripped me tighter, lifting his hips to grind against me. I widened my thighs, opening myself to him, allowing him access to my swollen clit.

He drank and rubbed and my mind unraveled, head spinning at the sensation coursing through me.

Sev gripped my wrist and brought it to his chest, angling my hand so my nails scraped his skin.

It took a moment to realize what he wanted, what he needed, but as soon as I did, I gave it to him without question, digging my nails into his flesh hard enough to break skin. He bucked beneath me, cock breaking free of his pouch to press against my heat. To fit perfectly between my lips even through the thin fabric of my panties.

I clawed him again and he growled, mouth vibrating against my jugular. I rode him as he swelled, desperately chasing the friction, the cold, tell-tale burn of an epic orgasm.

He pulled aside my panties, lifting me slightly. What? Oh, fuck. He entered me with his tail, sinking in deep and curving to hit my G-spot while I continued to ride the length of his cock.

Yes. Fuck, yes.

I came in a rush of heat, body going stiff in the grip of the orgasm. I breathed through it, allowing it to consume me, and barely felt him retract his fangs and seal the wound with a flick of his tongue.

"Nyx..." His voice was raw and hoarse.

I pushed up to look down at him, and for the first

time in a long time the urge to instigate a kiss rushed through me. Instead, I pressed my forehead to his and breathed in time with him, inhaling the coppery scent of my blood and the musky scent of our sex.

"You beautiful fucking nightmare." I raked my fingers through his silken hair, gently scraping his scalp and earning a purr of pleasure in response. "I'm never letting you go."

"Do you promise?" he asked gruffly.

I slid my cheek down the side of his face and pressed a kiss to his jaw, then his neck. "I fucking promise. I can't believe I almost lost you." I kissed below his ear. "I'm so sorry."

For our fight, for not understanding what he was and what he needed. For everything.

"I'm sorry too. I should have explained... understood it sooner."

I sucked and nipped his earlobe and his hips jerked upward.

"I'm still hungry," he growled.

I looked at him in surprise. "You are?"

"Not for blood or pain..." He reached down and sliced my panties off with his talons.

I sat up. "You want to fuck?"

"I want to rut. I want to be deep inside you."

His eyes blazed with desire and need, and my stomach flipped. I rubbed myself against him, sucking air through my teeth at the tingle that shot through me. I was so fucking ready for more.

I lifted my hips off him and gripped him, angling him and positioning him at my entrance.

"Fuck yes." His eyes were bright, gaze flicking from my pussy to my face then back again.

I licked my lips and sank down onto him.

He sucked air through his teeth. "Fucking earth and stars."

Euphoria expanded in my chest because his tail was one thing, but his cock... Oh, fucking perfect.

He sat up, bracing himself with one hand and wrapping the other around my waist. "Now you get to make me come." His eyes blazed in challenge.

I rolled my hips, sliding back and forth on his cock, then leaned back slightly. "Watch me. Watch me fuck you."

He groaned, chest heaving as I rode him, tipping my head back and surrendering to the sensations rocketing through my body.

He swelled, thickening, stretching me. "Fuck!"

He flipped us, pushing me into the mattress as he took over, hips snapping against mine. He was monstrous and glorious hovering over me, body connected to mine, not just physically but on a level that I doubted either of us fully understood. But I felt it in my chest, in that spot at my solar plexus, a delicious thrum of completion, as he pinned me to the bed and pushed us both over the edge into wicked oblivion.

Chapter Nine

Turned out that although Sev was bound to me, he didn't have an invite to enter the Court of Flame. Neither did Chase.

Leaving them behind wasn't ideal; I could have benefited from the extra eyes and ears on my mission to find Veena's tormenter. But I was sure Keelan and I —with Ignatius's help, once we got him on board— would be enough.

The gray light of dawn filtered into the room as I dressed for my meeting with Ignatius.

"I don't like that I can't come with you," Sev said from the bed behind me. "How can I protect you when I'm here and you're there."

I slipped a dagger into my boot, then pulled my hair back and began to braid it, tutting under my breath when my thick hair tangled between my fingers. I fucking hated doing braids, but I needed my hair out of the way just in case I got into hand-to-hand. "Do I look like I need protecting?"

He chuckled softly. "You look like you need help with your hair."

I flicked a glance at his reflection in the mirror, noting how bright his eyes were against his shimmering gray skin. He'd fed, and the difference in his aura was startlingly apparent in the way he glowed; even the silver strands of his hair seemed brighter. I raked him over unabashedly, drinking in the vision of corded muscle built for speed and power. The memory of how he'd felt beneath me, trapped between my thighs, then on top of me, claiming me, then behind me...Fuck, we'd had a marathon all right. I exhaled to shake off the carnal images flitting through my head.

Head in the game, Nyx. "How long before you need to feed?"

"A few days. I'll be fine. Will you?"

"I have Keelan with me and Ignatius's protection. We'll be okay." I met his gaze again. "If all goes to plan, I'll bring back the head of the bastard that fucked with Veena."

I'd filled him in on Veena's situation, on the creature who'd held her captive all these weeks and made her kill her siblings. He'd been silent for a long time, his eyes filling with shadows.

"Killing leaves a mark," he'd said. "It's a stain that changes you."

It reminded me that although Veena was free of the

creature, it would be a long time before she'd be free of the things it made her do.

"Be wary, Nyx," Sev said, drawing me out of my thoughts. "A creature that can hide itself so thoroughly is a powerful one indeed."

"Hide itself? Veena knew she was possessed."

"But none of us, not even any of the dukes, sensed that thing inside her."

I turned away from the mirror. "And they should have?"

"Yes. They should have."

There was a knock on the door.

I strode across the room and pulled it open to find Zinichi holding a tray. "Breakfast, sweet ones." I stepped back as she bustled into the room. "I have an extra-large bowl of that porridge you enjoyed so much the last time." She beamed at Sev. "With extra fruit."

His eyes lit up. "Syrup?"

"Of course." Her brows came down in a frown and she gnawed on her bottom lip, looking torn, as if she had something to say but wasn't sure she should say it.

"What is it, Zinichi?"

She exhaled. "Is it true what the zuni are saying?"

For a moment I thought she was talking about Veena and her secret, and my stomach bottomed out. "What?"

"I think she's referring to my graceful swoon in the portal chamber last night," Sev drawled. "Duke

Ignatius and some zuni keep residents found me, but as you can see, I'm all recovered."

Her shoulders sagged in relief as he took the bowl of porridge from the tray she'd set on the bed. "Oh, and here's the whetstone you asked for yesterday morning." She handed him a wrapped package.

Sev beamed at her. "Thank you."

She blushed. "My pleasure."

I glanced between them. What the hell was this dynamic?

She looked over at me. "Oh dear, if you're going to braid your hair, then you must do it right." She hurried to stand behind me and started unraveling my hard work. "Now see, you have to brush it smooth, leave a few tendrils to frame your sweet face."

Sweet? I was a lot of things, but sweet was not one of them.

I tried to catch Sev's eye, but he was too busy stuffing his face with porridge.

"There, all done." She gripped my shoulders and turned me to face the mirror. "See?"

Okay, I had to admit, her braid was much better than my slightly bumpy, lopsided attempt. "Thanks."

"Keelan is all fed too. He told me you two were headed out today?"

"Yeah, we have...stuff to do." I couldn't let anyone else know what had happened with Veena.

"Is Sev going with you?" she asked.

"Um...no, why?"

"I was wondering if I could borrow him to put up some shelves in the kitchens."

I looked to Sev. "That's up to him." His gaze flicked up in surprise. "What?" His throat bobbed, but he didn't say anything. Tension was suddenly thick in the air. "What?"

"You own me," Sev said flatly. "*You* get to decide."

I was beginning to hate the hierarchy and power dynamic in this place. "Look, Sev, I did the whole blood debt thing to save you. I don't want to own you or anyone. It's icky as fuck. So please, from now on, just do what you want with your time. If I need you, I'll ask. *Ask* being the operative word, okay?" I gnawed on my bottom lip. "In fact, why can't we just break the blood debt thing?"

"The debt won't be paid until I shed blood to save your life."

I gave him a small smile. "I see why you wanted to come to the Court of Flame now."

His eyes widened. "No. That wasn't why." He set his bowl down. "It's complicated...this *desire* to protect you." Shadows filled his eyes. "Primal and primitive almost as if it's sewn into the fabric of my being."

Our gazes locked and a connection thrummed between us. Not the debt, something else, something new and deep.

"A blood debt does not create such feelings," Zinichi said.

Sev and I both started and looked at her. Shit, for a moment I'd forgotten she was there.

I cleared my throat. "Sev makes his own decisions."

The corner of his mouth tipped up. "In that case, I'll help, but in exchange I'd like a basket of muffins."

"Deal." Zinichi gave him another beaming smile before bustling out of the room.

I crossed my arms and arched a brow. "What *was* that?"

He picked up his porridge bowl again. "What was what?" He spooned food into his mouth, the corners lifting slightly.

"You and her?"

He swallowed and smirked. "Jealous?"

Was I? The cold prickle at my nape...Was that jealousy? Like hell. "No."

"Good, because there is no need to be. I sensed her pain around me several times and inquired as to the cause. I remind her of the son she lost a decade ago. Not in appearance, of course, but in...demeanor. Her feelings toward me are... maternal."

He said the word as if it was alien to him. As if he didn't fully understand what it meant, and it hit me that he hadn't spoken of his mother at all.

I opened my mouth to ask when there was another knock at the door. "Come in."

Keelan stepped into the room, his broad frame blocking the doorway. He'd dressed in a fitted black tunic and loose crimson pants. Leather woven bracelets were twisted around his wrists and his dark hair was swept back to leave his polished horns bare. He cut an imposing figure. Black wings gleamed in the warm dawn light. Wait, were those red stripes across the ridges of his wings? How had I not noticed them before?

He followed my gaze, glancing over his shoulder, then grinned. "It won't be long now."

"Long until what?"

He snorted and clomped into the room on gleaming hooves. "You have so much to learn."

I arched a brow. "Then enlighten me."

"Minorax have wings but cannot fly until their colors appear. It can take a century or more." He puffed out his chest. "But I will have mine sooner rather than later. A true mark of power."

I grinned up at him. "I would expect nothing less from my brother."

His hard gaze softened, and he snorted again. "Come, we have a bastard to hunt."

He headed for the door to the Court of Flame. I made to follow just as the door on the other side of my room flew open.

"Where do you think you're going?" Zepar demanded.

Chapter Ten

Zepar's formidable presence reduced my spacious chamber into a box. The fallen's energy was a physical pressure against my skin, hot and probing as he raked me over with his tawny gaze. "Where do you think you're going?" he said again, as if speaking to an imbecile.

His tone immediately had my back up. "Excuse me?" My eyes narrowed to slits and my jaw tightened. I hadn't forgotten how he'd stood by and let Charod die. How he hadn't moved to speak up on my behalf, and the fact that it bothered me, bothered me even more.

"You know..." Sev said in his smooth, lilting tone. "You should knock before entering this chamber. Who knows what you'll see. The shit we get up to...it's enough to blind a fallen and make a white wing weep."

Zepar ignored him, making me the focus of his derision, lip curled. "You're fucking the nightmare?"

Oh, he did not just... I breathed through my nose to hold onto my composure, and when I spoke my tone was cold and even. "Who I *fuck* is none of your business."

He lifted his chin. "You'd be surprised how much of what you do is now my business. I'm your sponsor, and I get a say in how you conduct yourself. Your actions are a reflection of the Court of Ivory. A reflection of me."

His words were potential shackles, and I didn't like them one bit, but before I could retort, Keelan had stepped up beside me.

"You are a sponsor only as long as Nyx chooses to remain in the circle of your protection," he said. "You are also not her only sponsor."

Zepar blinked sharply and I smirked. Nice going, Keelan, reminding him that I had options. I guess accepting both offers of sponsorship had been a smart move after all.

I crossed my arms and tipped my head to the side. "So...do we have a problem, Duke Zepar?"

His jaw flexed. "If you want the Satan seat, you'll need to make sacrifices. Look and act the part. A nightmare lover is crass and does not fit the role."

I shrugged. "Then maybe it's time to change things so that the role fits the person who claims it, rather than the other way around. Because, you see, I don't believe in the classist bullshit spouted in this keep, and if I make Satan, that shit is going to change." I locked gazes with him. "So, the question remains...do *you* still want to offer *me* your sponsorship, or am I too *crass* for your highborn sensibilities?"

His tawny gaze was unreadable as he considered my words and then he slow-blinked, lips curving in a smile. "Satan must also be willing to stand up for his or her convictions. Well done, Nyx."

"I don't need a pat on the back, I need to know why you're here."

He inclined his head slightly. "I came to invite you to dine with me tonight, but I see you have a prior engagement." His gaze flew to the door behind me. The door to Ignatius.

There was no way I was telling him that the visit to the Court of Flame was personal business. I kept silent, letting him draw his own conclusions.

His leonine gaze seemed to harden a little. "Very well. I would invite you to visit me, once you return."

"Okay, I'll see you then."

He stiffened and I realized I'd inadvertently dismissed a fallen angel. Standing up for my convictions was one thing, but alienating a powerful ally at a time when we could use him was foolish. Zepar had boundaries. I was learning the limits of those, and I had a sneaky suspicion I might have overstepped slightly. But he stepped through the portal before I could do or say anything to soften my words.

Fuck.

Keelan confirmed my conclusion a moment later.

"Fallen think they're better than everyone else. Still, they do hold the power, so we must observe the niceties."

But my attention had dropped to Sev, who sat silently, head bowed, shoulders tense. My throat tightened with an emotion I couldn't define. I crossed the room on impulse, pushed one knee onto the mattress, and pressed a kiss to the corner of his mouth.

"I'll see you later, lover." I breathed the words against his lips and felt his smile.

My nightmare lover was an enigma, hardy and able to take a beating that would reduce most anyone into a sobbing, begging mess, built with edges and angles and a slave to pain, but there was a vulnerability in him too, a need that resonated as an echo within me. One I'd denied for the longest time. Sev was a mirror of my twisted psyche, and maybe by healing him, I'd find a way to heal myself.

I wasn't sure what I'd been expecting from a portal. Probably the same gut-wrenching nausea my first trip had evoked, but this time the disturbance in my stomach was minimal.

We appeared in a short corridor with walls made of shimmering golden stone and a smooth, black, marble-like surface for the floor. There was a single door in front of us. The wood was painted gold with an ochre pattern climbing up it. Keelan and I exchanged a look and then he strode forward and opened the door, leading us into a room that looked like it belonged in an exotic holiday getaway magazine. The air was warm, hitting me in the face and clogging my lungs.

"Give it a moment," Keelan said. "You will acclimatize."

Damn, it was hot in here. Make-your-vision-blur kinda hot. I blinked to clear it and took in the room once more. The huge bed parked in the center of it told me this was a bedchamber, but it was large enough to house a seating area made up of floor cushions and a low table. One wall was taken up by floor-to-ceiling arched doors leading out onto a balcony that overlooked...Was that a desert?

I crossed the room toward the balcony, but Keelan gently gripped my arm to stop me.

"You'll fry out there at this time."

I noted the shimmer rising off the ground, a tell-tale sign of extreme heat. "Wow. This is a far cry from icy Morningstar."

"The Court of Flame is ruled over by an efreet, and it mimics their home world. The demon realm is not like this."

"You've seen it?"

"Once or twice with my bearer. As a general in Prince Levistus's army, she is often stationed between the court and Iram."

I cast my mind back to my conversation with Artimus just over a week ago even though it felt like much longer. He'd given me the rundown on the remaining princes. Prince Levistus was the fallen associated with wrath. He'd put Ignatius in charge of the Court of Flame because Ignatius had saved his life or something. Up until last night, I wouldn't have thought Ignatius capable of any excess of emotion. He came across so cool and unfazed, but his anger at Sev's condition had cured me of that misconception.

"This must be Ignatius's room."

"It stands to reason that he would want the portal to you to be close to him," Keelan said.

"What about the one to you?"

"I wager it's the same doorway."

"Ahem, excuse you."

I spun toward the voice to find empty space.

"Hello?" the voice said.

I dropped my gaze to the ground, to the two-foot creature with blue hair floating up from his head and purple eyes. Wait, the hair wasn't hair, it was fire. Blue fire.

His mouth turned down in a wince. "The duke told me to expect you. I've been waiting, but I had to leave for a moment and then I came back, and you were here." He wrung his hands. "He will be so upset to know I left my post." He drifted closer. "You won't tell him, will you?" He held up his hand and shook his head so that the blue flame wavered back and forth.

"No. No, of course I cannot ask you to lie on my behalf." He dropped his head down but peered up at me through his lashes.

He was so freaking cute, despite the killer blue flame hair. I bit back a smile. "I think we can keep that between us. What's your name?"

"Flintlimelia, but everyone calls me Flint." His cheeks bunched in a smile. "I'm the duke's personal assistant and now I will take you to him."

"Wait." I was here to find a killer who could be anywhere or anyone. If he saw me, he might bolt. I needed to speak to Ignatius here in private and form a plan.

Flint stood looking up at me expectantly.

"Can you bring the duke here? Tell him it's urgent and private." I smiled warmly at Flint. "I don't want anyone else to know I'm here yet. Can you do that?"

"Of course. I can do it. I will do it right now." He winked out.

"Whoa, what did he do?"

"Many demons can transition between places with a thought," Keelan said. "Sprites are particularly good at it." He looked out at the desert and took a deep breath so his chest swelled. "I have missed the court air."

"This is your home?"

"It was, yes."

Was that why Ignatius had sponsored him?

Because he belonged to his court? "Have you spent much time with the duke? Do you know him well?"

He snorted. "About as well as any member of the court. Although as a child I would sometimes accompany my mother to court meetings. The duke was always...kind."

I was suddenly curious to know more about my sponsor and his court, about the efreet and the demons who lived here.

The air by the bed shimmered and Ignatius materialized. As usual he was dressed in a tunic and loose pants, and golden slippers graced his feet. His spun-gold hair was brushed off his face and his ember eyes glowed softly against his shimmering skin. He was formidable and statuesque, and his presence made my pulse quicken involuntarily.

"Important and secret?" He tipped his head to the side. "What could be so important and secret enough for you to call me away from a court meeting?"

The corner of my mouth lifted wryly. "How about murder."

Chapter Eleven

ARTIMUS

I lounge in my seat at the council table. Council, *pah,* what a joke. There is no real council here. Just the Erinyes, Satan's advisors, who now wanted to *be* Satan.

Erinea has insisted on calling this meeting, dragging us all to this room at the crack of dawn to lay out her disconcertion.

I've heard it all before.

Last night.

I'd finally shut her up with my cock, providing her with something else to do with her mouth. But as she'd set to work sucking and taking me deep, I'd closed my eyes and summoned another face to my mind, hand tightening in her feathers, imagining them to be dark, silken locks.

I'd allowed her to have my body, hoping to distract her once again, but Erinea is single-minded when it comes to the pursuit of power.

Now, hours later, I can still smell her on my skin, even after the hottest shower known to a demon.

I sip my tea, something spicy prepared by the zuni who serve the Erinyes, and wait for the others to arrive. Erinea throws a terse smile my way. She's nervous, as well she should be.

What she's about to propose goes against the nature of the trials.

Zepar enters first, his tawny gaze troubled. I rake him over. The cream T-shirt and the ripped jeans. Why he insists on dressing like a mortal is beyond me.

"Erinea." He lifts his chin at her.

"Apologies for summoning you so early," she croons.

Fucking bitch. Didn't apologize to me after keeping me up all night by bouncing on my cock. Her gaze falls to me, and I give her a warm, intimate smile, allowing it to bleed to my eyes.

She simpers.

Actually fucking simpers.

I imagine wrapping my hands around her throat and squeezing. The knot in my belly eases and I sip my tea and relax. What is the winged wanker saying? I tune in.

"Saw her going to see Ignatius with the Minorax sibling." He takes the offered cup from Erinea.

My ears perk up. "Nyx has gone to the Court of Flame?"

"*Harumph.*"

Does it bug me that she didn't consult me first? No. It doesn't bother me at all. But I bet it bothers Zepar. I look him over. I bet you hate that, don't you. You don't like to share your toys. You want them to stay all shiny and pristine so you can violate them yourself.

Zepar looks across at me sharply, and for a moment I wonder if I've spoken out loud, but then he says, "Have you spoken to her since the trial?"

"I have." I lean back in my chair. "She's extremely set on her plan. Admirable, actually."

"Ridiculous," Erinea says bluntly.

"Oh?" Zepar arches a dark brow.

Erinea ignores him, muttering to herself. "So she's visiting Ignatius. That might explain why Ignatius has not responded to my summons."

Or it could be because he thinks you're a cunt. I stifle a smirk at the thought.

The air crackles and our final guest appears. Not invited by choice, but only to remain within the parameters of the ascension rules.

Loke pulls out a seat and sits, aware that he's here only as an observer.

"Tea?" Erinea offers with a beaming smile.

God, her duplicity makes me sick.

Loke shakes his head. "I'm good, thank you."

The air crackles again and our final guest enters the room. My stomach tightens at the sight of Umbrane. The fallen makes my skin crawl, but I understand why Erinea has summoned him. Umbrane isn't a fallen to be crossed, and leaving him out of this assembly would be foolhardy, especially if one was angling for power of Morningstar. Erinea is banking on Umbrane's support above the others, probably because they share the same goals.

"Ah, spiced tea," Umbrane purrs. "I will take a cup, my dear."

My dear? Earth and stars, he makes me sick to my stomach.

Erinea gives him one of her sexy smiles and hands him a cup. I zero in on how his fingers caress hers, lingering as he takes the tea.

Stupid woman is playing with fire. You don't dangle your cunt in Umbrane's face and not expect to get fucked.

But maybe that's her plan? Ice trickles in my belly followed by an injection of adrenaline. Have I missed something in our late-night chats? Have I been sleeping with the enemy for nothing? My jaw tenses and I force myself to relax.

Umbrane takes a seat and sips his tea, dark horns gleaming in the sunlight. He's gone for his habitual black outfit to reflect the darkness of his soul. How has a fallen become so corrupt?

"So what do you want to discuss?" Zepar asks.

"The Nephilim." Erinea takes a seat at the head of the table. "I want to discuss Nyx and her ridiculous plan to petition the princes to alter the contract."

"Oh?" Umbrane's brows shoot up. "She plans to attend the conclave?"

Erinea's lips thin. "She does, and our seneschal has made all the arrangements." She shoots daggers my way.

Interesting. The daggers were absent last night, buried beneath her moans of pleasure. Maybe I've underestimated her.

"I'm sure we can all agree that drawing the princes' attention to Morningstar and the ascension would be an unwise move," she says.

"Would it?" Umbrane sets his cup down. "For whom?"

"For us all," she says. "Thus far the princes have steered clear of Morningstar affairs, allowing us to govern without interference. Taking the contracts to them could nudge them into coming here. Into paying attention."

Zepar tucks in his chin, lips pressed in a thoughtful pout, but Umbrane merely chuckles, a low, raspy sound that makes the hairs on my arm tingle.

"Oh, Erinea, let's drop the act, shall we? This isn't about us. It's about you. About *your* desire to maintain control of the seat."

"Do you really want Prince Merihem to come sniffing around the Court of Shadows?" Erinea snaps. "I doubt he'd be accepting of your methods."

Umbrane's smile is cold. "I have no issue with the prince visiting my court. In fact, I'm quite intrigued to see what the little Nephilim can achieve with her visit to the conclave."

I'm confused. This is not what I expected. Umbrane willing to risk princely intervention?

"We can't stop her," Zepar says. "The ascension is about allowing the spawn to find themselves, to flourish and to exhibit their strengths and weaknesses. I would have thought you'd advocate her petition; you have, after all, lost a son to these trials, and if the contracts stand, you risk losing a daughter."

She flinches and sits back. "Which should demonstrate how strongly I feel about this."

"You don't want your son to be the only casualty of this ascension," Loke says softly.

Her gaze whips to his. "This isn't about casualties; it's about upholding the sanctity of Satan's wishes. It's about keeping Morningstar a neutral ground. I would sacrifice a thousand offspring to achieve that."

Silence follows her declaration.

Zepar is the first to break it. "Regardless, we will not interfere. If the spawn wish to petition, then we shall allow them to do so."

Erinea's eyes flash with anger, and she drops her

gaze to hide it. "So be it. But mark my words. No good shall come of this."

Foreboding trails a finger up my spine, and for the first time since Nyx voiced her plan, doubt unfurls in my mind.

Chapter Twelve

NYX

I'd always thought of myself as physically flexible, but sitting on floor cushions wasn't easy. My body protested when I crossed my legs, so I ended up sitting with them tucked to one side, knowing I'd have pins and needles eventually. But I was surprised to see how easily Ignatius was able to arrange his huge body on the ground. The guy had to be close to seven feet tall, but he moved with a fluid grace that put me to shame. Even Keelan managed to sit cross-legged with ease. I guess floor seating was common here.

I recounted what had happened with Veena in detail and Ignatius listened without interruption. He was silent for long seconds once I finished.

I studied the smooth, golden planes of his face as

he absorbed what I'd told him. "This is a serious allegation," he said finally.

"It's a fact."

"I don't doubt what you witnessed or that your sibling may have been possessed. I'm merely questioning if the entity responsible belongs to my court."

There was enough evidence to suggest so. "Veena mentioned ember eyes and the smell of ash and sulfur before it invaded her. She said it hated you and that she sensed her family was being held here. I believe what she sensed is true."

"Unless it wanted to trick her and allowed her to see and feel those things."

Crap, I hadn't considered that option. My face must have shown it because the corner of Ignatius's mouth turned up wryly.

There was one more thing, though. One piece of evidence that might help us decide.

I lifted my ass to tug the drawing Veena had made from my pocket. "Veena said she saw this symbol in her mind. Do you recognize it? Is it associated with a location here in the Court of Flame?"

He took the paper but didn't look at it. "You're thinking this symbol could be linked to where your sibling's family is being held?" I nodded and his gaze dropped to the drawing of a circle with spokes tipped with arrowheads jutting from it. His face drained of color. "Veena drew this?"

He recognized it. My pulse sped up. "Yes."

He inhaled sharply. "Then I have no choice but to believe you."

"You know that symbol?" Keelan asked.

"Unfortunately, yes. But it's been lost for the longest time. Eons, in fact. This symbol is a remnant of our old world." He scrunched up the piece of paper, eyes glowing with an emotion I couldn't define. "If this symbol is here, now, then we have a serious problem."

I HADN'T SEEN Ignatius rattled before, and to be fair, signs weren't that prominent now. Only because I'd made a point of honing my observation skills did I note the slight tightness around his eyes and mouth indicating signs of mental strain or stress.

I picked up the crumpled paper and smoothed it out. "Why is this symbol so bad?"

He dropped his gaze to the image, mouth flattening. "So many reasons. Reasons that after so long, feel like a dream." He took a breath and settled his gaze on me. "I'm sure you're aware that my people are not from your mortal or demon realm."

"Yes. You came from...somewhere else."

"There are an infinite number of realties, layers upon layers. A multiverse. Our world was a mirror of your human world in many ways. We would have settled there, but when we arrived, your mortal world was still so primitive. The demon realm was more inviting."

"So you settled there."

"Yes. But our world didn't die of its own accord. It was ravaged by war. Two sides with different goals, as is the premise for all wars. The efreet, the marid, the hinn, and the jann fought against the followers of a force called Shaitan. Every world has its good and evil. Its angels and its demons. In some cases, there are clear-cut parameters, but in others there are too many shades of gray. Shaitan was a djinn with great power, but that wasn't enough for him. He wanted more. He wanted to rule every oasis and he recruited an army of shiqq, ghouls, palis, and sil'at to attack the seven cities."

I had no idea what any of those creatures were and I didn't bother to hide my confusion.

He smiled thinly. "The creatures' natures do not matter save to say that Shaitan followers had a lust for mortal flesh and blood. The marid, the giants of our world, gave their lives to create a chasm between Shaitan's forces and our cities. But the chasm caused damage to the fabric of our universe. We were forced to flee, leaving Shaitan and his forces to die, thus ending the attack by the fawda." He sighed. "But it isn't over." He stared at the symbol. "This was their mark. Their banner. And if it is here now, that means the fawda movement is rising once more."

"But why now after so long?" Keelan said. "The efreet have been in this world for centuries. If the fawda were here, surely they would have risen earlier."

I knew the answer to that. "Maybe they were weakened. Needed time to recruit. They had to bide their time and now...Now we have an open Satan seat. They want control of it." My breath caught. "Wait...you don't think that they're—"

"Responsible for Satan's death," Keelan finished for me.

We exchanged shocked gazes.

"If they're here, then it's a real possibility they were involved," Ignatius said. "But they would need a leader. Someone powerful."

"You don't think this Shaitan dude is here, do you?"

"No. That can't be."

But he didn't sound too sure.

"But possessing Veena wouldn't get them the seat," Keelan reminded us. "Veena wouldn't be able to sit on the throne with that thing inside her."

Ignatius nodded slowly. "She would not get the power held in the seat. We will take this one step at a time. First, we'll find the culprit. Then we'll take our time interrogating him to find out how large this movement is, and if..." He trailed off with a sigh, so I finished his sentence for him.

"If this Shaitan guy managed to find his way into this world?"

His expression was grim. "Yes. Shaitan followers

were given the ability to possess mortals. They offered power and riches to recruit mortals as cannon fodder into their armies. It fits. It all fits." He stood in one fluid move and held his hand out to me. I took it and he helped me to my feet. "Tonight, you will be announced as a guest of the court. This creature has seen you. It knows you. It will either attack or attempt to flee. It won't escape. The exits to the court will be closed to it." His lips curved in a cold smile that promised pain. "We will find it, Nyx, and it will pay, in blood and pain."

I grinned up at him. "You know what, Ignatius? I think you and I are gonna get along just fine."

Chapter Thirteen

Nyx giving me full autonomy means that for the first time in my life I *feel* free. Yes, the blood debt is still in place, but with a few words she elevated me from possession to equal. Now there is something I must do for her, and for those she cares about.

Chase is at my heels as I approach the zuni's door.

He chuffs softly as I hesitate.

I've never hesitated over anything. I've killed on command, inflicted pain when ordered to, and in more cases than I can recall, submitted to it. I've been a puppet all my life, which is why I need to do this.

I knock softly and wait.

The door opens a few moments later and Tristeene

looks at me with a gentle frown. Her gaze slips over my shoulder, looking for Nyx, no doubt.

"I wish to speak to Veena."

Her expression hardens. "Nyx spoke to you?"

"Yes."

Her lips tighten. "And? What do you want to say?"

"I will say that to the zuni."

"She's not up to seeing anyone."

"Tristeene, let him in," a small voice calls from the gloom beyond the succubus.

I flash a smile at Tristeene, who raises her chin, somehow managing to look down her nose at me, even though I'm taller.

"If you upset her..." She leaves the threat unfinished and I'm curious.

"What?"

"Excuse me?"

"What will you do to me if I upset her?"

Her eyes narrow and she leans in. "I'll hurt you, nightmare. Bad."

I can't help but smile wider at that. "I came here to help, but with a promise like that I'm tempted to renege on my plans."

She blinks in confusion and then her brow clears. "Of course, you're a sadomasochist."

"It sounds so dirty."

I like it.

She steps aside to let me in. Chase trails after me,

rounding the bed to lay his head on the comforter beside the small female's hip.

She puts her hand on his head and smiles, but it doesn't reach her eyes.

She's damaged. In pain. I can smell, feel it like a buzz against my skin, but I'm sated and the urge to draw it into me is absent. Even if I was hungry, her pain would do me no good.

"Say what you came here to say." Her throat bobs. "I can take it."

It strikes me that she believes I've come to berate her. A wry laugh breaks from my throat.

She flinches.

Tristeene takes a step closer and tension spikes in the air.

I sigh. "I'm sorry. I wasn't laughing at you."

"Then what were you laughing at?"

"At your assumption that I'm here to berate you."

Her brows flick up. "You're not?"

I approach the bed and crouch by it, locking gazes with her. "I'm in no position to look down on anyone, Veena. I'm a murderer who was controlled by a puppet master, ordered to inflict pain and take life. The only difference between us is that I was in control of my body when I made those kills."

She blinks rapidly to hold back her tears and ducks her head. "I was there, though. I felt what he did, his... love of it. The desire for it. It was almost..."

"Sexual?"

Her gaze whips up to mine. "Yes..." She catches her bottom lip between her teeth.

"And you liked it. In that moment, with him in control?"

Her eyes well, tears tracking down her face with her next blink. "I can't get it out of my head. I can't get clean."

Her words echo inside me, finding that hidden part of myself that I've buried for so long, latching on to it. I realize this is why I've come here. Not for Nyx, not for Veena, but for me. I need to remember what it was like, before, at the beginning, to remember my conflict before...before I'd shut it away and hardened my heart and senses.

Veena is an echo of my younger self.

"It's over." I reach for her hand. "You're free, and in time, the stains on your soul will fade. The pain, the memories will be buried beneath new, pleasant ones."

She sobs and squeezes my hand. "Do you promise?"

"I promise."

She leans forward and wraps an arm around my neck. An emotion swells inside me, one I believed myself incapable of feeling. Something soft and maternal. An instinct that I'd believed died with my lyncat.

An instinct Umbrane tried to kill.

It's still here.

Still inside me.

Maybe there is hope for me yet. Maybe I can be worthy of the woman who's slowly capturing my heart.

Chapter Fourteen

Ignatius decided it was best for us to remain in his personal area of the keep. The Court of Flame was a sandstone whitewashed building, topped with domed towers, surrounded by desert land dotted with settlements.

Keelan had requested permission to utilize the combat room, whatever that was, and left with instructions to meet back at Ignatius's chamber in two hours.

Meanwhile, Ignatius offered to give me a tour of his area of the keep.

We strolled along a sandstone walkway that connected two sections of the fortress, sheltered from the arid land either side by walls broken up by tall arches and a vaulted roof.

Heat pressed in on me, but it was no longer unpleasant. "Keelan said I'd fry if I stepped out there."

"Probably," Ignatius said. "The heat is intense for efreet, demons, and abyssbloods, but for someone with mortal blood it could be lethal. It will cool in a couple of hours, and if you like, I can take you to our nearest settlement. There will be a market this afternoon, running until the evening. Males and females will be purchasing trinkets for the twin flame ceremony tonight."

"Twin flame? What is that?"

"An annual event where efreet solidify their mating bond before our sacred flame."

I wanted to ask more but I lost my train of thought as we stepped off the walkway, through a door, onto a mosaic tiled floor. Ochre, red, and yellow spread out across the large expanse, stealing my breath with the intricate beauty of the pattern.

The windows were high up on the walls and sunlight lanced down to dapple the patterned floor. Bookcases filled with colorfully bound books were set against the wall and wreathed in shadow, protected from the sun. Gilded framed paintings filled the spaces between each bookcase. A cluster of low chaise longues sat on a rug in the center of the room surrounded by more floor cushions and several tables.

"This is my personal library," Ignatius said. "We were not able to save much from our world, but what we do have is kept here."

I wandered over to the nearest painting, a cityscape

with towering buildings and huge, bird-like shapes in the sky.

I felt him come up behind me, felt the heat of his body mingling with mine, and breathed in the scent of his honey breath as it whispered against my cheek.

"That's the city of Arihem." He reached out to touch the frame. "It was my home."

By my calculations, the efreet had come to the demon realm several centuries ago, and if he'd been alive back then, that would make him... "How old are you?"

"Old enough to remember that the air smelled like nectar, and that the colors were so vivid they made my heart ache. The colors here are muted in comparison."

"For some reason I expected deserts."

"There were deserts in between the cities, yes. Each city was built around an oasis. Seven cities. Seven oases connected by underground rivers."

"Wow, it's...beautiful." And it was. The sky was a bruised purple, the spires and domes of the buildings were eggshell white, reflecting hints of that soft purple. It gave the whole image a dream-like air.

My chest ached for this world lost to war. I moved to the bookcase, scanning the crimson leather pressed with gold and silver foil, titles I couldn't read, and onto the next painting. Ignatius moved with me, my shadow as I devoured it. This one was filled with green leafy trees, trunks bowing inward toward a shimmering lake dotted with tiny vessels and the impression of people, smudges of color on the blue and gray expanse of water.

"The triannual boat races," Ignatius said. "The water elementals would always win; efreet steered clear completely, of course. But the air and water elementals would battle it out." There was nostalgic warmth in his voice. A soft pulse of longing.

I pressed back my words and my questions, not wanting to pull him out of this moment. But I itched to see the next painting, the next window into his world.

I broke away from the lake landscape and he sighed softly as I moved on to the next painting.

Wait, this one was different. The sky was a swirling rose laced with violet. The buildings were silver and black, sharp towers connected by walkways with winding streets below.

"What is this?"

"The daimon realm."

Did he say daimon? "You mean demon."

"No, Nyx. I mean daimon. This"—he reached out to touch the silver frame—"is the abyss."

How could this be? How could this technologically advanced vista be the abyss? "I don't understand. I thought daimons were monsters that stole demons and forcefully procreated with them. I mean... the Chaos War happened because of them, right?"

He gave a heartfelt sigh and retreated, taking his heat with him. With a final once-over of the painting, I followed him to the chaise in the center of the room.

"Sit." He indicated one of the seats but lowered his body to the floor by the chaise, resting his arm along it, so close to me that the temptation to stroke it had me curling my hand into a fist. That skin, though, shimmery, golden, and velvety to the touch. I recalled it from our last two skin-to-skin encounters.

I wanted to feel it again.

"History is written by those with power," he said, pulling me out of my thoughts. "In this case, the fallen."

"You're saying it's a lie?"

"Not a lie exactly, but a truth riddled with holes."

Now I needed to know more. "Tell me." I slipped off the chaise and onto the floor so we were sitting side by side with his arm braced on the chaise behind my shoulders.

His ember eyes flickered, gaze coming to rest on my face like a warm caress. "Are you sitting comfortably?" His voice was a gentle buzz creating a tingle that ran up my spine to gather at my nape.

"Yes." Why was I whispering?

His gaze dropped to my mouth. "The daimon realm —or the abyss, as it was also called—was a place of great technomystical energy. A metropolis of power.

The creatures that lived there were like any other race, a mixture of good and bad, and everything in between. There was no demon realm. It all belonged to the daimons, and demons were merely a species who lived outside of the abyss, in smaller towns and settlements, traveling through the great gate into the abyss for trade. Many settled there, made homes, procreated with daimons to create abyssbloods."

"So it was all peaceful?"

"For a time, yes. When our world fell, we came here. Our numbers were small and the daimons took us in and gave us a home. They gave us a place to bury the seed of our power so we could continue to live and grow."

"Seed of power?"

His brow pinched as he searched for the words. "The ember of our world, of our life force. The seed makes us fruitful, feeds our power so that we can flourish, procreate, and grow. We lived among the daimons for half a century before the fallen came. They built their cities outside the abyss, taking the demons under their wing and building alliances with the daimons."

"Once again, it all sounds very peaceful."

"It was, for a time," he said again. "But curiosity and pride have always been the fallen's downfall, and eventually those two traits spawned a war none of us could win."

"The Chaos War?"

"Yes. There was a place on the outskirts of the daimon city. A holy place, cut off, guarded and off-limits. A gateway that they spoke of in hushed tones. A passage to a world they called Inferis. A place of great horror, great wonder, and immeasurable power. According to daimon history, the pit had been sealed eons ago by the messiah, a being from Inferis who'd brought the pilgrims to the abyss where they formed their first settlement."

"Wait, are you saying the daimons originated in this horrible place, Inferis?"

"That's what their history books say."

"And what has this got to do with the fallen?"

His mouth twisted bitterly. "It was the fallen who reopened that door."

Chapter Fifteen

ater cascaded over my body, spilling like raindrops from a ceiling that was one huge showerhead. The cool kiss was bliss against my overheated skin. It even smelled good, like jasmine and something sweet.

My mind was a hive of information and my ears echoed with the sound of Ignatius's dulcet tones. Alone in his library, nestled beside him on the cushions, I'd been transported briefly into another world.

He'd dropped me back at his chambers with instructions to freshen up before our trip to the market. Flint would be bringing me more appropriate clothing for our trip, and for the first time since coming to Morningstar, I was looking forward to something.

Guilt tightened my belly. I was supposed to be

hunting a murderer, not enjoying myself. But there was no denying the satisfaction that came with learning the truth.

Knowledge was, after all, power. And I'd learned a lot.

Turned out the Chaos War had begun because Lucifer bloody Morningstar himself had wanted to explore new worlds. Specifically, Inferis. He believed, in his hubris, that he was powerful enough to control what lay beyond.

He'd been wrong.

Monsters had spilled forth into the abyss along with a mystical virus that the daimons had been running from in the first place, one that turned them into daimon zombies. Okay, so Ignatius hadn't called them that, but the way he'd described it fit.

The Chaos War was the fallen's fault. But like all good politicians, they'd spun it in their favor, turning Lucifer's act of contrition in giving his light to close the pit into a sacrifice. They'd built Morningstar territory off the back of it and created a whole new system to ensure that shit didn't happen again, that one fallen's hubris, or need for power, didn't drag their carefully built empires down with him.

Lucifer's actions had resulted in the fall of the daimon empire.

None had made it out of the abyss before the great gates had been sealed off. Many efreet and abyssbloods remained locked behind those gates along with the efreet seed of power.

Tristeene had mentioned a curse on the efreet, one that meant they struggled to procreate, but the truth was that the loss of their seed of power had rendered them weak and vulnerable, forcing them into Prince Levistus's service. All they had left now was a small flame that was still connected to the seed trapped beyond the daimon gates.

I raked my fingers through my wet hair, then stepped off the silver tiled portion of the room. The water shut off. Warm air wafted down, and I was dry in seconds.

Bloody hell, why did Morningstar not have this feature?

I grabbed an oversized robe from a hook and shrugged it on. It was opaque but light material that wouldn't make me hot and sweaty.

Keelan waited in the room beyond, lounging on the floor cushions. He'd changed out of his tunic into a gauzy cream shirt, sleeves rolled up. His eyes were half closed. He looked...relaxed.

"Did you have fun in the combat room?"

He snorted softly as I approached. "I feel invigorated."

I eyed the floor cushions, but doubted I'd be able to arrange myself on them in this robe without flashing my sibling.

I padded to the bed and parked my butt on the end

of it, feet dangling inches from the ground. "What is the combat room?"

"Minorax and efreet built stamina in hand-to-hand combat with golems trained in every fighting skill."

"Golems? Those are real?"

I mean I'd read about such creatures. Beings made from earth and metal, forged together using intricate magic. But I'd never seen one before.

"Only the most powerful conji have the strength of allure to forge and command a golem. The Court of Flame has several affiliated to it, but there are rules." He sat up and looked at me. "Golems may be used to train soldiers to fight, but they cannot be used directly in battle."

"Why?"

He shrugged. "I don't know."

"Hello."

I jumped, hand going to my chest as Flint appeared in front of me.

He held out a pile of clothes. "The duke says to get dressed and then I will take you to him."

"Where are you going?" Keelan asked me.

"To the market. You wanna come?"

He snorted again. "I hate the market. Flint, can you smuggle me into the barracks? I would like to see my brothers in arms."

"Of course," Flint said, his eyes still on me. "As soon as I've delivered my lady to the duke."

My lady? "Please just call me Nyx."

He blinked sharply. "But that would not be fitting."

"Trust me, it fits me just fine."

I took the bundle of clothes and felt that they were wrapped around something hard. I headed back to the washroom to change, careful not to stand on the silver tiles. I tugged on a pair of loose pants and a baggy shirt that cinched at the waist with a ribbon-like belt.

The hard thing was a pair of boots made of soft, breathable material. I pulled them on, then strode back into the main room where Flint was waiting with his hands clasped behind his back.

"Ah, my lady looks well dressed."

"Nyx. My name is Nyx."

His blue flame hair flickered. "Nyx." The flame on his head dimmed a little.

"Are you all right?"

He blinked up at me in confusion.

I pointed at his head. "Your flame..."

"Oh. I do not wish to burn you." He held out his hand. "Now I am safe to touch."

"Okay." I looked over at Keelan. "Keep your ears open." He nodded. I took Flint's hand. "Take me to your leader."

Chapter Sixteen

I wasn't sure what kind of transport I'd been expecting to take through the desert, but it wasn't a sled pulled by two large, sleek beasts with tan hides and hooded eyes. Their skin was rough to the touch, and they had a vicious look about them, long snouts and pointed ears filled with hair.

The sled had a roof and netting over the windows, and the interior was blessedly cool. We whizzed across the sand, over dunes, across a desolate landscape that was all too vast and frightening.

"The karrak can go weeks without water," Ignatius explained beside me. "Perfect steeds for the desert."

His thigh was pressed to mine, warm and solid, and my shoulder was snug against his arm. I could have moved, but I didn't want to. I liked his proximity. The comfort of it. The familiarity.

"Don't you have camels?"

He frowned. "What are those?"

This really was a different world. I glanced out the window, viewing the world through the thin fabric of the fine net, and spotted a blur on the horizon. "What's that?"

Ignatius leaned forward to look out my window, forcing his body even closer to mine. I inhaled, sipping at his baked-bread scent.

"A jann moving across the desert. There are a few living here, but they rarely interact with anyone. Their species is almost extinct, and some say the journey from our world to this broke their minds. The daimon realm was not good for them. They need open spaces, heat, and sand. It fuels their life force just as the seed fuels us all."

"Is that why you had the Court of Flame fashioned after your world?"

He sat back with a small smile. "I suppose so. Here, in this pocket of reality, we can experience an illusion of home, and the demons and devils who choose to live here find it quite pleasing."

"Demons like Flint?"

"Sprites, imps, Minorax, and many Nephalem live here."

"What about fallen?"

He slid a glance my way. "What? And be ruled over by a lowly efreet?" His chuckle was full and warm. "My station as duke was not looked upon favorably by the fallen."

"But Prince Levistus gave you the title because you saved his life."

"Yes. The fallen do not like to be indebted to anyone, especially not a debt such as that."

The sky was now a rich orange threaded with purple. "The sun will set soon."

"Not for another two hours. We will be back at the keep by then, in time to dress for the twin flame celebration."

"Tell me more about that."

"We believe that a soul is born in two halves, forever searching for its twin. The flame helps us to find our twin soul."

"And what if you don't find them?"

"Then we choose based solely on our heart's desire. Not all find their soul twin, and even fewer since we were forced to flee our world and come here. Now the twin flame is merely a symbol of what was. Matches come together to ask for its blessing, a formality before they are bound."

"So no one has found their match since?"

"The last true twin soul bond occurred two centuries ago after we arrived in the daimon realm. There have been none since. Although each year we hope. Younglings are rare because we cannot procreate with demons, only with abyssbloods with strong daimon blood in their veins or other djinn." He fell into his thoughts and dropped into silence.

To be so old and yet never age, to carry a century of memories alone...I couldn't do it.

I studied his profile long enough that he must have felt my regard and turned his head to meet my eyes. The embers in his irises flickered, live flame that lived in his soul.

Whoa, I was getting fanciful.

"You study me as an artist would a subject," he said.

"You are pretty gorgeous." Fuck, had I said that out loud?

He chuckled again and the vibration rippled through me. What would he do if I swung myself onto his lap and straddled him right now? What would he do if I raked my fingers through his silken gold locks and rubbed my cheek against the planes of his hard jaw?

The flames in his eyes flared. "What are you thinking, little one?"

Usually I'd just tell him, but for some reason my cheeks warmed in a flush and I dropped my gaze.

What the fuck? I wasn't the shy type.

The warmth of his finger beneath my chin had my gaze shooting up to meet his.

"I would not object to your attentions."

And he could read me like a fucking book. I smiled and reached up to curl my fingers around his hand, ignoring the flutter in my chest and my throat. "It's not wise to mix business and pleasure." My voice came out breathless and husky and totally phone-sex line.

He leaned in slightly, delicious breath kissing my face. "I've never claimed to be wise."

Now I knew what panty melting meant. Sheesh.

His nostrils flared as if he could sense my arousal, and for a moment we were both suspended on the precipice of making a decision that would take us into hot, sweaty waters.

Messy, complicated waters.

I pulled back. "Are we there yet?"

His expression closed and his smile was cool. "Yes."

The sled came to a halt as if on unspoken command and relief warred with disappointment, because damn if those hot, sweaty waters wouldn't have been an adventure.

Ignatius wrapped his hands around my waist and lifted me out of the sled, setting me on the ground. I was lithe muscle and heavy bones, and to lift me so effortlessly...yeah, that was hot as fuck.

Several males appeared as if out of nowhere. Tall like Ignatius with bronze, sun-kissed skin and dark hair laced with streaks of sunlight.

They fell into step around us.

Efreet guards?

Ignatius inclined his head toward me. "Shall we?"

The market was filled with colorful stalls,

interesting aromas, music, and voices raised in a language that I didn't understand, and it struck me that Ignatius and Flint must have been speaking in the mortal tongue to me all this time. Now, in the midst of the natives of the Court of Flame, I was subjected to the true nature of this world and its people. The language was lilting and melodious, harmonizing with the wind instruments that played a tinkling tune. Pretty colored lanterns hung above, suspended on invisible string so they looked like they were floating in thin air.

The sellers and the patrons were dressed in bright fabrics that rippled in the breeze. There were imps wearing loose pants, a couple of sprites with purple and green flame for hair. Many human-looking demons—Nephalem, no doubt—and many efreet with skin that was various shades of sun-kissed and eyes like embers. I caught several of them look our way before glancing away again, almost as if they were trying not to be seen. As if looking at us was a crime.

My skin prickled.

We moved further into the market where scarfs hung from awnings and bangles jangled on ribbon. We strolled side by side, and although Ignatius seemed at ease, I couldn't help but notice that the people weren't. The music dropped in volume as did the chatter, and the furtive glances got more frequent.

"Ignatius?"

"Hmmm."

"Why do the people look terrified of you."

"Because they are," he said simply. "And they shall remain so."

Wow. "You rule through fear."

"I do what I must to keep my people safe. Some stories of my acts of terror may have been exaggerated."

Acts of terror. Really? "And you aren't bothered by that."

"I am not. My people know the laws and they abide by them because they recognize the penalty for breaking them." He sighed. "But I can see how my presence might make your visit here uncomfortable." I opened my mouth to deny it, but he forged on. "I will leave you with Hrath. He will watch over you while you peruse the goods. Feel free to take whatever you wish. Hrath will settle the bill."

He was leaving me? "I don't need anything."

"You will need adornment for this evening's ceremony and a dress. Choose them yourself or submit to whatever I provide." His smirk softened into what I was pretty sure was a threat.

"Fine."

The efreet with the dark hair and blond streaks broke away from the entourage and inclined his head while Ignatius moved off with his guards.

I looked up at my guard and then glanced around at the denizens who were eyeing him just as fearfully as they had Ignatius.

Great. "Look, can you trail me at a distance?"

He inclined his head. I backed away, and he remained. Okay. I headed for a stall decked with pretty fabric and bracelets. I'd never been a dress-up kinda gal, but getting dolled up for the Custodia ceremony had given me a taste, and to be honest, it was kind of nice to put away the battle gear once in a while. Although I'd need my daggers, so whatever I wore needed to hide those. I scanned the items: flowing skirts, beaded tunics, and bangles of every color.

A woman appeared beside me and started speaking to me in that gorgeous, lilting tongue. I shook my head and smiled, hoping to convey my lack of comprehension.

Her kind eyes warmed and she nodded and reached for a voluminous skirt made of feather-light fabric. She pointed at me, then to the skirt. There was something familiar about that gesture, about the way she moved, that I couldn't put my finger on, but it made me feel...safe.

She arched a brow, waiting for my nonverbal response to her offer.

I nodded and she unhooked it and held it against me, grinning from ear to ear. Gold patterns shimmered across her dark skin.

She said something more, plucking at the fabric so it flared out and swaying side to side. She was showing me how it would spin when I danced.

I didn't dance, but still. It was good to know that I could if I needed to.

My neck prickled with the sensation of being watched. I glanced behind me, catching only shadow and Hrath's hulking frame a few stalls down, ember eyes fixed on me.

Well, that explained the sensation of being watched.

The woman unhooked an off-the-shoulder blouse from the rack, grabbed a belt, and held them together, nodding eagerly.

"Yes." I smiled. The ensemble was perfect.

Her gaze slipped behind me, and her face crumpled into a scowl. She grabbed my arm and pulled me toward her, spitting words that sounded like curses.

A rumbling male voice returned them, and hands grabbed at me. I spun toward the intruder, meeting dark eyes and a snarl.

"Back off!" I'd barely spoken when the man was plucked off his feet and held aloft.

Hrath bared his teeth and shook the man, who squealed in horror.

The woman began to babble, pressing her hands together in what I construed as a pleading gesture.

What the fuck was going on?

The market fell into a hush, and the reason presented itself a moment later as Ignatius materialized behind Hrath.

He spoke in that lilting language, except coming from him, it sounded lethal and forbidding.

Hrath nodded and reached over his shoulder to draw a blade. What the fuck? Where had that come from?

Ignatius addressed the crowd, his voice a boom that had them quaking in their boots. Hrath set the man on his feet, and two other guards stepped forward and grabbed the man's wrists, pulling his arms out in front of him.

The man wailed.

Ignatius said something else.

"What is it? What are you saying?"

"No one touches what is mine," a raspy voice whispered in my ear.

I knew that voice. Had heard it only a day ago coming from Veena.

I opened my mouth to cry out as Hrath brought his blade down and cleaved the man's hands from his body.

Shadows wrapped around me, and the scent of sulfur filled my nose. The last thing I saw before the world shattered was Ignatius's ember gaze locking on mine in horror.

CHAPTER SEVENTEEN

IGNATIUS

Nyx's silent, screaming eyes fill my vision, but before I can move toward her, before I can shift through the air, shadows swallow her. The rage in my veins is extinguished by icy dread.

"Nyx!" I stride to the spot where she was standing a moment ago and am hit by the distinctive scent of sulfur.

Blood and gore and the battle cry of hardened soldiers fill my head as the scent takes me back to the battleground, back to a time of war. Back to my world.

This is the scent of a shiqq. A half-formed monster, twisted, cruel, and desperate to be whole. They'd given themselves to Shaitan, desperate for the ability to take hosts, to have whole bodies.

Ice crystalizes in my veins.

Our killer has her.

This is my fault. I brought her out. I left her side. I turned my back on her to punish a citizen for daring to touch her.

Stop. Think. Remember what they are, what they can do.

Their power lies in manipulation of the mind, but physically they are weak. In comparison to other breeds of djinn, they are of little consequence. But Nyx? She's mostly mortal, and to her a shiqq will be a threat.

"Please...forgive me, my lord. Forgive me." The man sobs from behind me and my rage returns.

I turn to him, a snarl curling my lips. "Get out of my sight before I take your head."

He struggles to stand, cradling his stumps to his chest. I have no remorse, no doubts about my decision to take his dirty hands. They will grow back in time, but the growth will be accompanied by agonizing pain and he will think twice before laying hands on any unwilling female again.

His head, however, will not grow back.

"Hrath, Ugar, take to the wind. Find her." The two sylphs, the last of their kind, mist into smokeless fire and shoot up into the air.

I make to stride away, but a hand grips my wrist. I look sharply at the old woman standing too close, sad eyes peering up at me with too many questions.

"What do you want?"

She holds out a package. "For the woman who shines. She will need it when you find her."

Something about her words, about the way she delivers them, makes my mind itch. "What is your name?"

She gives me an enigmatic smile and releases me. "Go quick, my lord, before the paths of destiny shift."

She walks away, and I resist the urge to go after her. I have a Nephilim to find and a shiqq to punish.

Chapter Eighteen

Sand, still warm from the sun but rapidly cooling, grated my palms. The sky was blood red, the world darkening swiftly, and I was in the middle of fucking nowhere.

I wasn't alone, though.

The creature who'd brought me here lingered, his presence a flitting shadow, first at my back, then to my side.

I sat up and dusted my hands, scanning the vast expanse of soft, rolling dunes around me.

The creature's breathing quickened, in either excitement or anticipation. I wasn't sure which, and I didn't care.

I turned my head to look at him, but he moved quickly to avoid being seen.

I sensed him behind me once more. "So, you found out I was at the Court of Flame?"

Silence greeted my question, and I was beginning to think he wouldn't respond when he finally spoke.

"I knew it the moment you set foot through the portal." Ah, that distinctive raspy voice, perfect for a horror movie villain.

He shifted so he was hovering to my right. I resisted the urge to turn my head toward him. He'd just move again anyway. He didn't want to be seen. Not properly.

I didn't need to see him to get the answers I needed. "What do you want from me?"

"I want you to die."

O-kay. "That's a little harsh. I mean, we barely know each other. A death wish seems a little excessive, don't you think?"

"Ah, humor to quell the rapid beat of your heart and stem your fear. I know this tactic."

Perceptive little fucker. Yeah, I'd be a fool not to be a little afraid. I was in an alien realm in the middle of the fucking desert with a murderer. But I had no doubt that Ignatius was looking for me.

He'd find me. I just had to buy him the time to do so.

I stood slowly. "I'm not afraid of you."

"Oh?"

"You're a coward who preys on the weak." I shrugged. "You attack from the shadows but you're too afraid to meet your opponent head-on." I sighed. "You're nothing to be afraid of."

"He won't find you. That is what you're hoping, right?"

"I was hoping for a margarita and some finger food at the ceremony later, but you've gone and thrown a spanner in the works."

He chuckled, the sound like nails on a chalkboard. "Ah, you have a spine and a strong will. A shame to crush it, a shame to end such fire..." He moved behind me again and my scalp tightened. "You would have made a promising addition to the fawda. In fact, there is still time to join us."

My skin tingled and pinched with awareness. He was close. Too close, and it took everything I had not to whirl around and try to catch a glimpse of him. Instead, I focused on his words, recognizing his play. He'd lost Veena as his puppet, and now he needed a new one. He wanted me.

Okay, it was time to play his game.

"What do you mean?" I kept my tone light and curious, shuddering as hot, rancid breath wafted past my ear.

Damn, he smelled bad. Do not gag. Do not fucking gag.

"In a few minutes the sand will erupt, and the weavers will come to feast. Beneath you lies flesh and bone they've amassed and buried to return to time and time again. Tonight, they will find live meat. But you can avoid the awful fate that awaits you by joining with me."

Yep, he wanted me as a host. "You want to possess me?"

He tutted. "Possession is such a dirty word. I prefer to call it a partnership with mutual benefits."

Pfft, like fuck. "You get a body and I get a parasite? I hardly see that as beneficial for me."

That dirty, rancid chuckle again. "Did the zuni not tell you of our nights of passion? How I made her writhe and moan in ecstasy. The things I made her feel." He sucked in a breath as if recalling decadent nights of pleasure.

My stomach turned. "You abused her."

"She begged me for it, time and time again." His tone grew high and soft, an exact mimicry of Veena's. "More. Don't stop. Like that. Yes. Please, like that. Ahhh, oh earth, ahh."

"Stop it!"

"The truth is a dirty thing, just like the little zuni and her sweet cunt. I guided her hands, you know, made her play herself like a fiddle, pushing her fingers so deep that they—"

"Enough!" I whirled around, catching nothing but a shiver of shadow as he moved again. Fuck, fuck, fuck. Keep it together, Nyx. Breathe.

I curled my hands into fists. "I don't need you to get me off. I have much more desirable options. You'll have to do better than that if you want my body as host."

"Power, then. I can offer you that. With me inside you, you will have strength and allure. You'll have an edge in the trials to come, and once you succeed, once you claim Satan's seat, you will have a place at *his* side."

"Who is he? Shaitan?"

He froze and I knew I'd fucked up. Shit, I'd given away how much we knew about him because there was no way I could have known that name, not on my own.

"I see you've been making deductions."

"I'm smart that way."

"Not smart enough to know that name. How much does the duke know?"

The jig was up. No point hiding it now. "Enough to come after you, find you, and drag the rest of the information from your bleeding, battered body."

He groaned softly. "So perfectly bloodthirsty. Shame that you must die. You would have made the perfect host."

"Is that it, then? You're done with the recruitment spiel?"

"There is no benefit in recruiting a compromised host."

"Good point."

Now that he knew Ignatius was aware of his existence and what he was, using me as a host would put him in danger. Ignatius would be on the lookout for such a thing.

I'd fucked up, revealed too much, and lost the chance of getting the intel we needed, and now I had nothing more to do than hope Ignatius would find me before these weaver creatures arrived.

If not, then I'd have to fight, and I wasn't sure a dagger would be enough against whatever was coming for me.

"They come." His voice thrummed with excitement. "The weavers come."

I braced myself, scanning the dunes around me. "You're not going to get away with this."

"It matters not. We are many. We are everywhere. He won't stop us. No one can. If one of us falls, another will rise in his place."

The sand beneath my feet shifted and the earth vibrated. Bloody hell, how big were these things? My heart squeezed with terror. I pulled my trusty dagger from the sheath strapped to my boot, the handle in my hand helping me to overcome the fear a little. I was fast, lethally stabby, and if these fuckers wanted to chow down on me, they'd have to work for it.

I had seconds, if that, before the weavers were on me. "What do you want? What do you people fucking want?"

"The world," he said softly.

The sand a few meters away exploded outward and my involuntary scream of shock sliced through the night.

CHAPTER NINETEEN

Two weavers bore down on me. The odds wouldn't have been so bad if the fuckers hadn't been gigantic, with armored skin and serrated mandibles that stuck out a meter from the soft flesh of their mouths, making it near impossible to get close enough to strike. They moved across the sand like they were skating on water, fluid and graceful. I tried to stay light on my feet, to not stay in one spot for more than a split second, because if I did, the sand sucked me in.

I kept moving this way and that to avoid the strike of curved barbed tails that reminded me of a scorpion. In fact, the creatures looked like a cross between a centipede and a scorpion with long, segmented bodies that curled up at the butt to form the stinger.

I had no doubt they would spear me and inject a

toxin into my body. They hissed with each attack, in a frenzy to get hold of me.

"You can't evade them forever," the raspy fucker said from a distance. "They're hardy creatures, and when it comes to prey, they are relentless."

Yeah, I was feeling the burn in my lungs and limbs. Muscles already tiring of staying on the move, staying fast and light enough not to sink into the sand their movements churned up.

My palm was sweaty around the dagger hilt but there was no break in the attack, no reprieve to allow me to address that. They moved too fast, synchronized.

Synchronized.

Wait a fucking second. There was a pattern to the movements.

A pattern that looped. And patterns could be intercepted. Where was the break in their defenses? There had to be a split second where one of them was vulnerable.

The potential of getting close enough to hurt one of them flooded me with a fresh wave of adrenaline. A second wind.

Time to use it.

I continued my evasion, scanning their moves, noting and latching on to the exact moment when the larger one shifted to the left, and then I saw it, a gleaming red pouch on the smaller one's side. An unarmored spot.

That was my target.

I let out a whoop.

"What? Why are you exultant?"

"Because I'm not dying today. Not here. Not now." I rushed through the gap between the two creatures, using the breach to get to the squishy spot and plunge my dagger in.

The weaver screamed, an inhuman, horrific sound that made my chest ache. As the larger one veered its body back toward the smaller one, I bolted forward, dragging the dagger through the fleshy expanse and pulling it free in time to leap and roll to avoid being crushed between their bodies.

A second scream rose in the air as the first petered out. I turned, expecting to see the creatures bearing down on me, but they were huddled together, the larger one hovering over the smaller.

Protecting it.

Her.

Ice trickled through my veins as I finally got a good look at my surroundings, at the shimmery gold and pink egg sacs churned up by the fight.

Younglings.

The weavers' younglings?

They'd been attacking me not to eat me but to protect their young. This wasn't a horde, it was a nest filled with their babies.

Oh, God... What had I done?

The larger weaver continued to wail, the sound heart-wrenching and awful.

"Kill her!" the bastard djinn yelled. "Avenge your mate."

The weaver turned its head toward me, red eyes filled with intelligence and sorrow locking on me.

How had I missed that? How? I shook my head. "I'm sorry. I didn't...I didn't know."

The weaver groaned and folded itself around its mate—the mother of all these children sleeping unaware in their sacs.

"No! You need to die. This is not what is meant to happen. Creatures do anything to protect their family," the djinn screamed.

Just like Veena had done for hers. "Where are they? Where are Veena's parents? What did you do—"

His shadow form hurtled toward me. His hands wrapped around my throat and his weight threw me to the ground.

My dagger slipped from my sweaty grasp.

Dammit.

I twisted and kicked out, hands raking at his shadowy ones, trying to pry them off. "You can't have me. I won't allow it. I don't agree." I managed to slip my fingers between his palm and my throat, giving me enough leverage to yank his hand away and suck in a decent breath. "I don't give you permission to possess me."

He grabbed my hair, yanking back my throat. "Permission is only required if we wish to keep the mind and body intact. But that is not my goal. I will tear you open from the inside out."

"Fuck you, ass breath." I brought my knee up, hoping, praying that—

"Argh!" His grip on me slackened.

I shoved him off and rolled free. "Looks like you've got some balls after all." I scooped up my dagger. "You want a piece of me, you're gonna have to fight for it, bitch." Rage buzzed under my skin like a hive of fucked-off bees.

I caught the flash of crimson eyes buried in the malformed, shadowy form of my adversary before he rushed toward me again.

This time I was ready, ducking and slicing across the air to elicit a bellow of pain. Black shit spattered the sand as he reared back. Looked like shadows could bleed.

Perfect.

"Come on!" I beckoned with one hand. A gust of wind blew my hair forward over my shoulders. "Come on."

But instead of attacking me, the fucker vanished.

What the hell?

The wind howled and moaned. I looked over my shoulder across the rapidly darkening dunes to see a shape hurtling toward me.

A whirlwind. A sandstorm.

Fuck.

I looked to the weaver, who was busy churning up

the sand. My boots began to slide as a sinkhole opened.

Hell no. I scrambled away from the weaver and his family, away from the churning mass of sand as it bubbled and swallowed both creatures and their young.

The air whipped and sliced at my skin as the sandstorm grew closer.

With no shelter in sight, I'd be cut to ribbons.

I was so screwed.

I dropped to the ground and curled into a ball, tucking my face and arms under my body to protect the exposed skin from the worst of the assault.

I had no clue if that was the right thing to do or not. This was my first desert sandstorm.

The world howled around me, drowning out the rush of blood pounding in my head. It was almost on me now. Almost over me.

And silence.

Absolute.

Complete.

What? "What the fuck?" I tried to move but there was pressure on me, holding me down. Panic exploded in my chest.

Tahiyat Malikati.

The rumbling voice was all around me. "What... who are you?"

He said something more that I couldn't quite catch.

But his voice soothed my panic. I was safe with this creature. Whatever it was.

It continued to speak, low and rumbling and soothing, and my muscles relaxed, my breathing slowed, then I heard my name.

"Nyx! Nyx?"

Ignatius?

I tried to sit up, and the pressure around me loosened its grip.

Ignatius called out something I didn't understand. But he was close now. Louder. The pressure around me melted away and a hand fell on my shoulder.

"Nyx?"

I looked up into Ignatius's ember eyes, relief flooding me with heat that turned my limbs to noodles. "What took you so long?"

Chapter Twenty

Ignatius paced back and forth across his chamber, his body a mass of agitation. "The filthy swine. I will find him. He will not escape."

I'd showered. Again. But it had taken ages to get the sand out of my hair. It coated my skin, fine grains clinging to my pores, and washing it off had been almost painful. A sand exfoliation I hadn't banked on.

Still, it would have been a lot worse if the jann hadn't come to my aid. According to Ignatius, they were loner djinn who made the desert their home. They rarely intervened in other people's affairs, but this one had shielded me from the storm and kept me calm. Ignatius had sounded almost stunned when he'd told me this, studying me as if the reason for the jann's actions might have been written on my face.

"Did he speak to you?" he'd asked. "Can you recall what he said?"

I'd been frazzled, able to recall only two words that seemed to have stuck in my mind. *Tahiyat Malikati.*

I'd said them out loud and it was hard to tell, due to the darkness in the carriage, but I could have sworn Ignatius had gone pale.

He still hadn't told me what that meant. Wait, had I asked? I'd been shaken, still in shock from the weaver attack and the storm.

But I was more myself now. Alert as I processed it all.

I'd survived being killed by weavers, then being strangled and torn inside out by the shiqq. Yep, according to Ignatius, that's what ass breath was.

I was alive, and that was something to be celebrated. Usually with a stiff drink, but I guess I'd have to make do with whatever passed for alcohol in this place.

I sat on the end of Ignatius's bed, skin still tingling and flushed from my shower, smooth as silk beneath the robe Flint had provided, and tracked the duke as he prowled back and forth across the room like a caged panther. Nah, a panther was too small, he was something bigger, more dangerous. Damn, I wish I knew my big cats better.

"He knows that I know about him," Ignatius said. "But it matters not. Soon he will also know my wrath."

I wanted a good chunk of that wrath to be mine. I'd killed a weaver because of him. The bastard had put me in a position where I'd had no choice, and he'd pay for that on top of what he'd done to Veena.

"Do you believe he will attack again?" Keelan asked from his spot by the balcony.

"We can only hope." Ignatius's eyes gleamed. "And when he does, we shall be ready."

Attack? They meant attack me. "You know, if you're gonna use me as bait, you should really ask my permission."

His eyes narrowed and then his shoulders relaxed. He ambled across the room to stand before me. Seated as I was, I was eye level with his crotch and the Adonis belt that promised special magical treasures. I dragged my gaze up his chiseled torso to his face.

He smiled down at me thinly. "Nyx of no family name, may I use you as bait?"

"You can use me however you like." It was meant to be a quip, a smart-ass comment, but I regretted it as soon as it was out of my mouth.

His eyes lit up. "Oh, really?"

"Ahem." Keelan cleared his throat, reminding us that we weren't alone in the room. "He will expect us to be watching her."

Ignatius stepped away from me. "Yes, but his kind are single-minded in their pursuits, and being bound to the court, unable to flee, will fuel his rage. If we push him, then he will lose his temper and act rashly."

Sounded like a plan to me. "Then we do what we have to. When does the ceremony start?"

"In an hour. Flint, take Keelan to the guest chamber and provide him with appropriate attire for the evening's festivities. He shall be among my guard tonight."

Keelan allowed Flint to take his hand and they both vanished.

I stood and rolled my shoulders, the exertion from earlier finally hitting me. "You need guards at a party?"

His ember eyes dimmed. "There are enemies in every shadow, now more than ever."

Was this how he lived? Having to be guarded, afraid of attack. Were there that many enemies at his court?

Maybe it had something to do with his ruling style. "You had that man's hands cut off in the market."

His expression smoothed out, the look of someone who was prepared to stand by his convictions. "Yes."

"Because he touched me?"

His eyes flinched. "Yes. But they will grow back, eventually."

"A little excessive, don't you think? I mean, maybe you'd have less enemies if you were more of a benevolent ruler."

"Efreet are not benevolent. Fallen and demons are not benevolent. We rule with an iron fist because to do anything less is to show weakness."

"Kindness is weakness?"

He made a sound of exasperation. "Yes. A kind heart can be manipulated and tricked. As a ruler, that part of you must be set aside when passing judgment. Swift, decisive action will earn you the respect of your people."

"And also their fear."

Flames flickered in his eyes. "I cannot control how the people feel about me, but I can ensure that they are safe. That criminals are brought to justice swiftly. I took that man's hands because he touched without permission." The flames in his eyes glowed brighter. "He touched what was mine. I don't share."

Wow...well... I waited for my inner feminist to roar and be like, what the fuck, I do not belong to you, but she sat there stunned, kinda hot under the collar, and more than a little intrigued. "What about Zepar? He's my sponsor too."

He smirked and ambled closer. I backed up until the backs of my knees hit the bed, blood surging to the surface of my skin. He stopped less than a foot away, but it might as well have been inches, because his presence was a physical force, a caress that ran the length of my body.

"Does Duke Zepar make you feel like you do right now?" He slow-blinked and canted his head, waiting for my response.

He wanted an admission that I was turned on by him, attracted to him, and I wasn't about to beat around the bush. "No. In a different situation, a different world, you and I might have some fun." I glanced at the bed behind me. "More than a little fun.

But like I said before, I don't mix business with pleasure."

"I'll hold you to that, and once the business is done..."

Oh boy. I was in so much trouble with this one.

I UNWRAPPED the package on the bed that held my outfit for the evening, wishing I'd managed to secure the skirt and blouse from the market.

Wait, this *was* the same skirt and blouse. The belt was there too, and a pair of soft silver slippers, and... what the... I held up the thigh holster containing a small silver dagger.

How the hell?

A flicker at the periphery of my vision drew my attention to the dresser, where a sprite with purple flame for hair had appeared.

"Mistress. Have underthings for you," she said, jade eyes wide as she took me in with open curiosity.

I arched a brow, unable to hide a smile at her overt perusal.

She dropped her gaze quickly. "Apologize. Not mean to stare."

"It's okay. You can stare if you want."

She raised her attention back to my face. "Not seen a Nephilim before."

Ah, the whole Nephilim thing. "It's no big deal, trust me." I eyed the package in her hands. "Is that for me?"

"Yes, yes." She hurried over and held out the package.

I unwrapped the gauzy fabric to find lingerie inside. Black, lacy, and definitely my size. "Did you..." I pointed at the garments.

She made an "o" with her mouth, then ducked her head. "The duke pick them out personally."

"He did, did he?" An image of Ignatius fingering lacy slips of fabric to find the best one for me filled my head. I liked it. The duke had taste. Although I preferred a sports bra and cotton briefs for everyday workwear, I'd have picked out something just as decadent for a night out.

Fancy lingerie beneath my clothes always made me feel sexy. It had been a while since there'd been an opportunity for anyone to appreciate it on me, though.

I dropped the robe and began to dress, aware of the sprite ogling me. I didn't care. Nakedness was not a huge deal to me. I was comfortable in my skin. The lingerie fit like a glove. Ignatius had guessed my size perfectly, and damn if that wasn't a turn-on.

The skirt flowed easily against my legs, fabric shimmering when I swayed. The material of the blouse was silken soft, cut to flatter, and left my one tanned shoulder bare. Coupled with the belt, the whole ensemble looked effortlessly chic. No one would guess I was carrying a weapon.

"Mistress let Tipta do her hair?"

Tipta? That was her name. Cute. "Sure."

She led me to the dresser, and I took a seat.

She held her hand a few inches from my head and ran it downward inches from my hair, leaving it dry in her wake.

"Wow, that's a neat trick."

She beamed at me, showcasing tiny sharp teeth. "Mistress has pretty hair." She brushed it through before holding her hand over it again. This time, when she ran it over my locks, they tightened into soft waves tumbling down my back and over my shoulders like an inky waterfall.

My hazel eyes looked lighter, swimming with gold flecks, and my skin seemed to glow. I looked good. Pretty, even. I wasn't used to feeling this way but I liked it.

The air popped behind me and Flint's reflection appeared in the mirror.

"The duke awaits," he said.

It was time to take my sexy ass out for a test drive and hopefully provoke a shiqq into trying to kill me.

Bait never looked so good.

Chapter Twenty-One

Flint transported me to a set of golden doors that had to be at least eleven feet tall. Ignatius stood to one side with Hrath and Keelan at his side.

My sibling looked impressively forbidding in a black fitted tunic with armored shoulders that accentuated his broad frame. His dark hair was pulled back into a braid and his horns were painted with gold patterns. His dark wings were folded sharply against his back, the crimson stripes visible, and if I wasn't mistaken, looking thicker than they had earlier that day.

I couldn't imagine anyone daring to try and bypass him to get to Ignatius. His jaw was set in that mulish way I'd come to know as his back-off expression, but when he caught my eye, it softened.

Hrath wore a similar outfit, except the gold patterns

on his skin weren't paint, they were a part of him, moving beneath his skin like a living entity. His ember eyes were filled with storms, his broad granite features set in forbidding lines.

Yes, Ignatius didn't need any more guards than these two.

Speaking of Ignatius…He was a jewel set in a sturdy crown and no less lethal and forbidding than his companions when it came to stature and aura. He was dressed simply in loose black pants and a black shirt, but it was the way those clothes fit that made the difference. The black shirt stretched across his wide chest and shoulders, the short sleeves hugging his biceps and accentuating the bulge of muscle. The dark material made the shimmer in his skin more pronounced, the golden hues more defined. His sun-streaked hair gleamed in the lamplight, brushed back off his forehead and held there by a slender band like an Alice band, except there was nothing feminine about the item on him.

There was nothing feminine about Ignatius at all. The efreet exuded dangerous masculine energy.

My mouth went dry at the sight of him.

He smiled knowingly and held out his hand, palm up, to me. "Are you ready?" he asked softly. "The shiqq will undoubtedly be beyond those doors. You'll stay close to me."

It wasn't a question. It was a command.

I didn't do orders, but in this case I'd make an exception.

I was no fool.

The shiqq was dangerous, but the whole point of playing bait was to be attacked. "He won't attack me if I stay close to you."

"No, he won't, which is why when the time is right, a commotion will occur, and I will leave your side. The shiqq will believe I have been distracted and will make his move. But you will always have eyes on you. You'll be safe. We will capture him."

"You make it sound easy."

"It can be. Shiqq are not powerful, and they are not smart. But they are single-minded in the pursuit of a goal. This one wants to end your life. It will attack you when it is given an opening. Our job is to control that window."

I liked the way he thought. The cool calculation. The confidence. It was sexy as hell. I took a deep breath and his gaze dropped to my parted lips before dragging back up to my eyes. My mouth tingled as if he'd touched it.

This guy was dangerous in too many ways.

His grip on my hand tightened a fraction. "Shall we?"

"Yes."

The golden doors swung open and he led me into the room beyond.

THE ROOM beyond the golden doors was no room at all, but an enclosed courtyard. Three floors of balconies rose around us, and demons and efreet stood about drinking and laughing. Colorful scarves hung from railings, fluttering in the breeze. Lanterns floated above us, amber lights competing with the starlight above, and the air smelled of cinnamon and spice. Music played, soft and lilting like the language of this world, so that the conversation and the melody wove together to create its own unique symphony.

For a moment my senses were overwhelmed and I instinctively gripped Ignatius's hand tighter.

He leaned in slightly. "Take a moment. Breathe."

I did just that, using his grip to anchor me. I was going to play bait and then hunt my predator. I needed to be sharp. I needed to acclimatize. I breathed, logging the different sensations until they became familiar, until the vibrant sensory vista settled around me, becoming a backdrop.

I relaxed my grip on him and he moved us forward.

Conversation dropped into a lull as the revelers realized their duke was here. I felt hot gazes on my face too, drinking me in. I didn't mind being the center of attention, but this was almost as overwhelming as the backdrop had been.

I looked to Ignatius, watching how he dipped his

chin here and there to acknowledge those watching us and how they were quick to lower their gazes once they'd been spotted gawking.

I supposed this was normal for him, for any duke in his court, to be watched, dissected, whispered about.

I couldn't do it. Being the center of attention in a club or at a party was one thing, but the rest of the time the shadows were my friend. You could learn a lot from within the shadows.

We descended a flight of stairs into the mosaic-tiled courtyard. Demons parted, creating a path to let us pass.

The buzz of conversation became a hum and then stopped altogether. An impressive throne-like chair sat on a platform up ahead, all gold and ivory frame with a plush crimson cushion. The back was tall and sturdy to accommodate someone of Ignatius's height.

There was no seat for me.

Ignatius's grip on my hand flexed. "I was specific about the seating," he said coolly.

For a moment I thought he was speaking to me, but then Hrath responded.

"I'll see to it." He didn't leave our side until we'd climbed up three of the six steps leading to the platform. Ignatius brought us to a halt and turned to face the gathering.

Keelan remained beside the duke, his hands loose at his sides but in easy reach of the sword at his waist.

Ignatius gave him a look and he switched sides to me.

The duke began to speak, words that I couldn't understand, flowing, ebbing, his tone rising and falling in a way that felt right even though I couldn't comprehend them.

"Welcome to the twin flame ceremony," Keelan said softly beside me. "Where many matches will be solidified and, I hope, some may be found."

He was translating for me. I shot him a grateful smile.

Ignatius was talking about the possibility of a twin flame match, something that hadn't happened for centuries, and there was no ignoring the frisson of excitement that skimmed across the room. A frisson that screamed hope.

I scanned the crowd, picking out the efreet from their ember eyes and varying golden and bronze skin tones. There were so many other creatures here too, horned and hooved like the Minorax, and dark-eyed and svelte, exuding sex appeal like an incubus or succubus would, except these creatures had intricate patterns moving across their skin. I had no idea what kind of abyssbloods these were.

"And now the flame," Keelan said, translating the duke once more.

Everyone moved back to create space, and I noted the pattern on the ground properly for the first time, how the mosaic tiles were absent in a five-by-five space. This spot was rock, sprayed gold.

It rose with a rumble, pushing up out of the earth, becoming a huge, cubed unit made of thick glass. Inside the glass, glowing steady and sure, was a deep blue flame threaded with purple.

The rumbling stopped and the structure settled. Silence fell, thick and heavy.

Ignatius spoke again, looking from left to right.

"Those who wish to be blessed may step forward," Keelan said.

Several couples moved toward the flame. With some, the efreet and djinn traits were obvious; in others, not so much.

Once again, the crowd parted to let someone through. I craned my neck to see who, but the crowd was thick, and the person was hidden until they broke through and came to stand in front of the flame, facing us.

It was a sprite with purple flame hair threaded with silver and gold. His eyes, iridescent, like the film on a puddle reflecting a rainbow, held age and wisdom. And his golden robe spoke of stature and importance.

"That's the keeper of the flame," Keelan said. "The duke will invite him to speak."

Ignatius said something and the sprite inclined his head, closed his eyes, and began to sing.

The pitch was high and low at the same time, as if two people were singing in tandem. The air vibrated with possibility and the flame surged up to fill the glass cage.

A collective sigh rose around us.

The couples stepped forward, bowed their heads, and touched the glass to receive their blessings.

"That is the ibris flame," Keelan said softly. "A part of the seed of his power."

"Who is he?"

"The spark that spawned the djinn race. The first of them. He lives on in the seed and in the flame."

I couldn't take my eyes off that flame as it flared and kissed the glass. But that couldn't be glass, because glass would have melted at those temperatures.

The couples stepped back one by one, but the flame continued to bloom and the sprite continued to sing.

I leaned toward Keelan. "What's happening now?"

But it was Ignatius who answered. "The keeper is imploring the flame to call twin souls together."

I scanned the room. "How will we know?"

"*We* won't. *They* will. They'll feel it."

"How does it feel?"

He chuckled softly. "Only those who have experienced it can know for sure."

I watched the mesmerizing flames and my body relaxed, a sense of peace coming over me. The keeper of the flame's song resonated inside my head, beautiful and evocative even though I didn't understand it on a conscious level.

Did Ignatius feel the hypnotic quality of the flames? I turned my head to look at him and found his gaze fixed on me. Watching me as if *I* were the flame.

I wanted to laugh, to make light of that intense look. But the words refused to come and my chest grew tight and fluttery.

My voice was a whisper that caught on a breath. "What is it?" I wasn't sure what I was asking about—the strange, hollow yet full sensation in my chest or the fact that he was staring at me like he'd never seen me before.

The flame died down in my periphery. I wanted to look at it but couldn't break my eye lock with Ignatius. He held me captive with a look I didn't understand. A look that made my insides flutter and twist.

I registered the rumble of the plinth retreating below ground and the rise of conversation around me.

"What's happening?" Had I leaned closer?

Ignatius inhaled me, and when he spoke, his cool, collected tone belied the heat in his gaze. "There is essence of euphoria in the air. With your human aspect you must be affected."

Yes, that explained it, but what about him? Was he affected too?

"Your Grace." Hrath appeared beside us. "We have urgent business to attend to." He said it loud and deliberate, but Ignatius didn't seem to hear him.

"Your Grace, it is urgent. We must go now." Once again, he projected his voice so that others would hear.

It hit me that this must be part of the plan. The moment they were supposed to leave me alone to be attacked. To act as bait.

"Your Grace—"

"No." Ignatius blinked sharply and looked down his nose at me. "It can wait."

Hrath's brows pinched, but he didn't argue.

"A seat for Nyx," Ignatius said.

"Yes, we have it. The imps neglected to bring it through."

"Your Grace." A small, crimson-skinned man with a pointy chin and yellow eyes bowed at the foot of the steps.

Hrath sighed.

"What do you have to say for yourself, Rumi?" Ignatius demanded.

"Your Grace, I swear it. I placed the seats as you ordered. I ensured a plump cushion and a padded back to the seat. I even sourced the perfect footstool."

"And forgot to place them on the platform," Hrath added.

The imp bristled, his eyes sparking with controlled rage as they flitted to Hrath. "I assure you I did not."

"Enough," Ignatius said. "It matters not now. Go. Feast and enjoy. You have done well. One mistake does not detract from your efforts tonight."

Hrath's brows shot up and the imp sagged in relief.

"Thank you, thank you, Your Grace." He backed up while bowing.

Ignatius's attention was back on me, but his intense expression of a moment ago was gone. He looked down at me coolly and swept a hand up the steps. "Please be seated."

There was a second smaller seat besides Ignatius's now. It was just as ornate, cast in the same shades of gold and ivory. I climbed the final few steps, acutely aware of Ignatius behind me, and took my seat. At least my heart wasn't thumping any longer and my insides didn't feel all fluttery.

Ignatius's gaze was fixed on the revelers so I leaned in to get his attention. "What are we doing about the plan?"

"It's too dangerous."

"It's no more dangerous than it was a half hour ago."

"We'll find him another way. I will not use you as bait."

Annoyance flared in my chest. I'd come here to find Veena's tormenter, to save her parents, not sit around and watch people party. "You don't get to decide that. If I want to play bait, I will."

He turned his head and fixed me with a withering glare. "Not while you're in my care, at my court."

What the fuck? "What is wrong with you?" My palm tingled where it rested on the arm of the chair. I itched it absently. "This is the perfect opportunity to draw him out." I scratched my arm. "I can walk off, maybe go to the ladies' alone, and then he can—"

"What are you doing?" Ignatius was staring at my hands in horror.

I looked down at the blood covering the back of my hand and trailing up my arm. I'd scratched so hard I'd broken skin. Pain registered, rushing up my arm and sinking into my blood.

"Darkroot," Ignatius hissed. "Poison."

For fucksake. Not again!

Chapter Twenty-Two

Ignatius scooped me into his arms and carried me off the platform. Hrath and Keelan blocked us from view as we headed into the shadows of the nearest balcony and through a door into a room that I was too far gone with pain to scope out.

"Fucking hell." I arched my back. "I'm getting sick of this shit."

"Door," Ignatius barked.

Keelan stepped back out of the room and closed the door.

Hrath hovered. "Your Grace."

Ignatius's expression was dark, filled with an emotion I couldn't define.

"What is this. What's wrong with me?" I pushed the words through clenched teeth.

"It was on the chair," Ignatius said. "Smeared on the armrest."

"What?" I gasped.

"Darkroot," Hrath said. "It is deadly to all but the djinn."

Realization dawned. "You mean...I'm going to die."

"No." Ignatius held me tighter. "You will not."

I caught the look of surprise on Hrath's face but then another wave of searing pain stole my breath and concentration.

"Fight it, *qalbi*."

What was he saying? Oh, God. Fight it? How?

He gripped my jaw and pressed his lips to my cheek. Heat bloomed at the contact and for a moment the pain receded. For a moment there was nothing but his lips on my skin, moving, whispering words I didn't understand.

"Her arms..." Hrath said.

They were warm now, tingling beneath the pain.

Hrath said something more, but I was focused on my body, on the way it pressed to Ignatius's solid form. Of his breath, whispering, forever whispering against my skin and the heat spiraling in my chest and spreading, moving outward to my limbs where it turned cool against the awful buzz of pain.

Slowly, achingly, the pain ebbed. Ignatius tucked in his chin, pulling his lips away from my cheek, and a soft moan of protest lodged in my throat.

I looked down at my bloody arm to find it healed and...what was that moving beneath my skin? Golden lines? Patterns?

They dispersed as I watched. "What did you do?" I looked up at him.

Hrath made a small, inarticulate sound and Ignatius's head whipped toward him, sharp words falling from his lips.

Hrath sucked in a breath and the gaze he threw me before he ducked his head was filled with conflict.

"Ignatius?" I drew his attention back to me. "What did you do?"

"What needed to be done," he said tightly. "And now, we will find the culprit responsible." His eyes flashed with the promise of pain. "There is only one place that darkroot can be found. Here in the Court of Flame. In the conji gardens. And only one demon has access to it."

"You think that Milius helped the shiqq?" Hrath looked skeptical. "That demon is loyal to a fault."

"The zuni the shiqq possessed was also not a murderer," Ignatius said, "but he found a way to invade her and turn her into a killer regardless."

Hrath's brows shot up. "You believe Milius to be possessed?" His expression cleared. "If that is the case, the shiqq will not escape from his new host."

"How?" I looked to Hrath. "How will you keep him trapped?"

Hrath looked down his nose at me, pride simmering in his topaz eyes. "The conji of the Court of Flame are the most powerful."

Ignatius nodded. "Do it. Bring him to me."

A cold, ruthless smile curled Hrath's lips. "With pleasure."

IT WAS my turn to pace the floor, rage an inferno inside me. The need to do some damage had me clenching and unclenching my fists.

We were in a stone room equipped for torture. One wall was hung with blades and tongs, metal spikes and hammers. All sorts of torture devices. It was similar to the one I'd seen in the nightmare stables, but cleaner.

Less blood on the flagstones.

We'd soon fix that. "How much longer?"

The sound of bootfalls answered my question. I looked to the steps, heart leaping in satisfaction at the cries of protest of our culprit as he was dragged down them. Keelan appeared first, followed by Hrath, who had a demon by the nape of his neck.

The demon who'd given me darkroot.

Finally a male robed figure trailed after them. His presence filled the room with the crackle of power. This had to be the conji. His eye whites were black, irises silver, and his skin was a metallic blue with silver swirls decorating it.

Keelan took a position against the wall and Hrath shoved the demon, Milius, into the room. He fell to his knees, sobbing wretchedly. He was a slender demon, with short ivory horns and gentle blue eyes in a smooth, unlined face that seemed too young for someone in charge of a garden filled with deadly shit.

"Your Grace. Please... Please, I did not know," he pleaded. "He lied to me. He lied, and then it was too late."

The conji glided across the floor and around the kneeling demon. He made a full circle, and when he stepped back, the ground glowed with runic patterns where he'd walked.

Milius moaned. "What are you doing?" He squeezed his eyes shut. "You're hurting me."

He wasn't talking to us. He was speaking to the shiqq inside him.

The conji stepped into the circle and held out his hand to Milius.

Milius thrashed and gnashed, dropping his chin with a growl. When his head whipped up suddenly, his eyes were orange, and his face was crisscrossed with scars.

"You can't have him," he snarled. "You want me, you'll have to go through him."

I looked from Milius to Ignatius. "What's happening?"

"The shiqq knows that we can't hurt him physically while he's inside a host. But he senses that the circle the conji has created will allow the host to pass, but not the shiqq. He's holding on to the host to protect himself."

"It won't work," Hrath said. "Not for long."

He was right. The conji lunged for Milius, grabbed him by the collar, and dragged him out of the circle despite the way he bucked and thrashed.

The allure master was stronger than he looked.

A sizzle rose in the air and the circle flashed. Milius fell to the flagstones outside the circle, sobbing again, but something had been left behind.

My target.

The shiqq in all his glory.

Trapped in the circle of runes while his host scrambled away from him.

I was peripherally aware of Keelan speaking to Milius, of the demon's soft, watery words, but my attention was on the malformed thing inside the runic boundary.

It had half a head, one eye, and a twisted mouth that took up what slender jaw it had. It had a left arm, a right leg, and a withered torso, and the rest of it was slivers of shadow that shifted and adjusted to hold it upright.

It stood glaring at us with its one orange eye. "Death on you. Death on your spawn, death on—"

The conji raised his hand and the shiqq choked on his words.

Ignatius stepped forward. "You will die this day. That is a fact. But *how* you die is in your hands."

The shiqq's lips curled, his eye bugging as if he

wanted to spew curses, but the conji held him in his thrall.

"You can die slowly," Ignatius said. "In agony as we take pieces of you, or you can die swiftly with one strike. Which will it be?"

The conji opened his fist slightly.

The shiqq spewed a string of words I didn't understand but I guessed were curses.

"Then so be it," Ignatius said.

Hrath stepped forward, rolling up his sleeves.

"No." I walked up to the circle, energy thrumming beneath my skin. "He's mine." My voice was a low growl.

"Nyx?" Ignatius sounded surprised.

I kept my gaze on the monster in the circle. "He hurt my sister. Abused her. Used her. He tried to kill me twice. He's owed pain, and I want to deliver it."

I glanced his way now, eyes burning with determination. If he denied me this...

Hrath and Ignatius exchanged glances, then Ignatius inclined his head. "Very well."

The conji crossed the room and touched my shoulder, studying me with silver irises set in inky darkness like distant stars in the blackness of space. He muttered words under his breath and a tingle passed over me.

A protection. A ward.

He stepped back and released the shiqq from his grip.

"He's all yours," Ignatius said. "Feel free to use any implements in the room."

I dipped and drew the silver dagger the old woman had given me from the sheath at my thigh. "I have my own."

The shiqq's gaze dropped to my blade.

He scrambled back, hissing in pain as he met the barrier of the circle. "No. What...how did you get that?"

I held up the blade, eyes narrowing. "This? You're afraid of this?"

Ignatius muttered something softly beneath his breath. Then, "Where did you get that?"

I frowned at him. "From you. It was packed with the outfit."

His expression closed. "Yes. Of course it was."

"Fuck you, whore," the shiqq spat, drawing my attention. "I'm not afraid of anything. But your sister was. She sobbed when I violated her. Begged me to stop. 'Please. No more. No more.' Just like you'll cry out when I fuck—"

I rushed into the circle and buried the blade in his eye. He screamed, clawing at my hands but meeting only the crackle of the ward the conji had placed on me.

I looked down into his twisted face. "You were saying?"

I DIDN'T ENJOY INFLICTING pain on others, but I was single-minded in my pursuit of justice, and in this world, with this monster, pain was the key.

I cut away at him, piece by piece, blocking out his screams, stopping to ask him if he was ready to talk. Ready to tell me what I needed to know.

He was tough. I gave him that much. He held on until the moment I gripped his crotch and brought my blade down.

"No. Please no." He sobbed as I released him, falling to his knees amongst the slivers of his flesh. "I'll tell you. I'll tell you, but please, no more. Kill me quick."

He'd lasted longer than I'd expected. I looked down at the blood on my clothes. My pretty skirt and blouse were ruined.

Rage surged again but I tamped down on it. "Where are Veena's parents?"

"At home. They're at their home."

What? "You have them prisoner in their home?"

He looked up at me and I caught a glint of satisfaction in his eyes, a smug gleam at having gotten one over on us. "They were never prisoners. They were *accomplices*. They *gave* her to the cause."

Bitter wrath coated the inside of my mouth. "You're lying."

He shook his head. "You can see for yourself easily enough. They agreed to the possession, to the plan, so that the zuni may rise."

"But that isn't the plan, is it?" Ignatius said.

The shiqq hawked and spat blood.

"What is the plan?" Ignatius asked. "How would you possessing the zuni help your cause? You would not be able to sit on the throne."

He chuckled wet and raw. "I would not need to. I was merely the hands of death to get the zuni to power."

"Then what?" I kicked his knee. "What would happen then?"

"The pawn would be in place."

"Who is your master?" Ignatius demanded. "Who is the head of the movement?"

The shiqq stilled. "That I will not tell you."

He lunged so fast that I didn't realize what was happening until my blade was buried in his forehead. His eye rolled back in his head, and he disintegrated around me, turning to ash and dust.

I stared at the pile of carbon. "What the ever-loving fuck?"

He was gone, taking with him the chance of finding out who the real puppet master behind it all was.

I stepped out of the circle and turned to face Ignatius. "I need to see Veena's parents. They live on the outskirts of the Court of Shadows. I'll need access."

Ignatius tore his eyes from the remains of our only lead to the movement and fixed them on me. "Then you shall have it."

Chapter Twenty-Three

The rural lands that housed the zuni were neither under Umbrane's rule nor the rule of House Lunar. Turned out that zuni had been gifted domain by Satan for their dedicated service to the fallen over the years. Their humble, gentle nature was novel in this world and Satan had sought to protect them in what little way he could.

Learning this made me rethink my view of the father I'd never had a chance to know. It contradicted his bloodthirsty contracts when it came to his own flesh and blood. How could he pen laws that would murder his blood but provide a haven for a race that had no connection to him?

Hrath flew me to the zuni settlement.

The djinn was an air elemental, able to become the wind itself. I couldn't do that, but wrapped in his arms, cradled close to his chest, I could travel with him.

It was like being in a wind tunnel, loud and confusing, just the rush of blood in my head and the sensation of movement in my belly. Once we were in motion, his form was merely a suggestion. I was afraid that if I moved or squeezed his waist too hard, he'd vanish, and I'd plummet to earth with a crash.

I didn't look down, didn't look at anything. I kept my eyes screwed shut, praying for it to be over.

It would have been nice if Ignatius could have come, but the twin flame ceremony was still in progress. He had to be there. Put on a front and show his court that everything was in order. If news of the movement got out, there'd be panic and disorder.

Hrath was Ignatius's second.

"Having me with you is like having him by your side," he'd said.

It wasn't, though. Hrath didn't smell of honey and sunshine. Being close to him didn't make my stomach tremble and my knees weak, and what the hell was I doing feeling these things at all?

Ignatius was my sponsor. Nothing more.

You don't still think he could have killed Satan, though, do you?

No. I didn't believe that. Ignatius didn't believe in hidden justice. He believed in swift action, and he was unapologetic about it. If he'd wanted to kill Satan, he'd have done so openly, execution-style, and had a valid reason he'd have shared willingly.

No, it was more likely that this movement was

involved, and the mastermind, the person pulling the strings, was the murderer. I needed to find out who and stop him. Or her. It could always be a her.

But first I had to get closure for Veena.

Only when my boots touched the ground did I realize the flight was over. Hrath held on to me a moment longer.

"How do you feel?" he asked. "Are your legs stable?"

"Yeah, I'm good."

He stepped back, unwinding his arms from my waist, but cupped my elbows for a moment while I tested my own assertion.

"I'm good." I nodded. "Thanks."

He released me. "Then we are here."

Here was on a rise overlooking a moonlit village dotted with thatched roofs and winding streets.

"Do you know which abode your sibling's family resides in?"

Oh, crap. "I'm sure we can find out." I set off down the rise with the air elemental trailing behind me. "How long have you worked for Ignatius?"

He snorted.

"What?"

"I do not work *for* him, I am his..." He faltered.

I glanced over my shoulder to see him walking head bowed. I slowed my pace to match his. "His what?"

"I am his bond brother," he said finally. "I think that is the best translation."

"And what does that entail?"

"A vow to protect not only each other but that which belongs to each of us. We are family."

Ignatius had sent his family with me to watch over me. I wasn't sure what to make of that.

We entered the silent streets and I aimed for the nearest house with a tiny, neatly pruned front lawn, lit by the light of a lamppost holding an oil lamp aloft.

Everyone was bound to know the family of the zuni who was Satan spawn. Shouldn't be hard to find them.

I knocked on the door and waited.

"Zuni go to bed early as they rise before dawn to work," Hrath informed me.

"I'll make this quick."

The door opened and a rotund zuni dressed in a nightshirt and slippers looked up at me with bleary confusion.

"Where does the Satan spawn family live?"

He frowned up at me.

I sighed and repeated the question. Another zuni appeared behind the first, a woman with messy hair and a shawl thrown over her slender frame. She started babbling in a tongue I didn't recognize.

Dammit. Of course. They couldn't understand me. "Hrath, can you speak zuni?"

"No, but most demons and devils speak demon tongue as do the fallen. It is a universal language here."

He turned his attention to the zuni and fell into conversation with them.

A few moments passed, then the zuni stepped back and shut the door in our faces.

Rude. "I thought they were humble creatures."

"They're humble but they're also tired. It is late, remember."

I didn't have the luxury of guilt. The only guilt would come from failing Veena. "Did you get an address?"

He pointed across the street.

Great. I crossed to the house, identical to the one we'd just visited, knocked, and waited. No answer. I knocked again, louder. "Hey! Open up!"

Hrath placed a hand on my shoulder. "I know you are upset but we must respect the citizens."

I turned to him. "I don't have to respect anyone. These fuckers were probably all in on it. You think they don't know what was planned for Veena?"

His eyes filled with shadows. "Maybe. Maybe not. We cannot make assumptions."

"I'll assume whatever I like until I get answers." I hammered on the door again. "Open the fuck up!"

The door opened a crack, and beady eyes peered out at me.

Hrath took over, speaking in the demon tongue. The zuni's gaze flicked to me, fear filling his eyes.

Yes, you little fucker, you should be afraid. "Who is he? The father?"

The zuni attempted to close the door but Hrath pressed his palm to it and pushed, his jaw tense, dark eyes flashing. He said something else in demon language and the zuni shook his head, his mouth turning down. Another one appeared. A female. Her long dark hair, so like Veena's, was braided. Her eyes reminded me of my sister.

She fixed her gaze calmly on me and spoke, not in the demon tongue but in the mortal one. "What do you want from us? We did what we thought best to secure the zuni the status we deserve."

"Is that what the shiqq told you?"

"The fawda promise us freedom from drudgery. Freedom from serving the fallen."

Wait. "Are you telling me you're forced to work for the fallen?"

She gave me the kind of look a disappointed teacher would give a pupil when they got the answer to a question they should know wrong. "You are Satan spawn, and yet you ask me this? Have you learned nothing?"

I crossed my arms. "Enlighten me."

"We are slaves to the fallen and the demons. We are nothing to them. This land was given to us in a show of benevolence, but it is simply another cage. Another prison. Our gentle nature has been taken for granted for too long. The fawda promise us power and Veena will give us that."

Veena, my sweet sister. A pawn. A fucking object to be used. "Do you love your daughter?"

She blinked sharply. "Yes. Yes, of course."

I shook my head, unable to stop my lip from curling. "Nah, you're a fucking liar. A loving parent wouldn't do what you did."

She flinched. "I gave her power."

"You gave her to a monster to be abused. To be *used*. To be *traumatized*. Have you *any* idea what being trapped in her body and watching herself murder people has done to her?"

"I—"

"Have you any idea what that thing did to your daughter without her consent?"

She shook her head, her eyes wide with shock. "No...He promised she would be unharmed. That he'd shield her. Protect her. That he wouldn't allow her to see the...the..."

"Murders?"

She winced as if hearing the word was painful.

"He lied. He made her watch him kill and then he hurt her. *Used* her." I allowed the implication of that word to sink in and her face drained of color.

Her hand went to her trembling mouth. "No...That wasn't..." She exhaled shakily. "I need to see her."

My face felt like stone as I looked down on her, and when I spoke there was menace in my tone. "You aren't going anywhere near her."

"I'm her mother."

"You gave up that right when you allowed a shiqq to possess her. But your plan failed. The shiqq is dead, and Veena..." I lifted my chin. "Veena is now under *my* protection."

She let out a cry and moved toward me, but I was already walking away.

Chapter Twenty-Four

Hrath dropped me back in a courtyard at the Court of Flame. Flint was waiting for us and teleported me to Ignatius's personal library, where the duke stood staring at a painting. There was no sign of Keelan.

It was late, and moonlight shone through the high windows, lancing like silver daggers across the room to slice across the gorgeous tiled floors.

Ignatius was bathed in one of those shafts of moonlight. Tension rippled across his shoulders as I approached, telling me that he'd sensed my presence.

"She was formidable, you know," he said softly.

My gaze flicked to the painting. A depiction of battle where a slender female stood with her back to the painter, her dark hair whipping in a breeze. Three males stood with her, swords in hand, bodies clad in black and crimson armor as the world before them blazed with shooting stars and flame.

"Who is that?"

"The daimon queen. And that's the Chaos War. Soreena died protecting her realm."

Soreena. It sounded like such a soft name. Didn't fit the image of the warrior on canvas.

"She fought alongside her mates. Or maybe they fought alongside her."

"Mates?"

"Her consorts."

"She had more than one?"

I stepped closer to him to get a better look at the painting. The colors were washed gray and silver by the moonlight, but I could make out the embers dancing on the canvas, could almost hear the clang of metal on metal and the bellow of battle cries. But there on the rise, with her sword aloft, hair whipping out behind her like an inky flag, her mates by her side, it would have been quiet. The calm before the storm raging beneath her.

"Daimon females mated for life," Ignatius said. "But they often had more than one mate."

"Sounds a little greedy to me, not that I'm knocking it. Sounds pretty cool."

"When we came to their world it was strange to us. Efreet take one mate and we mate for life also. To see males share a female...To see a female capture the heart of more than one male and keep them was... novel. But that was their way."

I peered closer at the painting, noting the flames edging one of the male's fingers. "Wait, is that...Is that an efreet?"

He smiled. "Not efreet. Something...else. His name was Erebus. A powerful djinn with an incredible story."

"Oh?"

"He was no stranger to moving worlds. Our world was not his first. He'd lived a life before, but this..." He reached out to touch the canvas lightly with his fingertips. "Would be his last."

There was pain in his words. "He was your friend."

"He was my mentor." There was longing in his voice. A nostalgia for another age.

"I'm sorry."

He looked down at me with a frown. "For what?"

"For what you lost."

His smile was small and filled with shadows. "Me too. But life goes on and sometimes it can surprise you." His gaze skimmed my face. "Did you get the answers you were looking for?"

"Yes. Although I wish I hadn't."

"The shiqq told the truth?"

I nodded. "I'm not sure how to tell Veena."

"But you must. It's a betrayal that will hurt her, but it will make her stronger."

"I know." He'd gone back to studying the painting. "What will you do now?"

"Root them out. Stop them."

I smiled, liking the way he'd known exactly what I'd been referring to.

He sighed and pressed his fingers to his eyelids. "I cannot allow them to grow in number or strength. Now that we know they exist, we will fight. Again."

"What about the princes? Will you tell them?"

He nodded slowly. "I've requested an audience with Prince Levistus. It's imperative they be made aware." His gaze dropped to my bloody clothes. "You should change before you leave."

Leave. Yes, it was time to go back to Morningstar. Time to leave his side.

I didn't want to.

I ducked my head, confused by the feeling.

"Nyx?" His tone was soft, questing.

He placed the crook of his finger beneath my chin and urged me to look at him.

I met his gaze, conflicted, heavy-hearted. Strange. "Is it weird that I don't want to leave?"

Whoa, why had I said that?

He sucked in a breath, his ember eyes turning a shade like warm honey, gaze tripping across my features, searching for something. "What is it that makes you want to stay?"

You. It was on the tip of my tongue, but I bit it back

because that was crazy. I didn't do attachments, not this kind. It wasn't who I was.

Maybe you're changing.

Piss off.

"I like it here..." *With you.*

Oh, fucking hell. That annoying inner voice needed to die.

I swallowed and smiled. "You're an interesting male, Ignatius." He stroked my cheek with his thumb. Oh, God, he needed to stop touching me like that. "It's been...educational being here with you."

Yeah, keep it light. Keep the distance.

Just keep touching me too.

"Is that all?" Flames flickered in the dark depths of his pupils. "Is that all you feel?"

The urge to meet his lips with mine, to press them to his, to taste him, had my stomach flipping and panic blooming in my chest.

Hell no.

I stepped back, chasing my soft gasp with a breathless laugh. "Wow. You..." I wagged a finger at him. "You *are* dangerous."

He smiled but it didn't reach his eyes. "What are you afraid of, Nyx?"

"I'm not afraid of anything."

"Liar," he said softly, closing the distance between us.

My heart rate quickened, and I took a step toward

him, and before I could check myself my hands were on his arms, caressing his silken skin.

His chest purred and something inside me melted, warm and gooey with the need to hear that sound again. I stroked up his biceps, fingers curling over his powerful shoulders. Fuck, no one had the right to feel this damn good.

"Look at me," he demanded softly.

His gaze was a magnetic force, drawing mine. They locked with a snick. The connection was like coming home, and the warm, gooey feeling was now in my chest, swirling into a tight ball at my solar plexus.

He cupped my nape, thumb sliding up to skim the spot below my ear and flood me with a lethargic heat.

"You'll come back," he said with assurance. "This is your home now, if you want it." I could barely hear him above the buzz in my head. "Hrath will go with you to the conclave as your bodyguard."

"I have Artimus to protect me." It sounded breathless, the kind of plea that belonged inside a moment of passion.

His breath brushed my mouth. "The seneschal will protect you as long as it serves his interests. Hrath will protect *only* your interests."

My eyelids wanted to flutter closed, chin wanting to tip up to offer him my lips. The urge was so strong that I almost gave in to it, tipping my head up slightly to feel the brush of his warm mouth before his words registered fully. The fact that he was talking about my interests. The fact that everyone here had their own interests and agenda.

I wanted to believe Ignatius was different, that he cared for me, liked me even, but I needed more time with him to determine that for sure. Time to determine if I could let my guard down with him like this.

I dropped my chin with a smile. "My interests? You mean your *investment* as a sponsor."

The warmth in his eyes died and I wished I'd kept my mouth shut because losing that warmth didn't feel great.

He released me and slow-blinked. "Yes, Nyx. You're my custodia and I will not have you unprotected in such a dangerous setting."

"I'm not a fool to turn down backup." I shrugged to hide the disappointment that he was no longer touching me. "I like Hrath."

A small smile. "You'd be one of the few who do."

"Seriously? I mean, what's not to like? The guy practically exudes charm and humor."

Ignatius's smile turned into a grin. "If only everyone could see him the way you do."

We were back on even footing and I relaxed. "Thank you...for everything."

The air behind me rippled and I didn't need to look to know that Flint had appeared behind me, summoned by an unspoken command.

"Hrath will find you before your trip. Just send a

note to let him know when you plan to leave," Ignatius said.

I nodded as Flint took my hand. ""I'll see you soon."

"Soon, *Qalbi*," Ignatius said.

I turned to him. "What does that me—"

He dipped his head and claimed my lips, cutting off my words, my thoughts, my very breath. My heart lurched and I reached for him with my free hand, ready to fall into the kiss.

But the world shattered, taking me with it.

Taking me away from him.

Chapter Twenty-Five

ARTIMUS

"Oh, yes, yes, like that. Oh, earth and stars, please don't stop." Erinea's tits bounce as I fuck her.

My anger, my need to punish her, keeps me hard. I need to satisfy her, to remind her what she has so that she doesn't stray.

I can't lose her confidence, or I lose her ear, and that means satisfying her greedy cunt.

I pull out and flip her roughly onto her front, relieving me of the need to look at her face.

She moans and shivers in pleasure because she knows what's coming. I reach for the slick in the jar by the bed and coat myself with it, smearing it between her ass cheeks and pushing two fingers into her asshole to prep it.

She groans and pushes back. "Yes. Oh stars, yes."

The incubus in me rises and I'm throbbing now, aching to fuck that tight ass. The fact that I hate her doesn't matter. All that matters is feeling that tightness, that grip on my cock. All that matters is hearing her scream.

Yes, that part makes it all the sweeter.

I position myself at her entrance as she arches and widens her knees to brace herself. I grab her hips and slide my tip into her, pushing further, breath coming faster.

Her groan is long and protracted as I work my way in, back and forth, back and forth, further each time. My eyes roll back in my head the deeper I go.

She pants, pushing against me, urging me to hurry, to claim her. I'm in my head, in my favorite fantasy where it's Nyx beneath me. My cock is pushing into Nyx's ass. Fucking hell.

Yes. Fuck yes. I sink in and she cries out.

Nyx cries out.

I imagine her mouth parted, her eyes bright as she takes me, and when I withdraw she whimpers in protest.

Please. Fuck me, she says.

My balls tighten, my spine tenses, and I throw back my head and fuck her ass until she's screaming and sobbing and begging me to never stop.

Cold air drifts around the room, wafting over my naked skin and curling around my hot balls.

Erinea lights a cigarette and takes a drag, tipping her hair back to exhale liquorice-scented smoke into the air. She stands naked on the balcony despite the icy chill, dark plumes spilling down her back like an inky waterfall.

I want to dress and leave, but I remain naked on the bed, waiting to be dismissed, to perpetuate the illusion that I'm in her thrall. That she owns me.

"You were exceptional tonight," she purrs. "Such passion. It's been a while." She glances over her shoulder at me with an arched brow. "I was beginning to think your attraction to me was waning."

The non-existent attraction. I frown. "Why would you think that?"

She shrugs one slender shoulder and takes another drag on her cigarette. "You've been distracted."

She has no fucking idea.

I sigh and rake my hand through my hair. "This ascension is draining. My apologies if you've felt my absence."

"The ascension or the spawn?" I feel her dark gaze on me. "One spawn in particular."

A finger of ice trails up my spine, but I maintain a

relaxed posture and shoot her a confused glance. "I don't follow."

She studies me for a long beat and then sighs. "You really are oblivious, aren't you?"

It's my turn to arch a brow. "Enlighten me."

"The Nephilim?"

"What about her?"

She studies me for several beats. I stare right back, blank and confused.

She sighs and flicks away the cigarette butt. "Nothing."

"No, tell me." I sit up and pat the bed beside me. "If something is bothering you, I want to know what it is."

She enters the room, closing the balcony doors to join me on the bed. I gather her close, warming her chill skin with the heat of mine.

"You'll think me silly," she says.

"Never," I croon.

"I thought you had *feelings* for her."

I tense, then let out a bark of laughter. "Feelings?"

She tuts. "It isn't funny."

"Oh, but it is. Me and that...that thing? Erinea..." I tip her face up with a finger beneath her chin. "Why would I eat peasant stew when I can feast on venison." I snap my teeth at her, making sure to bare my fangs.

Her eyes light up with excitement at the move. The bitch loves it when I feed on her, but her blood, although sustaining, tastes like shit.

"Answer me." I squeeze her jaw slightly, taking

control the way I like, the way she craves. "Why would I want her when I have you?"

Her eyes glitter with pride and triumph. "True."

My hand drops to her throat. "You are all the female I need. Although..." I narrow my eyes and tighten my grip on her. I could snap her neck. I could do it, but then my line of communication with the powers that be, the princes, everything would be severed. Still, it's tempting. "I wonder if *I* am enough for you."

She smirks knowingly, unfazed by my hand on her throat, and my suspicions are confirmed. The bitch was deliberately flirting with Umbrane to get a rise out of me.

I give it to her, pushing her back onto the bed and pressing my weight into my hand. "Answer me."

Her eyelids flutter and she chokes slightly, her lips still curved in a smile. Her breasts rise and fall in excitement. Shit, if I'm not careful she'll want to fuck again.

I ease off on the choking.

She stares up at me. "I'm glad you noticed." She strokes a hand down my chest and hovers at my Adonis belt. "The fact that you're jealous tells me all I need to know." Her hand slips lower and grips my shaft. "You're mine, Artimus, and I am yours. Do not forget that. I do not share."

"And neither do I." I bare my teeth again. "Your cunt belongs to me."

"Show me." She parts her legs, and it takes everything I have to hide my revulsion.

I slide down her body, allowing my incubus nature to rise, to feed, because this is the only meal it will get.

The only sexual energy, the only blood, until Nyx is safe.

I will do whatever it takes to keep her safe.

CHAPTER TWENTY-SIX

NYX

I took the portal behind Ignatius's chamber back to my room. Keelan said he'd find me in the morning so we could speak to Veena together about what we'd discovered.

Ignatius's kiss was a brand on my lips, an unspoken promise that I was eager to explore soon. But for now, with dawn only a few hours away, exhaustion was clouding my thoughts.

I needed sleep, and my bedchamber had never looked better.

Sev rolled onto his side in bed, silver hair spilling across his cheek, and held out a hand to me. His chest rose and fell in even breaths, telling me he was between sleep and wakefulness.

I kicked off my boots, stripped off the clean tunic

and leggings Flint had provided, and climbed into bed with him.

I sighed as he pulled me close. "Where's Chase?"

"Outside the door." Sev kissed my forehead. "You smell sweet."

"I showered. A lot."

A low rumble of laughter in his chest. "Do I want to know why?"

"Oh, I have tales of adventure, but first I need sleep."

He tightened his grip on me and kissed my forehead again. "Roll over and I'll be your big spoon."

I obliged, exhaling and relaxing as soon as his body curved around mine.

"Sleep now." He kissed my neck, drawing me into the darkness and the inescapable arms of sleep.

"It's okay, Chase. It's just a storm. Just thunder."

The world flashes bright and thunder roars above the hammering rain. My stomach twists. Chase presses closer to me, lending me the warmth of his body.

"It's okay," I say again, more for myself than for him. He isn't scared. Chase isn't scared of anything.

I'm the one who's scared. Of the thunder. Of the shadows, of the weakness that comes with hunger.

Three days without a meal have left me lightheaded. Maybe I'll die and Chase can eat me. At least he'll live.

Chase chuffs, but it's an annoyed sound, almost as if he can read my thoughts.

I fancy that he can.

That he knows what I'm saying. That he understands me.

"I'm sorry." I wrap my arms around his neck and hug him tight. "I didn't mean it. I love you, Chase. I'm not leaving you. We'll be okay."

We're huddled in the spot we call home. A stairwell leading to a boarded-up building. I'd considered bunking in the building, but with only one exit, it felt too closed-in. The stairwell is enclosed enough, and we have tarp hung up to shield us from the worst of the rain. There are some blankets and my battered backpack as a pillow, a few supplies I've collected here and there, but we're out of food. Have been for days now. The restaurant where we'd get leftovers closed. The café owner who let me wash dishes for a meal died, and her daughter, the new owner, is mean.

There is a way to get food, but the thought of it makes my stomach turn and fear crawls up my spine. But I've seen others do it. The other street rats, older than me, males and females, sometimes go with men. They go for hours and then come back with coin.

I'm not sure what they do, but I know it's nothing good. I can tell from the dull look in their eyes.

Men approach me too, but Chase scares them off. He protects me except...maybe it's time for *me* to protect *him*.

I hug him tighter, noting the way his bones press through his skin.

He's starving too. Dying.

I blink back tears. He's saved me so many times, kept me warm, kept me sane. Maybe it's time for me to return the favor.

The sound of bootfalls is almost blocked out by the hammering rain. I tense and Chase growls low in his throat.

"No." I grab his face and turn him to face me. "No, you have to let me do this."

His eyes are large pools of comprehension. He chuffs again and presses against me to shield me before turning his huge head toward the person coming down the alley.

"Chase, no." I'm convinced this is our only chance of survival. Convinced it's the only way.

Chase makes a sound, low and menacing, and the hairs on my body stand to attention.

"Well, well, what is this?" a female voice says.

Chase cuts off the growl and whines.

"Oh, you poor thing. This is no way to live, is it?"

Chase chuffs in agreement and then shifts his body, revealing me to the woman. Pale blue eyes lock onto me.

I take in her weathered oval face and damp silver hair. She wears a bright blue raincoat and yellow wellington boots.

"Well, now, this won't do. This won't do one bit."

She purses her lips. "Now, you don't know me, and I don't know you, but I'd like to help if you'd let me."

Chase chuffs softly and nudges me.

He's a good judge of character. If he thinks that this woman is safe, then...

"What will you do?" My voice is hoarse and raspy. I clear my throat. "How will you help me?"

"Well, by getting you out of the rain for a start. A home-cooked meal and warm bed for the night. How about that?"

I can't help but be suspicious. No one does anything for anyone in the Fringe without a price. "Yeah? And what do you want in return?"

She sighs. "Well, I do need an errand girl. Someone to deliver messages and packages for me. A little help around the house with cleaning." She braces her hands on her knees. "My joints aren't what they used to be. So, what will it be, lass?"

I look to Chase, deep into his warm hazel eyes. He nods once.

I turn back to the woman. "Chase comes too."

She rolls her eyes. "Well of course he does."

She holds out her hand to me. "My name's Babs, what's yours?"

I take her hand. "Nyx. I'm called Nyx."

. . .

THE DREAM LINGERED in my mind as I dressed the next morning. I'd woken just after dawn to find Sev watching me with his eerie silver eyes.

"Well?" he'd asked. "Why the many showers?"

I'd filled him in on my visit, the heat, the desert, the attack, and then the torture of the shiqq. He'd listened avidly, focused on my every word. I'd seen anger in his eyes, turmoil, and something that resembled desire. He'd left soon after, claiming he needed fresh air, but he'd be back soon, falling into bed and sleeping away the day because daytime was his sleep time.

Chase had taken his place in the room with me.

Watching over me in Sev's absence. My first guardian.

The dream filled my mind again. "I dreamed about you last night."

He raised his brow in question.

"It was that day that Babs found us, remember? The storm and...Yeah, she found us."

He studied me silently, waiting for me to elaborate.

I pushed my feet into my boots. "I was planning on going with one of those men, you know."

He exhaled heavily as if to say, *you're an idiot.*

"I would have if she hadn't... I can't help but wonder..."

He stood and padded over to me, locking gazes with me in silent communication that told me he knew. That he remembered and he understood.

A lump formed in my throat, a cocktail of emotion for the child I'd been, the girl I'd become, and the woman I was now. Babs had saved me from an awful fate, from damage that would probably have never healed, but there was no denying the damage already done. The emotional damage that made it so hard for me to form deep romantic attachments. Giving my body over to someone else was one thing, but my heart...That was a different story. That was caged. Protected. It took time for that to be relinquished. Time Babs had put in. Time Orina and Quinn, my two best friends, had put in.

Just...time.

Chase tipped his head to the side and chuffed softly, as if to say, *I love you and you love me.*

"Yeah, buddy, I do. You're my heart."

He looked to the door, then back to me, as if to say, *what about the others?*

"Yeah, I think I'm falling in love with those fuckers too." Because there was a connection between us unlike any other. Blood, common ground, an understanding that went deeper than blood.

Maybe there was hope. Hope that I could let my guard down one day. Hope that I could love in that all-consuming, passionate way with the whole of my shattered, broken heart.

Maybe allowing my siblings into my heart was healing me.

The knock on my door dragged me out of my thoughts. "Yeah?"

"It's Keelan, you ready?"

I crossed the room and pulled the door open. "Ready as I'll ever be."

I wasn't sure what I'd expected from Veena when I told her about her family's betrayal. Nah, that was a lie, I'd expected tears. I'd expected her to call me a liar. To blame me for the shitty turn of events.

But what I got was the opposite. I got silence. I got eyes burning with rage and determination. I got acceptance.

Tristeene sat beside Veena, her arm around the zuni's shoulder. "Are you okay?"

Veena took a shuddering breath. "Yes. Now I know the truth. Now I know what they did and that he's gone for good."

I nodded slowly. "Oh, yeah, he's gone all right."

"But aren't there others out there?" she said. "Other djinn and demons who are part of this fawda movement?"

"Ignatius is dealing with it. He's contacting the princes, starting with Prince Levistus."

"And what if one of the princes is in on it?" Gus said.

The thought had crossed my mind. We had no clue who was pulling the strings or why, and my gut told me that the person responsible for Satan's death had to be connected to this movement.

"A prince could be in on it, so could one of the dukes. We don't know. But reporting it, bringing the existence of the fawda into the light, will make it harder for them to operate. It might shake things up, causing them to slip up."

"We need to finish the trials and claim that throne," Veena said. "We need to work together to stop them." All eyes were on her now as she lifted her head and flipped her hair over her shoulders, leaving her determined face exposed. "We have to do whatever it takes to stop them from picking us off. Whatever it takes to get rid of the elimination contract."

I loved her strength in that moment. "I will. I'll do everything in my power."

"No." Veena shook her head. "It's not fair that it should fall on you. If we're going to do this, we must show a united front."

"She's right," Keelan said. "We're stronger together."

It felt right. This, being with them, felt fucking right. I nodded slowly. "Then we do this. We all go to the conclave, and we petition together."

"As a team," Gus said.

"What about Mallini?" Tristeene asked.

"Mallini will be there too."

My head whipped round to the chamber door where Mallini stood, braced by the doorframe. Her crimson plumes were ruffled, and her eyes were bloodshot. She looked too pale, like a ghost of herself.

"I'm coming." Her knees buckled and Keelan caught her, swinging her into his arms and cradling her against his chest.

He looked down at her and snorted. "If you want to come, you will need to eat."

She stared at him defiantly. "Then we better order a feast."

The room broke into excited conversation. Plans for the trip. Things we could say to the princes.

My siblings were coming with me. I wouldn't be doing this alone.

Now all I had to do was tell Artimus about the change of plan.

Chapter Twenty-Seven

Zinichi led me through hidden passages toward the area of the keep that Artimus occupied.

"You can see the symbols for the west side of the keep." She pointed to a compass symbol, pointer indicating west. "This one brings you out behind the kitchens that serve the Erinyes."

"Artimus lives in the same wing as they do?"

"Oh goodness no." She bustled up a short flight of steps, holding her lantern aloft as the passage darkened. "The seneschal has his own quarters a couple of floors below Satan's seat. But you won't be able to use that dreadful contraption to get to that floor, no." She shook her head.

"You mean the elevator."

"That monstrosity. Dangerous, lumbering thing." She shuddered. "No, that goes straight up to Satan's seat. In truth, I have no idea why we have it. We have perfectly good staircases. Many of them, in fact."

I bit back a smile. "Maybe to transport heavy things?"

She paused for a moment as if considering it, then made a *pfft* sound. "We have Minorax for that."

She pushed open a door into a short corridor that smelled of peppermint and cloves.

It closed behind us, and when I looked back, it was gone. Wait...No, there it was, built so seamlessly into the patterned wallpaper that you wouldn't see it unless you were looking for it.

"You can't go back that way," Zinichi supplied. "That's exit only." She bustled down the corridor and I followed with a dirty smirk.

Exit only indeed.

She took me up a narrow flight of stairs and through another door. "Kitchens are to the left. They feed the Erinyes, but we go this way."

She took a right and another flight of steps onto cream tiled floors that morphed to gold, then opened out into a circular chamber with windows high above.

I was beginning to understand that the external structure of the keep was an illusion that hid an intricate interior filled with passages and wings and towers and way too many circular chambers and domed ceilings. Would I ever be able to find my way around this maze?

Probably not.

Zinichi stopped outside a set of black doors and knocked. The door opened a moment later to reveal an imp with an angry face.

"What is it?" His eyes widened at the sight of Zinichi and the anger melted into something that was more slight annoyance. "Zini, what are you doing here?"

Zinichi shook her head slightly and widened her eyes in warning, gaze flicking my way.

The imp cleared his throat. "Mistress Zinichi, how may I help you?"

"Satan spawn, Nyx of no family name, would like to—"

I held up my hands. "Whoa. Enough with the whole intro, please. Nyx is fine." I could live without the whole "no family name" spiel.

Zinichi smiled and nodded. "Yes, of course. Nyx would like to see the seneschal."

The imp glanced over his shoulder. "The seneschal is asleep."

I rolled my eyes. "Then wake him. This is important."

No doubt taking all the spawn to the demon realm would involve preparation, and I didn't want to give him any excuse to say no. I didn't want to fight him over this, but I would if I had to.

"I'm afraid the seneschal was...indisposed until dawn and has only just retired." The imp's smile was tight, almost a grimace.

Indisposed? Yeah, I knew what that meant. "You mean he was fucking till dawn?"

The imp looked at me in shock, as if the word *fuck* coming out of my mouth was an offense to nature. "Really? *Fuck* offends you?"

"Well, I...I would never, I..."

"It's all right, Blight," Zinichi said, then to me, "Blight is more refined in his choice of words than most."

I flicked both brows up. "Fine, but am I right?"

The imp sighed. "That you are, Mistress."

"*Nyx*, my name is Nyx, and Artimus's sexual exploits are not my problem. I have a real problem and he needs to hear about it." I pushed past the imp and strode into the room beyond.

He let out a yelp. "Mistress!"

"Nyx," I reminded him.

My boots clipped across the golden tiles, falling into silence when I hit the plush rug in the center of the room.

It was a nice room done up in gold and black with ivory accents. But I wasn't here to take in the décor. "Which room?" Several led off the main one.

Zinichi hurried toward me. "Nyx, maybe we should—"

"Which room?" I turned to Blight. "Look, the sooner I speak to him, the sooner I'll be out of your..." I looked at his bald head. "Horns."

He looked torn.

Fucking hell. "I could be the next Satan, you know..." I let that sink in.

He pointed to a door. "Through there. First door on the right."

"Thank you."

I pushed through the door into the cool corridor beyond, aware that I was about to invade Artimus's privacy, aware that he probably wasn't dressed, but not caring. Heck, he'd come into my bedroom and hung out when I wasn't there. He probably even went through my underwear drawer.

I shook away the thought, because, truth be told, the idea of the controlled seneschal riffling through my panties excited me.

I stepped into the dark bedchamber. The only light spilling from a gap in the drapes was cold and gray, barely illuminating the edge of a huge four-poster bed.

The sheets were rumpled, and Artimus was sprawled across them...naked.

I should look away.

I really should, but damn, that ass was a peach and a half.

Crap, he was stirring.

I walked over to the bed and grabbed the edge of the sheet, drawing it up over his lower half to hide temptation.

"Nyx?" His voice was gruffer than usual.

He hadn't looked at me yet. How could he know?

He inhaled and rolled onto his back and—

Oh. My. God.

I turned away before I could do something ridiculous like stare or drool.

A stillness filled the room, tension rippling against my back, caressing my nape.

"What are you doing here, Nyx?" That gruff, sleepy tone, words drawled and lazy, vastly different to his usual clipped notes, sent a shiver over me. "What do you want?"

Want? That word held so much possibility. I wanted to take a closer look at specific bits of his naked body. I wanted to touch him, to climb up onto the bed and bring my face close to his and...smell him.

What the ever-loving fuck? "This room is filled with sex mojo right now, isn't it?"

A long beat of silence. "Why would you say that?"

"Because I can feel it."

"And how does it make you *feel*, Nyx."

Motherfucker, was that his breath on the back of my neck? I made to turn around but his hands fell to my shoulders, holding me in place.

"Don't," he said.

"Why not? Are you shy?"

"No, Nyx. I'm just afraid of what I might do to you if I see your fuck-me eyes."

My mouth grew dry. "You don't speak like that."

"No?"

"Not usually."

"I believe I was quite clear about what I'd like to do

to you, Nyx, and the fact that you're here, in my bedchamber without an invitation, is sending all kinds of inappropriate signals to my very inappropriate parts."

I closed my eyes, breathing evenly through my nose. Do not think about it. Do not fucking go there. I kept my tone light. "I didn't come here to fuck you, Arty."

His grip on my shoulders slackened and his hands skimmed down my arms before releasing me.

I felt his retreat like the heat of a campfire going out.

"Why *did* you come?" he asked softly.

The rustle of fabric told me he was getting dressed and my heart sank just a little with disappointment.

"The spawn and I had a meeting."

"Oh?"

"There have been...developments."

We'd discussed what to tell Artimus. How much to tell him. Ignatius knew the truth of Veena's possession. What she'd done while under the shiqq's influence. I'd told him everything without too much thought because I'd needed his help, trusted him instinctually.

That same instinct told me to spill the beans to Artimus too, but he was fucking Erinea, and as much as he said it wasn't because he wanted to, I couldn't risk that I might be wrong. That the incubus might be playing me.

And damn, that would hurt, because the fucker

was growing on me. He intrigued me, stimulated me in a way not many people did. Still, there was that inkling of doubt in my mind that I wasn't prepared to ignore.

So I'd give him the half-truth.

"You can look now, Nyx, all the goodies have been tucked away."

Bastard. I turned to face him to find him in dark pants and a cream shirt, open to reveal the tanned expanse of his torso. An eight-pack. Nice. "Someone does their core exercises."

He ran a hand through his dark locks, the corner of his mouth lifting. "I'm tired, Nyx, and when I'm tired, I'm not so in control of my incubus." He padded closer and the air grew thinner. "And when that happens, people get fucked."

My pulse raced and stuttered, then raced some more. "You're saying fucking Erinea all night wasn't enough for your incubus?"

He flinched slightly, lip curling before he could stop it, sapphire eyes bleeding to crimson at the edges. "What. Do. You. Want?"

I sighed. "Veena was possessed by a shiqq that's part of some movement called fawda."

His eyes narrowed. "Never heard of it."

"It's a movement that started in the djinn realm." I filled him in on the shiqq and how it had wanted to influence Veena, leaving out the murder stuff and telling him about how the movement wanted to control Satan. Control the throne.

"You think this movement is responsible for Satan's death."

"Yes. I think the killer is allied with them. But it's now more imperative than ever that the spawn stick together."

He arched a brow. "Oh?"

"They want to come to petition the princes with me."

His eyes narrowed.

"Present a united front. Watch each other's back."

"Against possession and murderers?" he drawled.

I lifted my chin. "Yes."

He cupped his nape and rolled his neck on his shoulders. "Fine. I'll make the arrangements."

"You will?" My voice came out as a squeak of surprise. I cleared my throat. "Yeah, you will."

He smirked. "Get out of here before I lose the fight with my demon, throw you on the bed, and fuck you senseless."

Oh man, he totally knew how to sweet talk a woman. Would sticking around be so bad?

His eyes glowed bright, the crimson deepening, mouth parting to showcase his pronounced canines. "Nyx..." There was a thrumming note of warning in that tone that teased me in all the right places.

Usually I'd tease back, push the buttons, see how hot I could make a guy, but this was no *guy*. None of the males in Morningstar were, and I was beginning to realize that my brand of domination probably wasn't going to work so well on them. If I pushed Artimus, he'd happily snap, and then...I wasn't sure I'd have the willpower to resist. And that...

That would be bad for us both.

I took a deep breath and backed toward the door. "Fine. I'll go. But just so we're clear, it's not because you threatened to fuck me. I am not afraid of sex."

He took a step toward me.

I bolted out of the room, the sound of his soft laughter following me like a physical caress to my senses.

Chapter Twenty-Eight

Zinichi took me back toward the spawn quarters in silence, only stopping to speak when we were almost at the doors.

"You shouldn't antagonize the seneschal," she said.

I opened my mouth to deny the intention to antagonize Artimus but changed my mind at the look on her face.

Fear.

She was afraid. Of Artimus? For me?

I needed to dig a little on this one. "Why not?"

She chewed on her bottom lip, gaze dropping so her lashes shielded her hazel eyes.

"Zinichi, come on. If there's something that could hurt me, then—"

"The seneschal isn't who he seems," she blurted.

"O-kay..."

She pressed her lips together for a moment, then

continued. "There are stories of his demon. Of the incubus who shares his body."

"Wait...hang on. I'm confused. Incubus who *shares* his body? I thought he *was* an incubus."

She sighed. "Yes, yes, he is, but incubi and succubi are dual personalities that live in harmony. They are woven together, inseparable, but one is usually stronger than the other. In some cases, the part that must feed on sexual energy is stronger and must be wrangled and subdued. In others, that part is weaker and easily satisfied. The seneschal has great hunger." Her eyes grew wide. "There are stories of the seneschal being locked away as a youth. No one saw him for years, but the keep staff say they would hear his roars of rage. They say they felt his hunger. Then one day he was back by Satan's side. Composed and controlled and that was that. No one explained his absence and it was never spoken of again."

Hmmm, okay, interesting. "You're saying he could snap."

She eyed me, her gaze speculative, as if she was turning over the idea of speaking her thoughts.

Bit late for that now. She'd pretty much spilled the beans. "Just spit it out, Zinichi."

"I believe the seneschal *is* in control of his hunger. Has been for the longest time, but every creature has its Achilles' heel. And I fear that you, my sweet girl, might be his."

I LOUNGED on Tristeene's bed while she curled her gorgeous hair. Long, dark, and thick, her hair was something to be envied. I mean, it was like a silken sheet of sexiness. It was mesmerizing watching it go from poker straight to loose curls with each wrap of the heated roller thingy she was using.

Sev was asleep in my room, sprawled across the bed with an abandon that was admirable. He was a force to be reckoned with, contained in a package of lithe muscle and desire. And he was mine.

Had I been tempted to wake him with my hands and my mouth? Yes, for sure. But he needed his rest. So Chase and I were chilling in Tristeene's chamber. Watching her prepare for a dinner date with whatever male she'd be feeding off tonight.

I'd given the others the good news about being able to come with me to the demon realm and there was a general buzz of nervous excitement across the floor now.

Mallini was asleep after eating a decent meal and Veena had opted to stay with her. We had only a few days before we left for the demon realm, and all of us needed to be in top form. Alert, strong, focused. After the rough couple of days we'd had, we all needed some downtime.

Tristeene hummed softly to herself as she worked.

My conversation with Zinichi played in my head and I had to ask. "What's your hunger like?"

She met my gaze in the mirror and arched a brow. "Excuse me?"

"Just something Zinichi said about the dual nature of a succubi and incubi."

"Ah…" She went back to her curls. "Mine is easily controlled. She's happy so long as she feeds a couple of times a month, but I like to keep her topped up. There are some succubi and incubi who need to feast more frequently, and some prefer to binge." She frowned slightly. "How did this topic of conversation come up with Zinichi?"

I plucked at the duvet cover. "She was warning me about Arty." I filled her in on what Zinichi had said.

Her brows flicked up. "Arty?"

Is that what she'd fixated on? "Artimus."

Her smile bordered on a smirk. "Pet names are dangerous, sweetie."

I snorted. "It's not a pet name if it annoys the recipient."

"Oh, it so is." She turned on her stool to face me. "And yes, I've heard stories. But that's all they are. Stories. The past is not the present. And the youth who was locked away is not the man who protects you now."

"Protects me?"

She rolled her eyes upward. "Oh, Nyx, are you that blind?"

"What are you talking about?"

"Artimus's interest in you is more than academic. More than political. He wants you. I can smell it on him."

No news there. "I know he wants to fuck me. He told me as much. But he's banging Erinea, and apparently she's the jealous type."

"It's more than that." She leaned forward slightly and her newly formed curls slipped over her shoulders to frame her heart-shaped face. "When you fell through the gateway to Umbrane's court, when Artimus was summoned by Nugen, I smelled the seneschal's fear."

Fear that he'd lost an investment. "Look, Tristeene, he's kinda like a mentor. He wants me on the throne so he can have my ear, that's all." I waved a hand. "He gave me this spiel about wanting to ensure all Satan spawn got the same chance in the trials, but if that was the case, he could have latched on to any one of you. But I'm neutral. Not affiliated to any court. Practically human. He thinks he can control me." I flashed her a smile that was more a baring of teeth than anything else. "He wants me all right, but not for the reasons you're implying."

"Is that why Zinichi is worried you'll cause him to snap?" Tristeene arched a brow. "Is that why his fear was for *your* welfare, not for his own plans failing?"

I stilled. "You can't know that."

"Oh, I can. There are different kinds of fear and

succubi and incubi can tell them apart. It's what makes us powerful allies and advisors. It's probably why Satan kept Artimus close...Until he didn't."

Ah, the famous dispute that no one seemed to have details on. Still. I had to ask. "Do you know what happened between them?"

She shook her head and turned back to her reflection. "I doubt anyone but Artimus and Satan himself knows the story there." She shot a sly look my way. "But I do like the way you deflected from Artimus's feelings for you."

I ducked my chin. "I have no idea what you're talking about."

"Ah, sweet sister, this is why you and I get on so well."

There was a knock at the door.

"Enter," Tristeene called.

The door opened and Zinichi popped her head in with a wince. "Um, Nyx, Duke Zepar has sent a summons."

I sat up straighter. "A summons?"

"It says you're to dine with him this evening." She stepped into the room and held out a package. "He sent this."

I slipped off the bed and took the package.

"Well?" Tristeene demanded, curler abandoned, full attention on me. "Open it."

I peeled off the thick paper and stared at the shimmering fabric inside. "Oh, for fucksake. No."

Tristeene plucked the package from me and laid it on the bed before carefully, almost reverently, lifting the material from the paper. The jade fabric glittered as if a billion miniscule stars were sewn into it.

Tristeene held it against her frame and cocked her head at me. "You don't like it?"

It was pretty. "I don't like dresses, full stop."

"Put it on," she demanded.

What would it feel like against my skin? "Piss off."

She smiled sweetly. "Please."

Fucking hell. I snatched it from her and she made a soft sound of distress. "Sweetie, careful. That material is delicate."

I shot her a glare before stripping down to my underwear and stepping into the dress. Zinichi zipped up the back.

"Oh..." Tristeene clasped her hands together before hurrying over and steering me toward the full-length mirror on the other side of her room.

I stared at the frowning, dark-haired woman in the glass. The dress was sleeveless, with slender gold straps to hold it up. The neckline was a soft scoop that skimmed the top of my breasts and the back was too deep to accommodate a regular bra. It molded to my lithe frame, accentuating what little curves I had. My waist looked tiny and my tits much bigger than they were. I looked...feminine and soft. Fragile and delicate.

This was why I didn't do dresses. They didn't reflect me. Not the me I wanted to project. Dressing up while in Morningstar had become a thing, though, and although I was beginning to kind of like it, this dress made me look like someone else.

I wasn't sure I liked that. "There's something wrong with your mirror."

Tristeene appeared behind me and rested her chin on my shoulder. "No, sweetie, that's you. You're beautiful."

I opened my mouth to protest but she beat me to it.

"Beautiful doesn't have to be soft. Beautiful can be deadly. No one would suspect that death could come in such a pretty package. The nip of teeth and the brush of soft lips would be expected from someone wearing this dress, but *no one* would be expecting the bite of a dagger."

Yeah, I liked that. I liked the sound of that very much. "Fine, I'll bloody wear it."

Tristeene plucked at the strap of my bra. "This will have to go, though."

I shrugged. "Whatever works."

If Zepar wanted me to have dinner with him in this dress, he'd have to deal with a little boobage.

Chapter Twenty-Nine

It was almost time to head over to see Zepar. I'd hoped to catch Sev before leaving. He'd been gone when I returned to the room, the only evidence he'd ever been there his delicious scent all over the rumpled sheets.

According to Zinichi, Zepar had demanded I grace him with my presence at sunset.

I hated guys who demanded anything of me.

Maybe I'd tell him that.

Did I need his protection badly enough to kiss ass? I had Ignatius, Arty, Sev, Chase, and my siblings. We were a team. Zepar had power and influence, but he no longer had the same hold over me as when I'd first come here.

Yeah, I could tell him to kiss my ass if he pissed me off.

It had barely been a week, but so much had changed.

Too much.

Had Orina gotten my letter? Was Sin okay? The thought of the demon made my chest ache and longing spark in my belly. I touched my mouth lightly. That kiss.

Fuck.

That kiss.

The door opened and Sev ambled in. He froze at the sight of me and took a long moment to take me in.

His mouth parted softly, his eyes darkening. "Please tell me that's for me?"

I caught my bottom lip between my teeth and tipped my head to the side. "It can be, if you're very, very good."

"Oh, I'll be good, if only to be very, very bad later." He bridged the distance between us, hands going to my waist, head dipping so he could run the tip of his nose up the column of my neck. "You smell good." He brushed his lips against my pulse, teasing it into a canter. "I want to be inside you."

My core contracted in time to the flex of his fingers.

Tempting. So fucking tempting.

He parted his lips, dampening my skin with a flick of his tongue. I rewarded him with a moan and he sucked on my skin, fangs scraping my aching pulse.

"Sev... I can't. I have to—"

He cupped my ass and hauled me against his groin,

rolling against me, showing me how much he wanted me.

My breasts ached, nipples pebbling. "Fucking hell, you don't make it easy, do you?" I turned my head slightly and kissed his jaw. "Later. I promise."

He made a rough sound of exasperation, running his hands over my ass one last time before relinquishing his grip.

I pulled back, gaze dropping to his lips. "You can have me later, I promise. I have to go eat with Zepar now."

"If I was the jealous, possessive type..." His silver eyes blazed, trailing from my lips, down my neck, and then slowly skimming up to rest at the spot below my ear. "You have a beautiful neck."

Tristeene had insisted on putting my hair up for me. My hand went to my throat, and he tracked the movement.

"Don't fuck him," Sev said. "Save it for me."

I gave him a what-the-fuck look. "I don't plan on fucking him."

He pressed a kiss to the bare skin of my shoulder and ran his fingers down my exposed spine. The dress was pretty revealing, but in a sophisticated manner, leaving enough to the imagination to be decent.

"He is a fallen," Sev said. "They have a certain charisma, an allure that mortals cannot resist."

"I'm not just any mortal." I slid my hands into his silken hair, urging his head up so I could brush his nose with mine in an Eskimo kiss. His breath caught and mine stalled too as we both froze, so close, lips a mere inch apart.

"I don't think I've ever wanted to kiss someone as badly as I want to kiss you right now," he said.

It was a raw, vulnerable declaration that shook me enough to force me away from him.

"Hey, you're not getting all emotional on me, are you?" My voice quivered.

I expected, hoped that he'd come back with a quip, something dark and dirty. Something that would put us back on even footing, but he simply stared at me, his silver fathomless eyes drinking me in, speaking to me without words.

My pulse thudded hard in my throat, hands itching to claim him, mouth aching to—

"Go." He dropped his gaze with a wicked smile. "I'll be waiting when you get back. I'm beginning to get hungry, and this time, I think I'll have the full three courses."

My stomach flipped and I swallowed to moisten my mouth. "I won't be long."

As the final red rays of the dying sun winked out and the room fell into gloom, the doorway to the Ivory Court lit up, ready for me.

With a final look Sev's way, I made my way to the doorway and stepped through it without looking back, unable to shake the feeling that I was leaving something vital behind.

THE WORLD beyond the gateway was a lush green garden. The warm air smelled like summer. It swept over me, heady and intoxicating, curling around me and drawing me forward. The sky was a deep blue filled with fluffy cottonwool clouds. This garden was a blessed reprieve after the icy winter landscape of Morningstar and the sweltering, arid heat of the Court of Flame.

A zuni with short silver hair and kind cocoa eyes appeared beside me.

"The duke awaits." He bowed. "This way."

The zuni in Morningstar wore dark colors, but this one wore a crisp white tunic over dark leggings. I followed him onto a cobbled path, grateful for the ballet flats Zinichi had provided. Heels would have sucked on cobbles.

Tall clusters of blooms lined the path. I was no gardener and flowers weren't my thing, but they were pretty enough and probably what made the air smell so good.

I caught the sound of water and through a gap in the foliage spied a crystal waterfall gushing over a rocky hill and pooling into a brook below.

"What is this place?"

"The duke's retreat," the zuni said. "His personal haven."

Like the library was Ignatius's. Zepar had a garden with open skies so he could take to the air. Made sense.

The path widened and an ivory gazebo came into view. I spotted the fallen a moment later, lounging in a chair. The back must have been cut low to accommodate his ebony wings, which were visible today, tucked against his body but still impressively large. The feathers gleamed like burnished obsidian where the light touched them.

I wanted to touch them.

Would they be soft and smooth? Warm or cold? Or would they be tough like some kind of bastardized metal-feather combo?

He looked up from his cup as we approached. His tawny eyes, stunning against his tan face, locked on to me. He lowered his cup, a small smile tugging at his lips as he took me in.

The imp stopped at the gazebo steps and Zepar pushed back his chair and stood as I climbed up to join him.

His gaze continued to rake over me, assessing and appreciative. His smile widened. "I was right, that cut and color is perfect on you."

He pulled out a chair for me. The perfect gentleman.

I sat and he reclaimed his seat. "I'm glad you came," he said.

I arched a brow. "You mean I had a choice?"

His smile faltered and a sigh slipped from his lips. "Sometimes my requests can sound like demands."

I narrowed my eyes. "Excuse me? Was that an apology?"

He gave me a sheepish look. "It is no easy feat running a court. Being duke requires a certain...front."

I propped my elbows on the table and rested my chin on my laced fingers. "Are you saying you're not usually an imperious ass?"

His mouth twitched as he reached for the teapot to pour me some tea. "Take it as you wish. I hoped that if we met alone, away from prying ears and eyes, then maybe we could get to know one another a little better."

He passed me the cup of tea. "It's herbal. Refreshing before a meal."

I took it and sipped. It was sweet, almost tart, but not unpleasant.

"How was your trip to the Court of Flame?" he asked.

Ah, so that's what he wanted to talk about. "It was good." I sipped again, aware of his intense scrutiny as he waited for me to elaborate.

I wasn't planning on doing that. If he wanted more information, he'd have to ask for it.

"Just good?" he asked.

I flicked my gaze up to catch his. "Yes."

Was that a flash of exasperation in the depths of his leonine eyes? And why did it give me a thrill?

He recovered quickly and leaned back in his seat, lids at half mast, shielded. "Ignatius is known to be an absent host. Busy with court affairs. How did you pass the time?"

And now he was probing to find out how much time I'd spent with the duke. I shrugged. "Ignatius made time for me. Gave me a tour. It's a beautiful keep."

"I'm surprised he invited you."

He was fishing for more information. I wouldn't give it to him. But I wasn't going to lie either. "He didn't. I asked to visit."

His brows flicked up and he was silent for a long beat. "Maybe I haven't made my interest in you as blatant as he has."

I met his gaze. "Your interest in me as your custodia is perfectly clear."

"And Ignatius's interest?"

"What about it?"

"Is it simply the interest of a sponsor?"

The thought of Ignatius, of the warmth beneath his cool exterior, of the male beneath the duke's persona, made my skin heat. Ignatius's intelligence, his drive, his touch...The efreet was compelling in a way I didn't understand. He was under my skin, and I wasn't sure I was wholly opposed to that.

"Nyx?" Zepar prompted softly.

I smiled quickly. "Ignatius's interest is that of a sponsor and a friend."

"A friend..." He seemed to consider this. "And would you be open to a friendship with me?"

I sat back in my seat, noting the tension in his jaw, the preternatural stillness of his body as he waited for my response. In that moment there was something almost vulnerable about the tough, hard-as-nails fallen. It was almost as if he held his breath, waiting for my response. As if my answer *mattered* to him.

So I considered his question. Was I open to a friendship with him? He could be a killer. He could be in league with the killer. In league with the movement. He could be so many things. Artimus had advocated for my accepting Zepar's sponsorship but said he didn't know about fawda. I needed to be careful with these two. For now, until I had more information. And you know what they say: keep your friends close and your enemies closer.

"I never turn down the hand of friendship if it's genuine. If there are no ulterior motives." I gave him a hard look, one that warned him not to take the offer lightly.

The tension surrounding him melted. "I am always genuine, Nyx."

We'd see about that. "Even when you're being an ass?"

"Even then." He topped up my tea. "Let us toast to the beginning of a beautiful friendship."

We clinked cups and sipped.

Two imps appeared with trays of food, which they

arranged on the table. Delicious, enticing aromas filled the air. Cuts of meat, fresh rolls, tiny pastries, there was so much to choose from.

"I hope you're hungry," Zepar said. "This is simply the first course. Any friend of mine will need a ravenous appetite to keep up with me."

I didn't miss the double entendre there.

I grinned up at him. "Bring it."

CHAPTER THIRTY

"I think I'm about to explode." I patted my belly as we walked through the gardens.

The meal had gone on for five courses. Five courses of trays and trays of food, all delicious. Zepar loved his food, and he ate with an abandon that was contrary to his controlled nature.

I slid a glance his way, noting how relaxed his gait was. Even his wings seemed more relaxed, not as tightly tucked in. "I'm surprised you're not a blob."

He looked down at me with a smile. "The blessing of being fallen. We do not age physically, and we metabolize too fast to gain weight. Our bones aren't like most, they're lighter, but also stronger so that we may take flight." He looked up at the azure sky.

The sun was high despite the fact we'd been eating for hours. "Is time different here?"

"My garden is always daytime. But the moon is out above the clouds."

A wooden arch wound with ivy appeared on the path up ahead. Zepar slowed his pace. "Would you like to see?"

"The moon?"

"The Court of Ivory."

"Sure."

His smile lit up his face. I took the hand he offered, and he closed his fingers around mine, drawing me close and wrapping an arm around my waist to anchor me to him.

"Hold on to me." He let go of my fingers and slid his hand over my hip to rest at the small of my back. "You may need to pull your dress up and wrap your legs around my waist."

He said it coolly, as if it were a mundane request.

I arched a brow at him. "Was this your plan all along? Send me this impractical dress and then take me for a flight?"

His brows pinched slightly but a smile played on his lips. "That wouldn't be a very friendly thing to do, would it?"

I bit back a smile of my own. "Definitely outside the realm of friendly propriety."

He pressed me closer. "We don't have to fly if you don't want to."

I tipped my head to the side. "I'm no shrinking

violet, Zepar." I stepped back slightly and ruched up my skirt.

His sharp inhalation had my gaze whipping up to find him focused on my legs.

"Anyone would think you'd never seen a woman's naked legs before."

He blinked slowly before raising his gaze to mine. "Legs are one of my favorite parts of the female anatomy." He dropped his attention back to mine. "You have beautiful legs."

His tone was hushed, reverent almost. I'd never had someone compliment my legs before. Never really thought much about them, but I looked down at them now, toned, slightly more muscular than most women due to all the running and kicking ass, but, yeah, they were in nice shape.

"Thanks." I stepped closer. "Shall we do this?"

He nodded.

I wrapped my arms around his neck and hopped up, wrapping my legs around his waist. We were chest to chest, groin to groin, and fuck, this was way too intimate.

Our faces were so close that I could see silver striations in his tawny eyes, like fractures to another world.

His hands landed on the bare skin of my thighs like twin brands. He squeezed, his gaze locking with mine almost in challenge before he smoothed his palms upward, leaving goosebumps in their wake. He took his time, curving around the swell of my hips before settling on my ass as if he owned it.

My mouth went dry and my voice came out a little hoarse. "You're cupping my ass."

"All the better to brace you with. Unless... You're uncomfortable?"

He was challenging me. Pushing to see when I'd shrink away. He had no idea who he was dealing with.

I leaned in, challenging him back with my proximity. "You'll need to hold me tighter than that."

A flicker of surprise flashed in his eyes and then his grip tightened into a delicious squeeze that pushed a moan up my throat. I held it down with a thin smile. Yeah, this was not friend zone, but there was no denying it was fun.

"Don't let go." His tone was husky, breath warm as it mingled with mine, and the next moment we were shooting up into the air.

The world whizzed by, blue skies, fluffy clouds, then the blackness of night speckled with a kazillion stars. We hovered above the blanket of blue, and below that was Zepar's garden, trapped in mystical daytime.

We tipped away from it, flying in a direction I couldn't map for a few moments. He came to a stop, wings beating the air, once, twice. Lazily and easily, keeping us aloft. I turned my head, brushing his jaw with my cheek to view the Ivory Court from above.

A dark expanse of flora lay beneath us, a blanket of various shades of green kissed by night. Flat, rolling hills and teeny settlements and villages lay to the left. To the right, close enough for me to count the arched windows, were ivory towers, slicing up into the sky like silver teeth in an inky black mouth.

Walkways jutted off the towers, reaching into the night to connect it to the arched windows. I spotted winged figures looping around the towers and alighting on those walkways, wings snapping closed before they disappeared inside.

I looked up at him, pulling back slightly as I realized how close we were again. "Are all the occupants of this court fallen?"

"No. But most are. We have zuni here and a few imps to manage the keep. Devils and demons affiliated with the court live in the surrounding areas."

We dipped in the air, and my stomach dropped. He gripped me tighter, beating his wings to pull us higher again.

I couldn't help but tease. "Am I too heavy for you?"

His eyes darkened. "You are perfect."

My stomach dipped again, but this time for an altogether different reason.

His pupils dilated until only a sliver of tawny iris remained, and I could see my stunned reflection in the darkness threatening to devour me. I was suddenly acutely aware of all the places our bodies touched. The contact burned cold and hot at the same time, making my skin tighten in awareness.

When I spoke, my voice was a whisper that skated his lips. "I need to get back."

"Are you sure?"

Heck no. "Yes."

"A shame." His gaze dropped to my mouth. "I had hoped we could do some more *friendly* activities together."

The corner of my mouth tipped up in a smirk. "I'm curious to know what *friendly* activities you had in mind?"

His eyes glittered, a wicked gleam that spoke to my wicked little heart. "You'll just have to wait to find out."

He dropped without warning, and I cut off a yelp and pressed my cheek to his as he swooped with me clutched to his chest. I tightened my legs, gripping him hard with my thighs.

He exhaled softly, his chuckle vibrating through me. "I have you, Nyx. I won't let you fall."

The warm breeze brushed its fingers across my cheeks, raking through my hair, desperate to pull it from its pins. I tucked my chin in, mouth brushing the column of Zepar's throat. I lingered, allowing my lips to part, wondering what a fallen angel would taste like.

The vibration of his landing rippled through me, and I pulled away, chest heaving, to lock gazes with him once more.

"You'll come dine with me again." It wasn't a question.

"Yes."

ZEPAR WALKED me to the doorway back to my chambers in Morningstar. A strange tension I couldn't quite define had sprung up between us. He'd asked for friendship, but the moments we'd shared weren't the kind that friends shared. Still, I'd liked them. Too much.

"Are you sure about petitioning the princes?" He guided me along the path with a gentle hand to the small of my back.

I ignored the tingle it sent up my spine. "It's my only option."

He inclined his head, pillowy lips pressing together in thought. "I wish I could be there with you."

I slid a glance his way. "What's stopping you?"

His jaw ticked. "Prince Ramiel has not demanded my presence."

"So you can't go?"

His pout pressed into a thin line. "Correct."

Yeah, he didn't like being told what to do, even if a prince was doing the telling. Zepar liked to be the one in control. Heck, most of the males here shared that trait.

A stone arch with a wooden door built into it came into view at the bottom of the cobbled path. My way home.

"This is your stop," Zepar said. "I'll find you when

you return. Whatever the princes decide, we will have a trial to prepare for."

"Oh? I thought you couldn't help us prepare."

"There are loopholes and exceptions." He gave me a lopsided smile. "I make sure to know what they are." He reached out and tucked a tendril of my hair behind my ear, sending a pleasant shiver down my neck. "Until next time...*friend*."

Friends? What a load of bullshit. What a front. But I'd take it. I turned away with a knowing smile to mask my confusion over the attraction. The several attractions I'd found since coming here.

Before Loke there'd been a dry spell. Sex, yes, but not this simmering heat in the pit of my stomach kind of attraction. Not the yearning beneath my skin kind of pull.

Fallen and Nephalem, abyssbloods and efreet... They were fucking dangerous. I needed to get my shit under control, because I had a prince to charm and a contract to dissolve. A little fun was one thing, but my gut told me getting entangled with Zepar, Ignatius, or Artimus would be dangerous, not just to my body but to my heart.

CHAPTER THIRTY-ONE

Running away from Zepar, Ignatius, and Artimus was one thing, but there was no running away from Sev. Maybe it was the fact that we'd shared our deepest pain, dreamed together, slept curled up in each other's arms. Maybe it was because he was bound to me in a blood debt. Whatever the reason, I trusted him, mind and body, which made keeping him at arm's length impossible.

Not that I had much desire to do that.

As soon as I stepped into the bedroom, I knew tonight, with him, would be different.

He was awake, sitting in the dark, waiting for me.

I'd made him a promise, after all, but the way he was looking at me, as if he wanted to claim more than my body, spawned moths in my belly.

He rose and moved to stand in front of me, his aura a physical pressure against my exposed skin. That scent—cinnamon, leather, and moonlight—was pure pheromone, and it made my head swim with a thousand yeses.

Focus, woman. Fucking focus.

I searched his face, looking for familiar ground and finding only new terrain. Rocky slopes of longing that went beyond the physical.

"Sev..." I took a step back, but he matched it, maintaining the proximity between us. His eyes glittered like a challenge in the gloom. "What do you want?" The words came out hushed, like a secret. I needed him to be specific. To put his desire into words. To give it a name so that emotions could stay out of it. So that I could know I was mistaken. "Tell me what you need."

I expected him to say "to feed" or "to fuck." But instead he said, "You. I want you."

You. A small word could mean everything, too much, all the things I wasn't prepared to give.

"Sev." I turned away from him, conflict churning inside me. "I can't..."

He grabbed my shoulders and tugged me close. My head fell back, breath catching as his mouth found my throat, my earlobe, my pulse, throbbing, throbbing against his lips, melting into a gallop beneath the press of his fangs and the lap of his tongue.

Yes, this I could handle. This I could give him.

But he didn't take it. Didn't sink his fangs into me.

Instead, he kissed my flesh, sucking softly, moving upward across my jaw toward my mouth.

I needed to pull away. Turn away. Stop him. But I was frozen, heart in my mouth, as he inched his way toward my lips. My eyes fluttered closed, chest growing as tight as a drum. Could I do this? Fuck, I wanted it. I needed it.

His lips brushed mine and sipped at the moan that fell from them. I waited for the kiss, heart pounding so hard I thought it would shatter my ribcage.

It didn't come; instead, his hands cupped my face, thumbs sweeping across my chin, my jaw. Touching me, lightly, reverently.

"Look at me," he demanded.

I opened my eyes and drowned in his gaze. "Sev..."

"I have this feeling," he said. "It hurts. The sweetest pain in my chest. In my heart. This yearning for more. For everything I can take, and everything I can give. For you, Nyx. For you. Only for you."

Something inside me crumbled. A barrier, a dam, the wall that shielded my heart. There was a hole, a fucking hole, and this nightmare had found his way in.

"Fuck you, Sev." My words were a whisper. "Fuck you." I kissed him, claiming his mouth with the abandon I'd been holding back since meeting the fucker. That plump, delicious mouth of his, the lower lip fuller than the upper. I plucked at it, licking it, running my tongue along the inside of it before sucking on it hard enough to make him groan with pleasure and pain.

He didn't move, didn't try to grip me tighter, simply held me as I explored his mouth with mine, curling my tongue around his and drawing him into my mouth. I wanted to be closer. Deeper. I wanted him all.

SEV

Her hands are in my hair, nails raking my scalp hard enough to evoke delicious pain, but it's her mouth that I focus on. So fucking soft. Softer than I imagined yet hard and punishing as she devours me.

I'm afraid to move. To break this spell. Afraid that if I do, she'll withdraw and my heart will shatter.

This feeling.

This fucking feeling of fullness in my chest, of an expanding emotion unlike anything I've ever experienced. It's terrifying but I need it. I need it to last forever.

She breaks the kiss, her chest heaving, breasts pushing against my chest. "Fuck me, Sev. I want your cock inside me. Not your tail. Your fucking cock."

My groin is already tight, pouch straining as it attempts to contain my arousal. It fails now, and my cock breaks free, coated in my natural slick. Ready, balls aching with the need for release.

She grips me, sliding her hand up and down slowly, pressing her thumb to the tip on the rise.

I choke on a moan. "Fuck, Nyx. Fuck."

"I want to taste you."

She makes to sink to her knees, but I grip her hair, tangling my fingers in it and forcing her head back. "Not this time. I'm too close." I hate to admit it. Hate that I'm so weak in her presence.

"Then we go twice. As many times as it takes. All fucking night."

The shock of her words slackens my grip, and she drops to her knees and takes me into her mouth.

I can't think. I can't fucking think.

It isn't the first time I've had my cock sucked, but this is Nyx. This is the woman I—

She draws me so deep my eyes snap open and I look down at her, into her eyes, as she lets me fuck her throat.

My body is not my own. It belongs to her. Singing to her tune, to her command. It's a cold burn, a tight, twisted need, a beautiful pain lancing through my lower back straight to my—

I try to push her away but she holds tight, drawing me deeper, and I come with a guttural sob, hips jerking over and over as she digs her nails into my ass hard enough to draw blood.

NYX

He was mine. I'd claimed him. I wiped my mouth with the back of my hand and placed my palms on his chest, forcing him back onto the bed. I wasn't done with him. Not yet.

He fell onto the mattress, chest heaving, eyes glowing like pearls against his Aegean skin. His silver hair was stuck to his high cheekbones; perspiration beaded his top lip. I'd done that. I'd undone the nightmare and it felt good.

I looked down at his gorgeous cock, licking the salt from my lips. He'd tasted unreal, like salty caramel, and now he was spent but still hard.

He gripped himself, pumping slow. "More."

Just the one word. It was all I needed.

I tugged my dress up for the second time that night, but this time with a pulse-pounding purpose. My panties were soaked, stuck to my swollen flesh with need. I slipped them off, sucking in a breath as the cool air kissed my heated skin.

He looked down at my pussy, then touched his mouth. "Give it to me."

The thought of sitting on his face was tempting, but not tonight. "Tonight, my pussy needs cock."

I straddled him, the sensitive skin of my inner

thighs brushing the rough skin of his and heightening my arousal. I rose over him and lowered myself enough to rub against him.

His jaw tightened, eyes flashing. "You like to tease."

"I do. But not tonight."

I sank onto him, taking him as far as I could and then more. I was too full, straining, the sensation snug and edging on pain.

I fucking loved it.

I rocked, crying out as he hit that spot inside that was often missed. Not tonight, though. Not like this. I threw back my head and abandoned myself to the sensation of his body trapped beneath mine.

Mine.

Our moans mingled, becoming primal groans and growls as I began to ride him. He gripped my thighs, angling his hips up to meet me until there was nothing but sensation and sound and the scent of sex.

Chapter Thirty-Two

I watched Sev sleep. The harsh lines of his feral face were softer in sleep. The scars like silver strokes of a cruel artist's brush across his cheeks and forehead. I traced them lightly with my fingertips, knowing he wouldn't stir. It was mid-morning and he was deep in slumber, his body sated, and confident that it was safe.

So, yeah, I touched his scars and brushed my lips over each one because I could. Because I wanted to. Because he was mine to protect, to hold close, and to...I closed my eyes and lay back on the bed beside him.

I'd stepped onto a rollercoaster when jumping into the arena to save Sev. An emotional rollercoaster that had led me here, to this moment, and last night I'd shown him how much he meant to me with my body. With my mouth on his. With a kiss I'd instigated. A kiss willingly and freely given.

I'd held up the walls around my heart for so long, against Loke, against Sin, and then this nightmare, this dark, dangerous, twisted nightmare, had burrowed a hole in that wall. Being here, with him, with my siblings, with the males who challenged me at every turn, was changing me. It terrified me because there was no going back. Resistance wouldn't stop the change, it wouldn't reverse the effects, all it would do was buy me time to accept it, to embrace it and to hope...to hope that it wouldn't bring me pain.

I turned onto my side and traced Sev's profile with my gaze, silently mouthing the three words I wasn't ready to say yet. The fullness in my heart expanded and I sucked in a breath, releasing it slowly.

Sev sighed softly, the corner of his mouth lifting in a sleepy smile as if he'd heard me.

I slipped from the bed and into the washroom. There were only a few days before the trip to the demon realm. I should focus on that. The heart stuff, the changes, everything else would wait.

It had to.

Sev was on his front when I came out of the shower, his lithe body stretched out to take up most of the bed. Errant rays of sunlight filtered in through the gap in the drapes to lay across his skin like questing fingers, highlighting the twin dips in the small of his back and the long, powerful muscles of his flanks.

He was beautiful.

I plucked the sheets from the rumpled mess at the bottom of the bed and drew one up over his pert ass. I couldn't have some rando coming into my room and ogling what belonged to me.

I dressed quickly in black leggings, a thigh-length, long-sleeve navy knitted top, and my boots. I picked up my usual dagger, then changed my mind and switched it for the strange silver one that Ignatius had given me. I'd liked the way it cut, effortless, like a hot blade through butter. It was perfect.

I tucked it into the specially designed sheath in my boot and pulled my damp hair into a knot at the base of my neck before stepping up to my ugly ornate mirror. Loke's advice had helped me save Veena. Now that she was free and the shiqq was dead, I felt comfortable sharing the whole truth with him, plus it was an excuse to see him.

And I desperately wanted to see him.

I touched the mirror and said his name.

THE BEDROOM WAS EMPTY, but I could hear voices. I crossed to the door, which was slightly ajar, recognizing Loke and someone else. A female.

"No, I haven't seen her," Loke said. "I would know."

"Would you? She has many faces."

"And all those faces would harbor the same soul. I know what I'm doing."

The female voice dropped to a murmur, making it hard for me to catch what she was saying.

I stepped closer to the door, desperate to hear better.

"Surely that would be interfering," Loke said.

"It's called following orders," the woman snapped. "Do you understand?"

"Yes." He sounded weary.

The woman's voice dropped to an inaudible murmur again.

"No," Loke said. "I know the boundaries." His tone was tight.

Bootfalls headed my way. Shit. I backed up to the mirror and then acted as if I was stepping out just as the door opened and Loke entered. I glanced over his shoulder, expecting to see someone with him, but he was alone.

Where had the woman gone? Was she still out there?

His eyes flared in surprise at the sight of me and then narrowed slightly, flicking from me to the mirror then down to his hand, which clutched a pink crystal.

"Hey." I canted my head. "I hope it's okay that I came to see you."

His shoulders relaxed. "You can come see me anytime." He crossed to his bedside table, pulled open the drawer, and dropped the crystal inside it.

"Are you sure?" I arched a brow. "You weren't busy?"

He sighed. "What did you hear?"

I couldn't be bothered to lie to him and play games. Not with Loke. "I heard you talking to a woman. But I couldn't catch everything she said. Who was she?"

"Let's take this conversation into the lounge."

I followed him through the door into a neat lounge area with a huddle of sofas and a hearth dominated by its very own crackling fire.

"Take a seat, Nyx."

I parked my ass on a two-seater and he took the armchair opposite me. "I was speaking to the source."

Ah, that made sense. "Through that crystal thing?"

"Yes."

"What did she want?"

"To check up on me. To make sure I was doing my job."

"To make sure the trials are going well and the contracts are being adhered to?"

He pressed his lips together. "Yes."

"And you told her about my plan."

"I did."

"How'd she take that?"

"I have no idea. She never gives anything away and her rules on interfering in anyone's destiny are clear."

I cast my mind back to the conversation I'd overheard. "Unless it comes to a woman with many faces?"

He tensed. "I can't talk to you about that."

"Or about what my destiny is."

He sighed again. "I don't know the full details of your destiny, Nyx. But even if I did, I couldn't tell you."

"Couldn't or wouldn't?"

The light in his dark eyes dipped and the corners of his mouth turned down. "Couldn't."

"She has a gag on you?"

He looked down at his lap. "It is what it is."

"What are you, Loke. What are you really?" That same smile, a shake of the head. "You can't say."

"Don't worry about me, Nyx. You have your own life to focus on. Your path won't be easy."

"Tell me about it."

"No, *you* tell me. What happened with your murderous sibling?"

"Wait, I didn't tell you the murderer was a sibling."

"Not a hard conclusion to draw," Loke said. "Who else would you be so desperate to protect?"

I locked gazes with him. "Veena."

His brows shot up and then he smiled, his eyes lighting up. "The zuni?"

"Don't look so happy about it."

He shook his head slightly. "I'm not happy about that. Just pleased that you confided in me."

"I should have told you before. I'm not sure why I didn't."

"You don't owe me anything."

"Maybe not, but I feel like I do. I know I can trust you, I just needed to square things with Veena first."

"And?"

"Well, things turned out to be a little more complicated than I'd thought."

I filled him in on the shiqq and my trip to the Court of Flame, the desert attack, the poisoning, and the shiqq's death.

"All we know is that there is a force gathering that wants Satan's seat."

His brows came down. "I'll need to inform the source of this. A threat to the seat is a threat to Tarrifel."

"Oh? How so?"

He pressed his lips together in a smirk. "Nice try. But even if I wanted to tell you, I—"

"Can't, I get it."

I was also beginning to understand how much of a prisoner Loke was. How much of a lackey, a pawn. It pissed me off.

"I wish I could speak to the source. Say hi, you know, introduce myself? And ask her why she's such a controlling bi—"

"Don't ever wish that." He'd gone pale.

"Why not?"

"Because if you get your wish, it'll mean you're dead."

Silence settled between us for long seconds. Loke

was the first to break it. "I wish I could come to the demon realm with you."

I didn't bother asking him why not. The answer was obvious. "I'll be fine. I have Artimus, and Ignatius is sending Hrath, his right-hand man, with me."

Loke's brows flicked up. "Oh. You must have made quite an impression on him." Was that a flash of jealousy in his eyes?

I was tempted to tease that jealous spark into a flame but what was the point of rubbing the attraction between Ignatius and me in his face? Loke could never act on his attraction to me, so I'd only be hurting him.

"Ignatius was a gracious host." I smiled. "But Hrath and Artimus won't be the only ones with me. My siblings are coming too. It's safest if we stick together."

"A united front." He echoed Artimus's words. "And what does the seneschal think of this plan?"

"He's on board."

"When do you leave?"

"A couple of days." My stomach fluttered at the thought. "Got any advice?"

"Yes. Be wary. Do not trust anyone aside from those who have already earned your trust, and please try to keep your temper in check."

I frowned. "I do not have a temper."

His brows shot up. "Excuse me?"

I exhaled heavily. "Fine."

"The princes won't take kindly to insubordination. They demand and they expect respect and subservience. Play the game, Nyx, and you might come away with what you ask for."

Oh, I'd play the game all right, and I'd be playing it to win. There was no other option because the cost of failure was too high.

Chapter Thirty-Three

IGNATIUS

The sand sled moves too slow for my liking. The karrak pulling it are too slow. Why are they so slow?

"Your agitation is infectious," Hrath says from the bench opposite mine. "I can fly ahead and find whomever you're searching for if you wish."

I suppose it would be a relief for him to exit the confines of the sled and fly. It is cramped for the two of us in here, and I'm regretting my decision not to take two sleds.

But what is done is done. "No. She might bolt, but with two of us there we can corner her." I can't let Hrath alert her that I'm coming.

"Who is this female you're looking for?"

"A stall owner who gave me the package for Nyx."

He stares at me blankly, waiting for me to elaborate.

I sigh and roll my eyes his way. "The package contained a flimorian dagger."

His left brow twitches, the only sign that he's perturbed. "I assumed that you provided her with that."

"I did not."

I allow that to sink in and watch as he absorbs the information and forms a conclusion. Flimorian is an extremely rare element from our old world. One that does not exist in this one. As far as I'm aware, I'm the only efreet to possess any weapons made of the element.

Hrath's gaze mists in a manner that tells me he is mulling this over. When he speaks, his voice is hushed. "Any element that does not exist in this world would be considered priceless in the right hands. Any efreet who owned such a piece would not part with it easily, and yet a stall owner gives one away to a Nephilim she does not know." He presses his lips together. "A Nephilim who, as it turns out, happens to be—"

"I know."

"I am intrigued," he says.

My smile is mirthless. "As am I."

Efreet can heal, given time. They can grow new parts if the old are removed, but not if a flimorian blade is used. In the old world, the highest nobility carried such blades, procuring the metal to forge weapons for their elite guards and torturers.

Now Nyx has such a blade. Gifted to her by a... nobody? No, this woman is someone, and I'm determined to discover who.

Hrath leans forward to peer out of his window. "We are here."

The carriage draws to a halt.

It is not yet late afternoon. The sun is still high enough to set the sands ablaze and the air is hot as it filters in and out of my lungs. I revel in the heat, allowing it to become one with the hidden fire inside me.

As a sylph, Hrath does not benefit from the same resilience to the heat as I, and so he wraps a white shawl around his head and shoulders before stepping out of the carriage to join me. The karrak allow their legs to fold and fall to the hot sand, chests heaving.

Hrath calls out to a passerby, instructing him to provide the beasts with water before following me into the market.

With the twin flame ceremony over, the market isn't as busy. The night will bring more shoppers, but for now, the market stalls are simply setting up, preparing for the sun to dip and the trickle of buyers from the nearby settlements to arrive.

The air is slightly fresher here, and I can smell the water from the nearby oasis, where the closest settlement rests.

Djinn and demons either bow or hide as I pass, and for some reason the latter reaction bothers me. Nyx's words are vultures in my mind, picking away at my conviction. Her assertion that to rule through fear is wrong bites at me.

A man ducks into his stall as I pass, and I find myself veering toward him. "You. Wait."

The snap in my tone draws him to a halt. His back straightens rodlike, and his hands are starfish at his sides. It's almost comical but then he begins to tremble.

A knot forms in my stomach. I gentle my tone when I speak next. "Turn around."

He obliges, keeping his head down, his gaze averted. "Your Grace..." His voice is a whisper. He clears his throat and says a little louder, "Your Grace, how may I serve?"

I want to ask him why he is afraid of me. To ask what I have done that could possibly make him tremble so, but the questions are pointless as I already know the answers.

I have ruled with an iron fist. Black and white with no gray in between. I have kept order, believing that in doing so I preserve my people, but...this...this terror... Why save them if it is only for them to live in terror?

"Do not be afraid. I merely wished to offer you a good day."

The djinn, one with an affinity to the earth if the markings swirling under his skin are any indication, looks up at me in surprise. He masks it quickly, though, and I find my lips aching to smile.

I allow them to do so and the man's eyes widen in shock? Horror? I'm not entirely sure.

"You might wish to rein it in a little," Hrath says from beside me. "You look positively feral."

I shoot him a lethal glance and the man whimpers.

"Not you." I hold out a hand and then soften my smile. "You may go about your business and have a good evening."

The man bobs his head and hurries away.

My shoulders heave. "They're terrified of me."

"And that suddenly bothers you."

It's not a question but I reply anyway. "Yes."

I can hear the smile in his voice. "She is changing you already."

"I know." I take a deep breath. "And she should be with me to see it."

"I will keep her safe, Ignatius. I swear it to you."

"I believe you. Now let's find the female we came here for."

I spot the stall easily. The colorful scarfs fluttering in the breeze make it stand out from the rest like a beacon.

I pick up my feet, moving faster until I'm standing

by the shade of an awning that is too low for my lofty frame.

Hrath ducks inside, taking the lead automatically. My guard, my brother, my protector since we were younglings.

He emerges a moment later with a look of surprise on his forbidding face. I do not often see that look on my friend's face and yet I have seen it twice in as many days now.

"What is it?"

"I believe she is expecting you," he says.

I'd expected her to run but I'd been wrong. Her plan is now clear to me. The dagger was for Nyx, but it was also a message for me. I nod and duck into the space beyond the stall.

Hrath follows like a lethal shadow.

The space inside is larger than it looks with enough headroom to stand tall while leaving more space between the top of my head and the ceiling. There is magic here, an old allure that my bones recognize.

The room is gloomy, strewn with colorful fabrics that wrestle with the shadows attempting to smother their vibrant hues. The scent of incense burns strongly in my nostrils and nostalgia squeezes my chest in its powerful fist.

The old woman sits in a chair behind a wooden table. A larger chair has been placed opposite her. A space for me. The spot is illuminated by warm amber light that has no visible origin, almost as if...as if it's emanating from the woman herself.

"You took your time," she says.

Her voice is young and melodious. At odds with her elderly visage.

I need to know now, more than ever. "Who are you?"

She smiles, paper-thin lips stretching across the bones of her teeth. "Sit, *Amir.*"

Hrath hisses, a sound that is sibilant and terrifying.

I hold up my hand, ignoring the thundering of my heart. "You speak a title long forgotten and long lost. Who. Are. You?"

"An ally should you wish. I believe I have demonstrated that. Now, if you will sit, I will tell you all that I can. Nothing more and nothing less."

I take a step toward her, but Hrath halts me with a hand to my arm. He rounds the table and comes to stand behind the woman. Hovering over her, his presence a blatant threat should she try...anything. She doesn't flinch, merely smiles once more.

We are no fools. We know that death can come in many guises and this outwardly frail female is not what she seems.

I take the seat and watch her warily as she picks up a pack of cards and shuffles them.

"Some believe that the future is written," she says. "That fate cannot be averted and that only the path to your destiny can be altered, never the destiny itself."

"I have heard such things."

"Do you believe?"

"I'm not sure what I believe."

"I believed it at one time." She looks away as if recalling that time. "I believed it so vehemently that I was willing to die for it. But I soon learned the truth. That fate is cruel, and destiny is her bitch."

I flinch at the profanity falling from her lips.

She smirks, her piercing green eyes lighting up. "*I say that our fate should be determined by our actions. Our path forged by our will. I say that destiny should be free to thwart fate. To evolve and grow.*"

"What has this got to do with the dagger you gave Nyx?"

She shrugs one shoulder. "A tool to cut the ties that bind."

I think I see now. "Nyx has a destiny."

Her smile widens. "And you are now tied to it." The smile falls and her eyes go dark. "She also has a fate."

A shiver races up my spine because I see death in that look. "No..."

"Like I said, I do not believe that fate is ironclad, and neither should you, because if we truly allow that to be true, then I'm afraid we are all doomed."

My heart is beating too fast, and yet my pulse is sluggish. "What should I do?"

"When the time is right, you must follow your heart."

I open my mouth to ask her more. To ask who she

is and where she got the dagger, but she vanishes into thin air, leaving not even a whisper of her presence. The amber light dims and I lift my gaze to Hrath's as turmoil churns in my chest.

"I must be with her."

"You cannot go to the demon realm unless summoned," Hrath reminds me. "Do not fear, I will keep her safe. I swear it."

I believe him, but it's not his place to take on such a responsibility. It's mine. "You'll go, and you'll make sure I receive a summons."

Hrath's chin dips. "As you wish."

CHAPTER THIRTY-FOUR

NYX

I stood on the balcony of my room wrapped in a fluffy robe, watching the sun rise higher above the glittering, snowy landscape. A message had arrived from Artimus about half an hour ago, telling us to be ready and waiting for him at midday. I'd sent my own message to Hrath via zuni as soon as I'd received it.

The djinn had been in touch, checking in to find out when we'd be departing. Ignatius was making good on his promise of protection.

I felt Sev step onto the balcony behind me and leaned into his touch as he wrapped his arms around my waist, pulling me to his chest.

I rested my head on his shoulder and closed my

eyes, inhaling his scent. "Will you miss me when I'm gone?"

His grip tightened and his voice was a low growl as it teased the delicate shell of my ear. "I should be with you."

I wanted him with me too, but Artimus had explained that taking Sev could aggravate the princes. Nightmares weren't meant to be free, and even though Sev wasn't technically free as he was bound to me in a blood debt, seeing one walking freely could be a trigger that might lead to Sev being taken from me.

I couldn't risk losing him. "I won't risk your life by taking you."

He made a sound of exasperation but didn't argue. We'd already argued enough and there was only a handful of hours before it was time for me to leave and head to the demon realm. Neither of us wanted to waste that time.

"I don't understand why they'd keep nightmares locked away. You're sentient, skilled beings but Umbrane treats you like cattle."

"Fear," Sev said.

"Fears of an uprising?"

"He fears the truth."

I turned in his arms to face him. "What do you mean?"

He smiled and ran his fingers down my cheek. "The Duke of Flame told you the truth of the Chaos War and the daimons."

"Yes, I told you what he said. Did *you* know the truth?"

He smiled wryly. "Yes, I knew. But there's more. The duke left out a vital part of the true history. The part that the nightmares played."

"Tell me."

"The daimon queen had a royal guard made up entirely of nightmares."

I stared at him in surprise. "Nightmares served the daimon queen?"

"Yes. But we weren't called nightmares then. That name was given to us much later. We were called maras, a breed of morpheses, creatures able to dive into dreams. Some maras acted as muses for other daimons, entering dreams to provide inspiration; others, like the baku, were employed to devour bad dreams; and then there were the marasguard, warriors in a stealth faction that served the crown. We were trained in manipulating the shadows, in entering enemies' minds for psychological warfare so they could be easily taken down by the second battalion of powerful warriors commanded by General Dhuma, one of the daimon queen's mates."

"Why didn't you tell me this before?"

"It didn't seem important."

"And it does now?"

"Now you're going to the demon realm. Knowledge will keep you safe. You can't trust the princes and their lies. All they care about is appearances. They took the marasguard and twisted us into these...nightmares. People fear us, look at us in disgust, and our history is forgotten."

My lip curled in disgust. "They want to rewrite history and come out looking like the champions."

His smile was one of shadows and sadness. "People will believe what the majority tell them, and the princes have done a good job of spreading their lies, of hiding the part the abyssbloods and daimons played in the Chaos War, of hiding the truth of what we fought against."

His people were warriors, fighters. It made sense. It fucking made sense, and now he was a prisoner. I had to do something to change this. To free them and let the truth come out. We, the Satan spawn, had to do something, and we would.

We fucking would.

I cupped his face and drew him down for a kiss, a soft pluck of lips that was meant to be brief, but we lingered, and that soft kiss became two, then three, deepening into something that would lead to more.

I wasn't going to see him for a few days. I wouldn't get to touch him, kiss him, taste him, hear his sexy voice for goodness knew how many hours.

I pulled back and grabbed his hand. "Let's go back to bed."

WE GATHERED IN THE HALLWAY, dressed in outfits provided by Zinichi. Black and silver, the Morningstar colors. The females wore leggings and boots with sturdy, flat soles. We had black shirts and silver belts with dress jackets lined with silver furs to go over the top. The males had something similar, and we all had fur-lined cloaks with deep hoods to go over the top of our ensembles.

We looked like a mini army waiting for our first mission. Even Gus and Veena, the smallest of us, looked fierce. A silver chain hung around Gus's neck, pendant tucked beneath his shirt. The chain stood out because he didn't usually wear jewelry. Veena had her hair pulled back and braided. She'd even applied a little kohl to her eyes. She looked badass.

I glanced over at Mallini, standing between Keelan and Gus. She was still pale, but her eyes were bright and alert. She looked my way and the corner of her mouth tipped in an almost smile.

I returned it with a nod.

Nerves were tense. None of us had ever visited the demon realms; well, aside from Keelan, who'd been there as a child. The rest of my siblings had been raised in the courts or here in Morningstar. We were headed into the unknown.

"How much longer do we have to wait?" Tristeene asked. "The message said we'd be picked up at midday."

It was almost twenty past now and my gut was

squirrelly. Artimus wasn't the kind of creature to be late to anything. Not without a valid reason.

"The seneschal will be here," Nugen said. He glanced at the door where two Minorax stood guard.

I flicked my gaze to Sev, communicating my unease with one look. He pushed off the door jamb of our room and sauntered over to the Minorax. I expected the guards to block him, to sneer at him or look down on him, but they stepped aside to let him pass. He ducked through the door and out into the hallway beyond, returning a moment later with a frown that echoed my disquiet.

I stepped forward. "What is it?"

"Something's wrong." Sev looked over his shoulder. "There are Erinyes headed this way."

The door burst open a moment later and Erinea strode in flanked by two of her Erinyes. Mallini made a low, feral growl that had the hairs on the back of my neck quivering to attention.

The Minorax exchanged confused glances. Okay, so this wasn't part of the plan. Erinea's visit wasn't meant to be happening.

Sev was still by the doors, partially hidden by the Minorax's bulk, unnoticed by the Erinyes. I caught his eye with an urgent glance. He nodded, then slipped unseen from the room.

Nugen moved to stand between the Erinyes and us. "What is this, Erinea?" he demanded. "Where is the seneschal?"

"You will address me by my title, Weapons Master, or you will not address me at all," Erinea snapped.

Nugen's jaw tightened, and his dark eyes flashed. "Oh, there are many titles that I would wish to address you with. Which one is it that you refer to?"

Her jaw ticked. "Do not test me, faun. I will not hesitate to have you locked away."

"On what charge?" Nugen challenged. "Lack of appropriate groveling?"

Oh...I liked the weapons master even more now.

"The spawn are in my charge," he continued. "So I ask you again, what is the meaning of this?"

She smiled thinly. "*This* is an intervention. I understood that the Nephilim wished to petition the princes and I was agreeable to that. To *one* spawn leaving the keep to attend the conclave, but this...all of you? No. This will not stand. I will *not* allow it."

"You can't stop us," Tristeene said. "The seneschal agreed to us accompanying him."

"Without my approval."

"We don't need your approval." I took a step to stand beside Nugen. "And I think you're forgetting your place. You're speaking to Satan spawn, and one of us will be on that throne soon enough. *You'll* be working for *us*. Doing *our* bidding."

Her eyes narrowed. "One day, yes. But that day is not today. And it may never come if you all get yourselves killed."

"Killed?" Mallini scoffed. "What the fuck do you care whether we live or die?"

Erinea flinched and slowly transferred her icy gaze to her daughter. "You speak out of turn, daughter."

"Don't," Mallini snapped. "You don't get to call me daughter. You lost your daughter when you lost your son. And you better hope to the earth and stars that I don't get that seat, because my first act as Satan will be to demand your head on a silver platter."

Wow, well...just wow.

The room fell into utter, absolute silence, and yep, Erinea went pale with that threat.

The bitch recovered super quick. "If that day comes, I will gladly place my neck on the executioner's block to serve my Satan."

I snorted. "You're full of bullshit."

She arched a brow at me. "Excuse me?"

I leaned in and enunciated. "You're. Full. Of. Bullshit. And we all know it. Where is Artimus? He doesn't know you're here, does he?"

Her lips thinned. "No, he doesn't. And by the time he finds out, it will be too late for him to do anything about it."

Keelan stepped forward. "You think you and three Erinyes can stop us?" His muscles flexed. "I'd like to see you try."

The Minorax by the door made grumbling noises and stood taller. I looked across at them in alarm, but they had their eyes on Keelan not in challenge but almost in reverence, as if they were waiting for his command. As if they were ready to follow his lead.

The Erinyes with Erinea glanced nervously at the door, but the plumed bitch was unfazed.

She lifted a cool gaze to meet Keelan's. "Oh, I don't have to *try* and stop you. I already have."

My pulse quickened, a feeling of dread pooling in my belly.

"What do you mean?" Gus asked.

Sev burst into the entranceway, chest heaving. "You have to go. You have to go now."

"What is it? What's happened?" Tristeene demanded.

"The port to the demon realm can only be opened from the demon realm side. It was opened today to allow Artimus through. It closes in less than half an hour."

I stared at Erinea, a horrible realization seeping into my mind. "Where is Artimus?"

She smirked smugly. "Probably making his way through the port if he has any sense. You were all meant to meet him there."

"But the message..." Veena looked confused.

"She sent it." My hands curled into fists as I faced Erinea. "You sent us the message to wait here, didn't you. You switched it with the one Artimus sent."

She shrugged a slender shoulder. "I did what needed to be done. The seneschal must attend to represent Morningstar, but you will all remain here where it is safe."

"Safe?" Mallini screeched. "How the fuck is it safe with the contracts active?"

Veena wrapped her arms around her sister's waist, making soft sounds to soothe her. Mallini's eyes were black, her body trembling. "You've doomed us. You've fucking doomed another one of us to die, you stupid fucking bi—"

"Is there another way to get into the demon realm?" I looked to Tristeene.

She shook her head. "Only by port or by a direct summons from a prince."

I wanted to smack the smug look off Erinea's stupid face. Instead, I finished Mallini's sentence. "Mallini's right. You're a bitch, Erinea."

My bedroom door opened and a large figure stepped through, bringing the scent of sunshine and deserts with him.

Hrath looked down his nose at us. "Apologies for being late."

Fuck, in all the commotion, I'd almost forgotten about him. But he was here, and damn if his presence didn't give me a stellar idea.

"Nyx?" Veena asked. "Why do you have that strange look on your face."

"This, sweet Veena, is my *idea* face." I canted my head and peered up at the sylph. "Hrath, how many people can you carry when you fly?"

Chapter Thirty-Five

ARTIMUS

Ten minutes left until the portal access closes. This is my fault. My fault that Nyx and the spawn aren't here. I should never have agreed to run a last-minute errand for Erinea, forcing me to allow Cerinea to arrange the spawn travel.

But Erinea had insisted with a smile and a touch, wanting my help and wanting to help me in turn. To show she was onboard with my decision.

It's obvious I've been duped.

My message to the spawn was probably switched, giving them a later meeting time. One that will be too late.

I've been a fool to trust Erinea with this. Arrogance is a dangerous thing.

The bitch has played me and there is no time to go back to get them. My duty, first and foremost, is to Morningstar.

I have no choice but to leave.

The equinex tethered to the carriage paw at the ground, sensing that time is almost up. I climb out and look up the dusty, winding road that leads to the keep, miles away.

Damn my short-sightedness. Damn me for trusting that she was agreeable to all the spawn coming with me.

She'd faked her assent well last night, writhing and moaning and agreeing to whatever I asked of her.

The light of day must have brought her senses back, and with me gone, with my allure miles away, she was able to thwart me.

Five minutes.

I can feel the energy around the port waning. I need to leave. Now.

"I'm sorry, Nyx."

I make to turn away when something in the air catches my eye. A shimmer that grows larger, closer. What is that?

I back away as it comes hurtling toward me. It's a mini tornado of air. It lands several meters away and the scent of sea and storms assault my senses. A gust of wind hits me hard, tearing at my hair and my clothes with icy fingers. I grab at the carriage as the equinex screech in confusion.

The wind drops as suddenly as it rose, and in a blink the swirling vortex is gone. In its place stands a large male with dark hair, bronze skin, and eyes like an abyss. Clutched to his side like a precious prize is the woman who haunts my dreams.

Nyx.

She's here.

But she isn't the only creature clinging to the male. The other spawn are attached to him also, holding on to him in some manner. The Minorax clings to his back, with Erinea's daughter latched onto him. The zuni is wrapped around the large male's leg, the succubus is pressed to his other side, and the imp perches on his shoulder like a grotesque bird of prey.

Nyx grins and steps away from the male and I realize who he must be.

A sylph.

This is Hrath, Ignatius's right hand.

I have so many questions, but there is no time. "Hurry, get in the carriage."

We have minutes, if that, before the portal closes.

Everyone piles in without a word, squeezing into a space made for five at the most. I pull Nyx onto my lap and wrap one arm around her, willing my cock to behave.

There's barely room to breathe, but as the carriage lurches forward toward the port, I find myself inhaling her scent deep into my lungs.

She made it.

And she's with me.
Mine for the next few days.

Chapter Thirty-Six

NYX

The world blurred and tipped, evoking the same kind of sensation as being teleported, but Artimus's arm around my waist was an anchor holding me in place and centering me. I focused on that pressure, solid and real, and closed my eyes as we made the dive through the port into the demon realm beyond.

Part of me wanted to see how the obsidian pillar etched with runes would pull us through to another realm. Was it activated on contact? Did a tear open in this world for us to drive through? But another part of me didn't care, just wanting this to be over, grateful we'd made it.

We'd come close to missing out because of the bitch Erinea, but with Hrath present she'd backed off.

Hrath was Ignatius's eyes and ears, the duke's confidant, and fucking with us while he was there was a no-no, even for her.

Thank fuck Artimus hadn't told her the djinn was coming with us. She'd probably have found a way to delay him or sent a contradictory message to him too. Thank goodness Hrath had arrived in time to sweep us all off our feet and to the port on time.

Now, as the world righted itself and the carriage and its occupants came back into focus, my gaze tripped to the djinn, noting how pale he'd gone.

I leaned forward slightly in Artimus's lap and his grip on me tightened. "Hrath, are you okay?"

Hrath nodded. "I will be fine."

God, did all the males from this world have a stiff-upper-lip problem? "But you're not fine now. You just flew us all for miles. What can we do to help you recover?"

He shook his head slightly. "I will be recovered soon enough."

"He needs willing breath," Gus said.

Hrath's gaze zeroed in on my impish sibling and his brows pinched in a frown.

Gus didn't look away, his stunning blue eyes locking with Hrath's firmly. "Don't deny it. I know these things."

I bit back a smile, pride swelling in my chest at Gus owning his intelligence.

"Time will do just as well," Hrath retorted.

"And how much time will it take?" Artimus asked.

"Several hours," Gus replied for Hrath. "Maybe a day."

Hrath made a sound of exasperation. "I am able to speak for myself."

"I'm afraid we don't have that kind of time." Artimus sounded strained.

I twisted to look down at him, but he had his gaze fixed on the view out the window. I tracked it to the gloomy, dark forest surrounding us.

A shiver ran up my arms. "Artimus, where are we?"

"Somewhere we shouldn't be."

The carriage rocked as Gus climbed over Keelan to get a look outside. "Oh...Oh dear..."

"Where are we?" Mallini echoed my question.

"Are we in the old forest?" Gus asked.

"I believe so," Artimus said. "Something must have gone awry during the transit."

I ducked my head to peer out the window, straining my eyes to see into the thicket beyond the edge of the trail we were on. The beasts pulling the carriage were ominously silent.

My pulse quickened in warning. "Does this... getting dumped in the wrong place, happen often?"

"No." He pressed his lips together. "It does not."

"Deliberate sabotage," Hrath said.

"Most likely," Artimus said, and he and the djinn locked gazes.

"Wow, someone wants us dead. Great."

"Yes, but how many people knew all of us were coming?" Gus pointed out.

They didn't. I looked down at Artimus. "Maybe this isn't about us...maybe it's about you?"

His nostrils flared. "I wouldn't be surprised. But whoever has done this has put the fate of our realm in jeopardy by putting all your lives at risk."

Okay, so we were definitely in danger. "How much danger are we in? Is it the kind we can fight our way out of?"

"No," Hrath and Artimus said at the same time.

"Fuck," Gus whispered. "Isn't this place haunted? Filled with dybbuk and all sorts of ancient nasty things?"

"You're the only one who can get assistance for us," Artimus said to Hrath. "Take the willing breath."

"What do we need to do?" Mallini asked. "What is willing breath?"

Hrath opened his mouth to reply but Gus beat him to it, sitting forward eagerly on Keelan's lap, eyes bright as he recited the facts.

"Djinn can metabolize the carbon dioxide other creatures produce and convert it to energy. Willing breath involves someone exhaling into their mouth."

Hrath frowned down at the imp. "Hmmm." His lip curled slightly.

Gus grinned up at him. "Am I right?"

Hrath responded by looking out the window.

There was more to this. "Hrath, what is it? Why don't you want to take the willing breath?"

He made a low sound in his throat. "Willing breath is not an everyday practice but an ancient one between a warrior and his mate. An act to invigorate the male before battle." His throat bobbed. "It is considered...intimate."

"Oh..." Gus blinked in surprise. "The books don't tell us that."

"Your books and knowledge of my kind are filled with holes."

Gus pressed his lips together. "Then maybe you'd like to patch them up." His eyes lit up. "You can teach me about your people."

"We don't have time for this," Artimus said. "Hrath, can you take willing breath from one of us? I understand it's not a usual request, but—"

"I will do it." His gaze fell to me. He nodded curtly. "I will do it because we have little other choice."

Now, the question was, who would do this intimate act with him?

Artimus's grip on me flexed in warning. He didn't want me offering. I was about to offer regardless but Tristeene beat me to it.

"I'll do it," she said with a smile. "I'd be happy to."

Hrath's gaze dropped to her, squashed up against the window beside him. His eyes darkened. "I would prefer not."

Tristeene flinched as if he'd slapped her. "Excuse me?" Her dark eyes flashed.

He pressed his lips together and looked away, but not before I caught the bob of his throat.

Shit...He found her attractive. He didn't want to be close to her because of it.

Fuck it. "I'll do it."

Artimus's chest rumbled, a warning sound of displeasure that had gooseflesh pricking my arms.

Hrath's eyes widened. "*You* cannot."

It was my turn to balk. "Why not?" I knew he didn't find *me* attractive. I had a nose for these things. There were cues, body language, and a certain way a man looked at you when he was attracted.

Hrath had given me none of those. So what the hell was his issue?

"I would prefer not," Hrath said. "You." He pointed at Mallini. "You will do."

"My name is Mallini and you can ask nicely."

"Mallini," Veena said, eyes wide. "He's doing this to help us."

Mallini shrugged. "Whatever. But keep your hands from roaming." She was squashed between Keelan and Artimus and wriggled free now to stumble onto Hrath's lap. He didn't touch her as she perched on his thigh. "What do I do?" she asked.

Once again Gus spoke for Hrath. "Place your mouth on his, inhale through your nose, and then exhale into his mouth."

This time Hrath threw him a grateful look.

Mallini cupped Hrath's face. "Damn, you're warm."

"He's a djinn," Gus said.

"Just get on with it," Keelan said gruffly, his attention on the view outside our carriage.

Hrath made an incoherent sound, probably because Mallini's mouth was already over his.

Long seconds passed in which Mallini did the breathing thing.

Tristeene sat with her chin tucked in, the tops of her cheekbones red with embarrassment. I wanted to nudge her and tell her what I'd made of Hrath's rejection of her offer, but now wasn't the time.

My gaze flitted to the window instead. Was that a shadow beyond the treeline? Shit, was it getting darker?

"We need to hurry," Artimus said tightly. "I can't hold the carriage in shadow for more than an hour or so."

His allure? That's why it looked darker out there. He had us wreathed in his shadowy allure.

The veins beneath Hrath's bronze skin began to glow in a soft, pulsing manner and he slowly raised his hand to place it on the small of Mallini's back. She pulled away, breaking lip contact.

"You good?" she asked.

"I am good," Hrath confirmed.

Mallini climbed back into her seat, and I noticed

how Hrath's gaze slid to Tristeene, lingering for a moment as if waiting for her to see him.

She kept her head down, delicate jaw set as if determined that she wouldn't look at him.

"So now you can fly us out of here?" Veena asked expectantly.

Hrath flexed his hands and tore his gaze from Tristeene to look at Veena with an apologetic smile. "The distance is too far for me to transport you all. I can be at Prince Merihem's fortress within the hour if I go alone. I will bring back help. Do not leave this carriage."

Artimus chuckled dryly. "Trust me, Hrath, I'm not that arrogant."

There was a new, underlying timbre to his usual smooth drawl, a tightness, like a spring wound too tight, and it hit me.

Artimus was afraid.

For the first time since I'd known him, the seneschal was scared.

Hrath squeezed past Veena, cracked open the carriage door, but hesitated. He threw a final look my way, his expression torn. "I will be back," he said softly. "Do *not* leave this carriage, Nyx, swear it to me."

There it was again. Fear. The djinn was afraid too.

"Swear it, Nyx."

I nodded. "I swear, I won't leave the carriage."

He exhaled and then slipped out the door and into the gloom.

Keelan pulled the door closed and latched it quickly.

A chill shot up my spine, because if some of the most powerful creatures I knew were scared, it meant whatever was lurking in the forest around us was bad.

Really fucking bad.

CHAPTER THIRTY-SEVEN

With Hrath gone, time crawled. I'd moved to the bench opposite Artimus. Tristeene had shuffled over so I could sit facing the seneschal. His eyes were closed, his head tipped back and braced on the plush crimson lining of the backrest.

Gus muttered to himself, toying with something dull and metallic in his hand—the pendant attached to the chain around his neck.

"Are you all right?" Veena asked him.

"No," he said. "It's one thing to read about all the creepy, scary stuff, it's another to see it. To be trapped in the middle of it."

I smiled. "You know, to some people, we *are* the creepy, scary *stuff*." I'd hoped to get a smile out of him, but he just looked at me with a fearful expression.

"Nyx, you have no idea... There are things in these

forests. Dead things that refuse to stay dead. Spirits called dybbuks hungry to possess live flesh so they can feed on...flesh. Ancient, lost things. They say the forest itself is alive. It's on the edge of one of the lost realms. A finger of land that was never fully cut off."

I was intrigued. "What do you mean?"

"The history books say there was a sickness that plagued some of the realms after the Chaos War. Powerful conji were employed to put up shields to cut off these lost realms. The old forest still harbors remnants of those sick creatures."

This had to be the sickness that Ignatius had told us about. The one that came from the pit. Looks like it had spread out of the abyss. I still hadn't told my siblings what Ignatius had shared with me, and now wasn't the time for a history lesson from me.

"Won't it spread?" Veena asked, wide-eyed. "The sickness inside this forest?"

"The creatures can't leave, and no one is fool enough to enter."

"Except someone sent us here to die," Keelan snorted.

"Not us," Tristeene said. "Artimus."

I looked at Artimus now. He was so pale I could see the blue veins beneath his skin. Beads of perspiration had broken out on his brow. He wasn't going to be able to hold up the allure much longer, and when it fell, we'd be fucked. "How long has Hrath been gone?"

"Just over an hour," Mallini said. She glanced at

Artimus and gnawed on her bottom lip. "He doesn't look good."

"I can hear you," Artimus said. "I'm not dead."

"Yet," Tristeene added. "But if you keep expending energy to hold the allure, it won't be long until you are."

"Don't be so dramatic," Artimus drawled. "It won't kill me."

"It'll knock you out, and in this place, that means you'll be as good as dead."

The thought of Artimus dying made my chest hurt. "Hey." I grabbed his hands. His skin was cold. So fucking cold. I squeezed his fingers, then rubbed them between my palms. "What can we do to help?"

"Give him blood," Tristeene said. "He needs to feed."

"No," Artimus snapped. "No blood."

I exchanged glances with my siblings. Fear and concern were evident on all their faces.

"Artimus, you know it's the only way," Tristeene said.

He growled another no and tried to pull his hand free of mine, but I gripped it tighter. "Dammit, Arty, why the fuck not?"

His eyes snapped open, irises ringed in crimson, pupils large and dilated. "Because I fucking say so." He slumped back in his seat, chest heaving with the exertion of being angry.

Gus spoke next, his tone tentative and non-confrontational. "We need you, Artimus."

Artimus's brow pinched. "Hrath will be back soon. I can hold on till then."

But could he? I looked to Tristeene and saw my doubt reflected on her face.

"If you fall into unconsciousness, it'll be too late for us to feed you," Tristeene pointed out.

"What about sex?" Mallini said. "Will that work?"

Artimus was silent, his chest rising and falling erratically.

"I doubt he'll be able to get it up in that state," Tristeene said.

I expected a smart response from Artimus, but he didn't speak. In fact, his head lolled to one side.

"Arty?" I sat forward. "Artimus?" No response. I slapped his cheek. "Hey!"

"Wha..." He cracked open an eye. "Did you just hit me?"

"I'll do more than that if you get us killed. You need to fucking feed. I don't care what hang-up you have. None of that matters right now. Understand?"

"There's something out there," Keelan said, his voice a soft rumble that had the hairs on my arms quivering. "It's circling us."

Fuck. "Arty, you need to feed." I tugged my sleeve up, determined to make him feed.

The buzz in the air I'd come to recognize as Artimus's allure dropped suddenly.

Keelan sat forward, his gaze on the window. "What the—"

He moved fast, yanking Veena away from the door just as it slammed open.

Something burst into the carriage. All I got was the impression of twisted, corded muscle.

A limb reaching for Keelan.

I cried out and threw myself toward him, hands outstretched to grab hold of him.

But I was too late.

My fingers closed on air as the thing yanked my brother from the carriage and into the night.

Veena's scream echoed in my ears for long, aching seconds and then silence, dead as the night beyond the open doorway, filled the carriage.

"It's gone," Mallini said. "The allure is gone and something has Keelan."

My chest heaved, panic squeezing my lungs and tightening my throat. Think, Nyx, think.

I looked to Artimus, dead to the world, then back at the door. We needed the allure back up, and for that we needed Artimus juiced up. But Keelan was in trouble and there was no way I was sitting here playing blood bag while something chowed down on my brother.

"Tristeene, Mallini, get some blood down his throat. I don't care what you have to do. Just do it."

I scrambled to the door.

"No!" Veena grabbed my arm. "You can't."

I smiled down at her delicate upturned face. "Honey, I have to. I'll be back, I promise."

"Hrath said not to leave," she reminded me. "You promised him."

"I know." But keeping that promise to him would mean breaking an older one I'd made to myself. To protect my family at all costs. "Keep the door shut. Stay back from it. Okay?"

Gus leaned forward and draped something around my neck. I looked down at the pendant on the chain. Just a finger of metal.

"It's iron," he said. "The things in the forest don't like iron."

"Thank you."

He leaned in and pecked my cheek and my heart swelled. "Come back to us."

Veena let out a cry of distress and then released me. "Don't die...please..."

I kissed her head and dove out into the night.

The forest seemed to surge up to close in around me, the silence like a muffler against my ears, eerie and unnatural. My skin pricked with awareness.

I wasn't alone. I glanced back at the carriage, a solitary structure planted in the middle of the trail.

The beasts that had drawn it were gone, and the ground was smeared with dark stains.

Blood.

Don't look. Focus.

Find Keelan.

I scanned the treeline looking for the trail—a disturbance in the flora, broken branches. There. I drew my silver dagger and moved fast, off the dirt track and into the darkness of the forest proper.

The world seemed to grow smaller, tightening around me. I got the impression that if I looked over my shoulder, I'd see nothing but unbroken treeline, no road beyond, no carriage.

I'd been swallowed.

But I wasn't someone who would go down easy. This fucking forest would choke on me and have to spit me out.

I didn't call for Keelan. I had no need. The trail was fresh, earth churned and kicked aside where he'd thrashed while being dragged by...whatever.

I followed, keeping low. Alert.

Deeper and deeper into the undergrowth where the air smelled of decay and death. The moon barely made it through the canopy above, but where it did, I spotted white gleaming things—the heads of mushrooms, clustered together, surrounded by tiny bones.

Not just one spot, but several.

I didn't understand it and I didn't care. The trail was all that mattered.

I heard a sound.

A wet slurping that made my stomach contract and my bowels weak. The coppery scent of blood hit me next. My gut twisted in foreboding and horror.

No...

I picked up speed, pushing past a cluster of bushes that swallowed the trail to find...

It took a moment for my brain to put the picture together.

The image of Keelan slumped against a tree, his head lolling to one side, eyes wide with shock and pain while something gray and green, sinew and vine, slurped at his torn-open abdomen. It looked like a tree branch with arms and a head. The tail end was a multitude of tentacles that shifted and thrashed against the earth like fat worms. Like roots that had come to life and freed themselves of the earth.

My breath caught in my throat, heart slamming against my chest as Keelan's gaze slowly met mine. There was a plea in those eyes.

I took a step, and he opened his mouth and made a strangled sound. The creature paused in its feeding.

Keelan sucked in a breath and forced one word from his lips. "Run!"

The creature's head snapped up, its dark, round eyes focusing on me. Its face was an oval that came to a sharp point at the chin, and its mouth was jagged, uneven teeth that looked like they were made of bracken and kindling. It was horrific and mesmerizing and fucking ugly as fuck.

"Run!" Keelan pleaded with me again.

And I did.

Right toward the fucker trying to eat my brother.

Chapter Thirty-Eight

NYX

My bloodcurdling cry split the silence as I launched myself at the tree monster. It whipped around to face me, hissing and spitting blood and black shit. Like that would stop me. I ducked a swipe of a tentacle, dropped to my knees, and slid forward a few feet to stab the fucker.

My blade cut through it like butter.

It screamed.

I stabbed it again and again.

"Nyx!"

Keelan's warning was followed by a wallop to my face. I saw stars and darkness and the inky nothingness of oblivion.

"Nyx, get up!"

I came to with a weight crushing me, pinching my torso. The creature was on top of me, squeezing me like a fucking tube of toothpaste.

"Fuck you!" I kicked out, thrashing and swiping with my dagger, desperate for the blade to get a bite. It hit, sinking into something soft and gooey.

The thing made a high-pitched wail and launched itself off me.

I scrambled up, blade clutched tight in my hand, even though it now dripped with icky goo.

The creature shook its head wildly from side to side, one eye a mass of bubbling, viscous fluid.

Okay, so that's what I'd sunk my blade into. I backed up toward Keelan, glancing at him then back at the monster to keep it in my sights. I needed to assess his injuries properly.

Oh, fuck, that thing had torn him open. His insides looked mangled. If this was a human, I'd say he was done for, but this was Keelan, a Minorax and my brother. There was no *done for* until he was done for.

"You go," Keelan gasped. "I can't...too badly..." His eyes drifted closed.

"I'm not leaving you."

I sensed movement and turned back to the creature in time for it to rush me. I dashed to the side, and it veered to match me. I feinted and darted the other way. It faltered, trying to correct itself, giving me the precious seconds that I needed to jump it.

I attacked, landing on it and scrambling onto its back, primal brain activating as I tore into it with my dagger, slicing and stabbing and tearing chunks off its body. Thick flesh, hardened on the outside like the bark of a tree but soft and alive on the inside.

"Nyx...stop. Stop."

Keelan's voice filtered through to me in increments, and it took a little longer than that to stop my hands from hacking. I sat back, still on the creature, except the creature was prone on the ground. Unmoving. Dead.

I climbed off it, thighs trembling, hands shaking, and allowed my feet to carry me back to Keelan.

I crouched beside him and took his arm to drape it around my shoulder so I could lift him.

He screamed as I tried to pull him to his feet.

That sound. That awful, brain scraping, heart-crushing sound had bile crawling up my throat. I released him and he sagged against the tree.

"I can't..." He looked up at me with bloodshot eyes. "You have to go."

Fuck, fuck, fuck. I couldn't carry him. He was too large. Too heavy. And his wounds... My gaze flicked back to the dead monster.

"Nyx, please...the others need you," Keelan said softly. "End me. The dagger to my heart will end the pain."

I cupped his face. "You're a stubborn bastard, but

you're noble and brave and you're my family. I'm not leaving you behind."

I stood swiftly and crossed the clearing to the dead creature. "You, fucker, are gonna serve a purpose, once I've repurposed you."

It didn't take long to cut him open and gut him to make a stretcher. I dragged the skin over to Keelan.

His eyes were closed now, head lolling. How much blood had he lost? Fuck, I needed to staunch that bleeding and pack that wound.

"Keelan?"

He groaned.

I grabbed his arm and tugged him toward me, maneuvering to tuck my arms under his. I took a moment to gather myself, then I lifted with my lower body, using thighs and hips to take his weight, drag him to the stretcher, and slide him onto it.

He cried out, eyes fluttering open to stare blearily at me.

"It's okay, buddy, I got you." I tugged my jacket off and pressed it to his abdomen, earning myself another scream of pain. I ignored it, looking around for something to hold it on with. Vines. There were vines all over the place. I grabbed some and wound them around him to hold the material in place, blocking out his cries of protest.

By the time I was done, he was sobbing and so was I.

"It's gonna be okay." I dashed the tears away and

moved round to grab the end of the stretcher closest to his head. "We're gonna be okay."

I dragged him out of the clearing, following the trail back to the carriage. It wasn't far. I hadn't come far. We could totally do this. And Hrath would be back with help. Keelan would be okay. We'd be okay.

We hit a snag, a bump in the ground that jolted Keelan, and he bellowed in agony. I stopped and looked back at him to find him unconscious.

It was for the best. Unconscious was good. At least this way he wouldn't feel the pain because the terrain was uneven and awful, and there would be more bumps all the way.

I had to keep moving.

The thunder of blood in my head and hammering of my heart filled the thick silence around me so that if not for the tightening of my gut and the pricking of my scalp, I'd have missed the new threat closing in on us.

But my body was honed for this. An alarm system in its own right, and I froze now. Listening, scanning the area around me. Reaching out with my senses. There, behind that tree. A shadow of movement. Up in the leaves too. I caught a gleam of eye whites, pinpricks of glowing red, like the tips of cigarettes, then the whispers began. Low at first, but then rising and swelling until they were inside my head, pressing in on me, scratching at my scalp as if trying to get inside.

No. I relinquished my grip on the stretcher to clutch my head. There was pressure, something trying to gain entry, to infiltrate my thoughts. My mind. I could sense frustration. Hunger. Rage. Desire.

I dug my nails into my scalp and squeezed my eyes closed, focusing on pushing them away, on keeping my mental barriers up.

You can have power.

You can save him.

He's dying but we can help.

We can make you stronger.

Faster.

Let. Us. In.

"Go fuck yourselves!"

Silence fell, thick and absolute. I opened my eyes and slowly dropped my hands to my sides. Were they gone?

I did a sweep of the surrounding area. Nothing. Fuck. I crouched to grab the stretcher and pulled. Something was wrong.

It moved too easily.

My gut clenched, skin prickling in a delayed response to threat as I slowly turned to look down at the stretcher.

The empty stretcher.

Keelan...

"Looking for this?" Keelan stepped out of the shadows to my left. His chin was tucked in as if he was studying the wound in his ruined torso.

"Keelan?" Even as I said his name, I knew it was all wrong. This wasn't Keelan. It was something else.

He raised his head slightly and tipped it to the side in a jerky motion. "Keelan is sleeping right now, but we...We are hungry."

Then the thing wearing my brother's body rushed me.

CHAPTER THIRTY-NINE

TRISTEENE

There are creatures outside the carriage. I can smell them, see the shadows as they circle us. The only thing keeping them at bay is the remnant of Artimus's allure and the iron bindings of this wooden carriage.

I'm not sure how long those elements will keep them at bay.

Gus echoes my concern a moment later. "I'm not sure how long the iron laced into the wood will keep the things outside at bay."

"It didn't stop that thing from taking Keelan." Veena's voice trembles.

"There are things with little aversion to it," Gus says.

We're all thinking the same thing now. What if more creatures with little aversion to iron come for us?

We need Artimus back in action.

We need his allure.

It shouldn't take much to provoke a hungry incubus to feed. The scent of blood will do it. But Artimus is falling into what we call the death sleep. I have no idea why he refused to feed. I don't know his psychological wounds, and I don't care.

Nyx is out there and so is Keelan. They're in danger and the seneschal can help save them if he's fed.

I know he has power.

I've heard the stories. Old tales of his incubus bloodline. The powerful allure passed down to each male. He's the last of them and he has that power. I've sensed it from time to time when his barriers dip.

Like now.

Now that he's vulnerable, I feel it thrumming against my power. Speaking to my demon in a language known only to them.

I have to act quickly if there's any chance of success. "Mallini, help me."

She shuffles forward, and together we pull and push Artimus into a sitting position. Mallini slips around him, straddling his form from behind to help hold him steady.

"Tristeene, I don't think this will work," she says. "The male's out cold."

I have my doubts too. "We have to try." I pull a

blade from my boot and slice open my wrist. It will heal in a few moments, but if I can get a few drops of blood into his mouth, then maybe I can activate his swallow reflex and he can take it from there.

I force his mouth open by pinching his jaw and press my bloody wrist to his lips. My blood trickles into his mouth achingly slow. "Come on, come on."

Mallini slaps his cheek. "Wake the fuck up."

Nothing happens for long seconds and then his throat bobs.

"Did you see that?" Veena says. "He swallowed."

She moves forward and Gus slides across the bench to press up to Mallini so we're all clustered around him.

He swallows again, but the wound in my wrist is already closing.

"Your neck," Mallini orders, grabbing Artimus's hair and yanking his head back so his mouth falls open.

If the seneschal could see this scene played back to him, he'd probably be mortified. The thought brings a wicked smile to my lips.

"What the hell, Tristeene?" Mallini stares at me in disgust. "It's not funny."

"It kinda is," Gus says. "Look at him."

Veena snorts and then covers her mouth, her eyes going large and dark. "We can't laugh. We shouldn't. Keelan and Nyx..."

I nod and lean into Artimus to press my throat to

his mouth, offering my slender neck like a gazelle to a lion.

Mallini slaps him again. "Hey. Drink."

I think she's simply enjoying the opportunity to hit him. I push harder against his mouth, closing my eyes when I feel his teeth scrape my skin, but it's his fangs I need. I turn my head slightly so that my jugular is pressed to his canine and then push up, wincing at the sting as his tooth breaks skin.

"His throat moved again," Veena informs me.

"Good, that means—"

I draw a sharp breath as his canines spear me. Pain slices down my neck as he latches on and sucks. I fight my instinct to pull away, breathing through my nose as he feeds.

This sensation of being prey is new. I'm usually the predator, the one sinking my teeth into a jugular while lowering myself onto a shaft. This...this is *not* pleasant. The endorphins that would make another creature weak and delirious with desire don't work on me.

He moans against my skin and his arms wrap around me, crushing me to his chest. He sucks harder, drawing fire through my veins.

I don't believe I've ever experienced such agony. "Fuck!"

"Tristeene!" Veena grabs my hand.

I can't see her, so I squeeze her hand and bite out the words she needs to hear. "I'm okay."

But I'm not. He's crushing me, squeezing me.

There's a crack, and a scream tears from my throat. My rib. Fuck, he broke my rib. The pain is a band of white flame cinching my chest. I can't breathe.

"Tristeene!" Veena begins to cry.

Mallini slaps Artimus. "Stop!" She hits him again. "Get off her."

They know better than to tear him from me. The damage to my jugular would mean I'd bleed out before I could heal.

Gus leans over us and grabs Artimus's jaw. Good. Yes, pinch it hard.

Artimus fights, latching on harder to me, his hold like a boa constrictor claiming its prey.

Gus growls. "Let go."

Artimus's canines retract. His grip slackens. I slip free, ass hitting the floor.

There's a pop inside me as my rib heals, allowing me to take a full breath.

I'm squashed between the benches, blinking back tears of relief, when Veena climbs into my lap and wraps her arms around my neck. I suck in a breath as she makes contact with the bite marks and she pulls away, eyes wide with horror.

"It's okay." I draw her back down and hug her. "I'm okay."

The air crackles and buzzes as the allure goes back up. Thank the earth.

"Finally," Mallini snaps. "What the fuck is your problem? Why didn't you feed in time?"

I look up at Artimus's flushed face. His eye whites are black, common for an incubus that's just fed, but the red pinpricks in his eyes are not. I slowly rise with Veena clinging to me and sit on the bench opposite him.

I keep my tone soft and unthreatening. "Artimus?"

He looks at me as if he doesn't see me and a low growl falls from his lips.

Trapped behind him, Mallini meets my wary gaze with a frightened one. She can probably sense the danger here. The fact that Artimus isn't fully in control of his demon right now.

Gus holds up his hands. "Seneschal, can you hear me? You're with the Satan spawn. We're trapped in the old forest. Do you remember?"

Artimus bares his bloody teeth and his hands fall to Mallini's thighs, gripping them tight as talons push out of the tips of his fingers.

Mallini presses her lips together, her body frozen in place.

Only Gus seems unperturbed. "You are Artimus, the seneschal to Morningstar. To Satan. Do you understand? Keelan and Nyx are in trouble and—"

Artimus's body flinches, eyes snapping in a sharp blink that clears the darkness from his eye whites. "Nyx... Where is she?"

His voice still isn't his own, but his gaze is sharp and coherent.

"Something took Keelan, and Nyx went after him," Gus says.

Artimus pushes away from Mallini and crosses the carriage to the door. He pauses but doesn't look back. "Stay in the carriage. I'll leave behind an allure to keep you safe. I'll be back before it wanes."

And then, just like Nyx had done before him, he leaps out of the carriage and into the night.

"So much for a fucking thank you," Mallini snaps.

I lock gazes with her. "It's good to have you back."

Chapter Forty

NYX

I backed away from Keelan. He was no longer in control of his body. There was something else driving him. Maybe more than one thing.

I'd felt the presence, seen several forms in my periphery, and now they were gone but not gone.

They were inside him.

"Let him go." I drew my dagger on instinct.

Keelan's gaze dropped to the blade in my hand. "What will you do with that? Hurt him? The one you fought so valiantly to save?" He smiled, a rictus of a smile that sat eerily on his face. "We think not."

"Keelan, can you hear me? Keelan, fight this."

Laughter echoed around me. "He cannot fight us. He is weak and we are many."

Many? Four at the most. I'd counted. "What do you want with him?"

"A vessel. A stomach with which to fill our own. A shield with which to escape the confines of this prison."

What had Gus said about this place? My mind was too scrambled to remember the details, but I recalled that this forest was meant to keep bad shit in. Was this why no one came here? So something like this couldn't happen?

Could these creatures use Keelan's body to escape this place? What would happen if they did? I had to stop them. I had to free Keelan.

Or kill him.

No. That wasn't an option.

What if it's the only way to stop them.

Fuck off. Focus, Nyx. There had to be a way to get them to leave his body.

Keelan made to turn away and staggered a step, a low moan slipping from his lips.

I took an instinctive step toward him to help him, but halted abruptly. What was I doing?

Keelan took another step.

He was leaving.

Off to find prey and a way out. I had to act now if I was going to stop this, and the solution was suddenly clear.

"Take me instead."

Keelan paused with his back to me.

"Look, that body is damaged. It won't last long if you push it to keep moving. You need me. Take me."

He turned his head, eyes blazing. "We cannot."

"I know I fought you earlier, but I won't this time. I'll let you have me." I wasn't sure what I was doing, only that I needed to stop them and save Keelan and maybe...maybe if I took them on, I'd be strong enough to fight them, to suppress them, long enough for Hrath to get here with reinforcements, and if not...

My hand tightened on my dagger.

If not, then I'd end their chance of escape with me.

A part of me was screaming at how stupid this idea was. That if no help came, if I died, then Keelan died too. But I had confidence that Hrath would come. He wouldn't leave me here, and even if he was too late to save me, he'd be able to save my brother.

The brother who'd saved me from a watery grave during the trials. I was here because of him. I owed him my life.

I choked back a lump of useless emotion threatening to tighten my throat. "Please, just take me."

"We cannot." It ground out the words in frustration.

Wait a second, did they mean they couldn't because they just...couldn't? "Why not?"

"Because you are—" He doubled over. "This body... This useless body."

"Then let him go."

"We will once we are done." It turned and ran.

"No!" I sprang at him, hitting him in the back and taking him down. "You won't have him. I won't let you use him up and spit him out."

We grappled, my chest to his back, and he arched, letting out a strangled scream. My chest burned where we made contact.

I pulled back and looked down at the iron pendant swinging between us. Wait a fucking second.

Keelan bucked suddenly and I lost my grip on him, sliding onto the ground. He scrambled up, ready to bolt, but I grabbed his ankle and pulled. He hit the ground again and I clambered onto him and locked an arm around his neck as he thrashed to be free.

I gripped the pendant and tugged hard enough to break the chain. Iron could hurt these fuckers.

"Scream for me, bitch!"

I slapped the iron to Keelan's forehead, and a sound like nails on a chalkboard tore at the air and burrowed into my skull.

They were screaming. Yes! They were screaming.

He began to buck like a fucking bronco.

I held on, the iron sizzling against my sibling's skin, the smell of charred flesh fresh in my nose. Muscles straining, ligaments aching, I held on as my lower body was whipped to and fro so hard that I was sure I'd have internal injuries once this was over. But the adrenaline lighting up my limbs gave strength to my inviolable purpose.

"Fight it, Keelan! You can do it. Come back to me, dude, come on!"

He slammed his head back into my face hard enough to bust my lip, hard enough to make me see stars, but I held on.

You violate us. You bitch, you dirty ichor blood bitch. Let us be. Let us...No...NO!

"NO!" Keelan roared.

His mouth yawned wide and black shit poured out. Flies? No, beetles. I wasn't sure. But there was a cloud of them. They rose above us, buzzing with rage. Eyes stared at me from the inky, buzzing darkness.

Ichor blood bitch. You will die. DIE!!! Curses on you, curses.

The beetle cloud whirled away and whizzed off into the trees.

I collapsed on top of Keelan, a sob of relief clinging to my throat.

"Nyx..." Keelan shifted beneath me.

Oh, shit. I released him and rolled off him, the iron pendant still clutched in my hand. "You okay?"

He didn't move, but his back rose and fell, telling me he was still alive. Alive and grinding earth and all kinds of bacteria into his wounds.

"Shit, shit, shit." I rolled him onto his back, and he stared up at me through swollen, slitted eyes.

"Leave...me..."

"Shut up." My crappy tourniquet had held. The bleeding seemed to have stopped. The burn in his forehead was fading. "We can do this. It's not far to the road."

He closed his eyes, mouth twisting in pain. "Stubborn fucking woman."

I grinned down at him. "You know it."

Together we managed to get him to the stretcher. He lay panting as I gathered the ends of my makeshift transportation device and began to pull.

Three or four meters and I was flagging.

The expenditure of energy had weakened me, and my limbs shook, perspiration popping on my brow with the effort. But I recognized this part of the trail. We were minutes away from the dirt track and that gave me hope. It loaned me strength.

I kept moving, and silence, blessed fucking silence, settled around me.

A couple more minutes passed before the crack and snap of branches pulled me up short. My hand had barely skimmed the hilt of my blade when three hunched creatures with tattered wings clinging to their backs stepped out of the treeline.

They stared at me with slanted eyes, snapping beaks covered in stains. They had long, tangled hair and the remnants of clothes clinging to their withered frames.

They reached for me with their dirty talons, eyes lighting up with desperate hunger.

"Oh, for fucksake." I adjusted my grip on my dagger. "Fine, bring it."

Chapter Forty-One

ARTIMUS

Nyx is in trouble and it's my fault.

My fault for being too weak to take what I need when I need it. The demon inside me surges up, wanting to take control, to be free, to feed, fuck, and feast. I can't allow that. I must remain in control.

I blink back the crimson haze threatening to cloud my vision. I'm an expert at control, except tonight I slipped up and overestimated my abilities, putting us all in danger. I should have fed. A little, just a few pulls from anyone...anyone but her.

The demon inside stretches beneath my skin, eager to take over.

I stop and breathe and will it into its box.

"Nyx!" I move through the undergrowth, following

her scent. There is fear and determination, but clouding it all is anger.

The corner of my mouth lifts. "Yes, that's my girl."

I forge on and catch a new scent. My belly trembles.

No...

Shit.

I break into a sprint, hoping I'm still on track. Hoping I make it on time, because if I'm too late, then everything I've worked to preserve, everything I've sacrificed to protect, will have been for nothing.

NYX

The tattered-winged creatures circled me and Keelan. A chittering, clicking sound filled the air. My gaze flicked down to their throats. To the bulge that inflated and deflated to make the strange sound.

Wait...I'd heard that sound before. Where had I heard it? The memory hit me suddenly, slugging me in the chest with horrific realization. I'd heard this sound coming from the Erinyes. Seen their throats bulge in the same way.

Could it be...

No, they couldn't be Erinyes.

But now that I'd made the connection, I couldn't

unsee it. The lithe muscle, the way they moved, that sound. The only thing missing were the plumes in place of hair.

"Hey." I held up my hands. "I don't want to hurt you. I'm with the seneschal. I'm Satan spawn."

One of them hissed and took an aggressive step toward me. My pulse spiked. She retreated, head bowed, neck jutting in and out so she looked like she was pecking at air.

My pulse had barely calmed when another one lunged at me and retreated, pecking at the air.

Another spike of adrenaline.

Again and again, they feinted attack, leaving me confused, leaving my body flooded with the flight-or-fight hormone and no way to do either.

"Argh, fuck you!" I lunged this time, slicing the air to the left and right.

The clicking intensified, and every hair on my body stood to attention, warning me, screaming at me to run.

If I ran, I might get away, but they'd have Keelan. I wouldn't let them have him.

All three lunged at me, and for a moment I thought this was it.

The fight.

The moment where I would have to give it my all. Win or lose. Live or die. But then they backed off.

Again.

Impotent rage clawed at my chest. "ARGH! Fuck

you. I fought a tree with teeth and a beetle cloud with eyes, so you three can take your saggy tits and fuck the pissing hell off."

The chittering grew louder, faster, and my heart pounded harder to match it, and suddenly it was impossible to draw breath.

I couldn't breathe, I couldn't fucking—

Something broke into the clearing with an inhuman roar and slammed into one of the Erinyes, knocking it off its feet.

The clicking stopped.

My pulse dropped. I sucked in a deep, much needed breath.

"Run!"

I blinked to clear the spots in my vision. "Artimus?"

He leaped away from the Erinyes, then lashed out, hitting one hard in the chest when it tried to move forward.

"Get back to the carriage," he ordered.

"I'm not leaving Keelan."

"I order you to go."

I would have rolled my eyes and told him where to shove it if we hadn't been in mortal danger, but this was not the time or place to argue. Didn't mean I was going to oblige and do as told.

"Dammit, Nyx!" Artimus spun and delivered a drop kick to the Erinyes on his left, then crouched and palm-punched the one in the middle. "I can't hold them off for—"

"Watch out!" I ran and shoulder-slammed the third Erinyes, knocking her away from him. Her beak snapped the air and she screeched like a fucking banshee, turning her rabid gaze on me.

I sliced the air, forcing her to leap back to avoid being stabbed. Again and again, I forced her away from Keelan.

Behind me, the sounds of Artimus battling the other two crazy bitches filled the clearing.

My heart sank, stomach clenching because my gut told me this would be a tight win, if that.

Artimus's bellow made my scalp tight. It was a bellow of pain, but there was no option to look his way, to know how bad things were. If I took my eye off this bitch, I was fucked.

She feinted left, then went right. I jabbed the blade into her side, catching her in the gut and slicing to open her up.

She made a gurgling sound and dropped to her knees. I slammed the knife into the side of her head, yanked it out, then spun to face Artimus.

He was on the ground, beneath two Erinyes. Both were making that fucked-up clicking sound again.

"Get off him!" I ran toward the cluster, but it exploded outward, sending the two Erinyes flying. One hit a tree with a sickening crunch; the other hit the ground with a crack.

Artimus rose, chin tucked in, suit shredded so it hung off his frame in ribbons that left his ripped torso exposed in too many places. His shoulders heaved and I couldn't help but think he looked bigger. Wider. Taller.

"Get. Back. To. The. Carriage." His voice rumbled through me, gripping my nape and shaking me. "Now!"

My feet obeyed, taking me halfway across the clearing before I could dig in my heels. "Artimus, what the fuck? I can't leave Keelan."

"I have him. I'm right behind you." He strode to Keelan and scooped him up like he weighed nothing even though Keelan was almost twice his size and a mass of thick, heavy muscle.

How the fuck? No. I wasn't gonna dwell on it. "Hurry, this way." Even with my head reeling, with my body aching to collapse, I found and locked onto the trail back. Okay, so the fact that Artimus had battered his own trail next to mine helped.

The road couldn't be much farther. I glanced back at Artimus, a couple of meters behind me, slowed down not by the weight but the size of his quarry.

He locked gazes with me, his sapphire eyes bright in the gloom. "Don't stop, woman. Keep moving."

His voice was different too. Deeper. More authoritarian. A shiver kissed my nape. I made to turn away when movement to his left caught my eye.

"Artimus!"

His head whipped toward the movement and a blur of gray and black slammed into him.

Chittering filled the air and two, no, three more appeared, surrounding him and Keelan, cutting them off from view.

"Run!" he yelled. "Go now!"

I ran toward him.

I was no fool, I knew when the odds were against us. Knew that I'd done everything I could to save Keelan. Knew this was insane, but I also knew that if I left now, if I ran away, it would eat away at me until it killed me.

Running away wasn't something I could live with. Not when there was even a small chance that I could help.

So I ran back to him with only one dagger and a shitload of determination. "Get away from him!" Something swelled in my chest, a ball of energy, an understanding, a confidence that was both cold and hot. "Get away!" My voice sounded odd, sharp and cutting like a blade. The energy grew and grew, ready to—

A howl filled the air and a tornado landed between me and Artimus. The powerful gust of wind flung me onto my ass. I rolled, slowly raising my head to see Hrath bearing down on the Erinyes.

More forms landed on the forest floor, winged beings with dark plumes for hair and silver armor.

Erinyes. But not psycho ones. These looked sane, if you could call sword-wielding bird women with plumes for hair sane.

I climbed to my feet, breathing through the pain in my side as my fractured ribs knit. Hrath appeared beside me with Keelan slung over his shoulder and Artimus by his side. His gaze was fiery rage as it raked over me, and I couldn't help but shrink from it.

"We must get to the carriage. There is a conji waiting with a portal to take us to the fortress."

I glanced back at the Erinyes fighting the…Erinyes.

Artimus grabbed my arm and hurried me away. "Move." His tone was saturated with anger.

"You left the carriage," Hrath said. "You vowed you would not. You broke your vow."

"To save Keelan."

"Nonetheless, you have proven you cannot be trusted."

Why did that bother me? "I did what I had to."

He looked away in disgust and continued walking.

Artimus's grip on me tightened and I yanked my arm free. "I can fucking walk just fine."

He made a sound of exasperation. "You could have died."

"Yeah, and you could have prevented all this by fucking feeding when we asked you to."

I expected an apology, an explanation, but instead he pressed his lips together, his expression closing off.

I shook my head in disgust and broke away from him, picking up speed to match Hrath and then surpass him.

I broke free of the trees and onto the dirt track with

them close on my heels. A hooded male stood by the carriage, which was now surrounded in azure light. Veena's face appeared in the window.

"Nyx!" Her face lit up, and she looked back into the carriage to address the others. "Nyx is back with Artimus and Hrath and they have Keelan."

The conji raised his hand and a door appeared in the azure bubble. I stepped through and into the carriage.

Veena threw her arms around me, and Gus leaned in to hug us both. Tristeene and Mallini came next until we were huddled together, rocking back and forth, breathing as one.

"You're safe," Tristeene said softly. "You made it back."

I closed my eyes and committed this moment to memory. "Yeah. I did. I made it home."

Chapter Forty-Two

The conji transported us all, carriage included, to a stone chamber with high, vaulted ceilings and several arches leading off from it. It took seconds. A dip in my belly, the world tipping, the sensation of Veena's hand in mine, and we were done.

I climbed out of the carriage to join Hrath and Artimus. The incubus tried to catch my eye but all I cared about in that moment was Keelan.

They'd propped him up against the carriage wheel but his body tipped to one side, as if desperate to give in to gravity. His face was bloodless, his chest barely moving with breath.

I crouched and gently adjusted him so he wasn't scrunched to one side.

"We need a healer. Now," Hrath said.

The conji inclined his head, then disappeared. Tristeene, Veena, Gus, and Mallini gathered around me and Keelan. Veena took his huge hand in both of hers.

"Please don't die," she whispered, blinking back tears. "Oh, Nyx, he's so cold."

A sob of fear lodged in my throat. I swallowed it and gave Veena a tight smile, forcing it to reach my eyes. "He's not going to die." Damn I sounded confident, even though my insides trembled with doubt. "He's gonna be fine."

Truth was he'd taken the kind of damage that to most would be lethal. He'd lost way too much blood. It was a miracle he was still alive. But he *was* alive.

He had to hold on a little longer.

Long enough for the healers to do their job.

"Where are they?" Gus bit out. "Fuck..." His mouth twisted as he took in my crumpled jacket, crushed to Keelan's abdomen. "How bad?"

I shook my head. "Bad. But he's strong."

He exhaled shakily. "Yeah, Minorax are strong. They heal fast. He'll be okay."

But he wasn't able to hide the doubt in his voice and my thoughts went there, acknowledging the possibility that we might lose him. That despite all efforts, Keelan might die.

I looked up at Artimus. "If he dies..." I clenched my jaw.

"Say it," he demanded. "Just say it."

Fine, fuck it. "If he dies, then it's your fault."

Silence reigned and no one objected. No one tried to correct me. They knew. They all knew that this could have all been avoided if Artimus had just taken blood sooner rather than later.

His throat bobbed. "I know."

"No," Hrath said. "This is the fault of whoever sent our carriage to the old forest. He or she is the culprit."

"You weren't there," Mallini snapped. "He could have kept the allure up if he'd fed. We begged him, and he refused, and then…" Her lip curled as she looked up at Artimus. "Why the hell didn't you just drink?"

Hrath looked at Artimus in confusion. "You allowed the allure to fall?"

"I made a bad judgment call. I didn't realize…" He inhaled, sapphire eyes flashing in anger. "What the hell took *you* so long anyway?"

Hrath stared at him for a long beat before speaking coldly. "You look to place the blame on me?"

"Enough!" Tristeene snapped. "Pointing fingers is a waste of time. We need to save Keelan, then find the bastard behind the portal diversion."

A woman in a purple robe carrying a bag appeared behind us. "You have wounded?" Hrath stepped aside and her gaze fell on Keelan.

She shooed us aside. "I need room to work."

We backed off and she crouched beside him, placed her bag on the ground, and opened it. She drew a pair of clippers and set to work on the vines I'd wrapped around his torso to keep my jacket in place, gently removing them before carefully peeling away one corner of the jacket.

I held my breath, expecting a trickle of blood, but there was nothing. She nodded and peeled the jacket away completely. Keelan's skin was raw and mangled in places but new flesh was growing over the wound and the bleeding had stopped.

"Good." She reached into her bag and pulled out a jar filled with yellow goop. "He's healing, but there is a risk of infection. The old forest is not the most sanitary place. But this should kill any dangerous bacteria and speed up the healing. It'll also help with the pain." She unscrewed the lid and began to smear it onto him. "The jacket was an excellent idea. It not only staunched the bleeding, it also protected the wound from further trauma and foreign entities."

I swallowed the lump in my throat. "He's going to be okay?"

She glanced over her shoulder with a smile. "Yes, I believe he will."

I sagged, blinking against the sting of tears. "Thank you." Tristeene hugged me and Veena let out a soft laugh that was also a sob. "He's going to be okay."

"Thanks to you." Gus looked up at me. "You saved him."

But I'd almost died doing it. Would have died if not for Artimus. My throat pinched, chest tightening with guilt at the way I'd spoken to him. Blaming him without knowing his reasons. My lack of gratitude...

I looked up, expecting to meet his gaze, to apologize, but the spot where he'd been standing a moment ago was empty.

The seneschal was gone.

CHAPTER FORTY-THREE

Hot water sluiced away the aches and pains, cleaning off the debris, dirt, and blood, but it did nothing for the icky feeling in the pit of my stomach.

Guilt.

I hated that bitch.

Keelan was safe, being tended to by the super sweet healer, Erantha. A conji in training. We'd been given quarters on an upper floor, east side of the fortress, away from the nobility and anyone else who might be a threat to our presence. Minorax guards were posted at the doors to the main chamber that split off into several smaller ones with interconnecting corridors.

This was a guest suite, but I'd been too exhausted to take in the details, needing to strip off the day and wash it all away.

But now that was done, and my brain was buzzing with questions that I needed answers to, like why had Artimus put us in danger? I'd exploded at him about it, but now that I'd calmed down, it was obvious that he'd have a valid reason. He wouldn't have deliberately let the allure die.

His objective was to keep us safe. To keep *me* safe.

And who the fuck had sent our carriage to the old forest. Who'd want to kill Artimus? Because that had to be the reason. Even if someone here had known the spawn were coming, why would they want to kill us all? That would leave the Satan seat empty, and all that power would go to waste.

So whoever did this was after Artimus.

I needed to find out who and why. I needed to speak to him. Problem was, we hadn't seen him since the healer had arrived. He'd vanished, leaving Hrath in charge.

The sylph had carried Keelan to these quarters and liaised with the fortress staff to get us all settled. He'd even arranged for fresh clothing for us all.

The bedroom was on the small side compared to my room at Morningstar, but it had a bed, a dresser, a mirror, and an ensuite bathroom, so as far as I was concerned, it was perfect.

I dried off, dressed in the leggings and fresh shirt someone had left on the double bed for me, and joined the others in the main chamber that was so large it could fit three tennis courts.

The furniture was shades of gray with orange and silver accents. No colorful tapestries here. Just a stone floor covered here and there in thick gray rugs. The vaulted windows were narrow with black shutters attached to each. It was a sparse, functional space, just like the bedroom, and it suited me fine.

Tristeene and Mallini sat on a sofa together and Veena was curled up in a large armchair. Gus was in the process of draping a throw over her.

I nodded in their direction, letting them know I'd be with them in a moment, then beelined for Hrath, who was standing by the window looking out at the sunset.

He'd been so pissed at me for breaking my promise not to leave the carriage. On the one hand, I got it, but on the other, he had to accept the extenuating circumstances that led me to do so.

We needed to talk it out.

I joined him at the window, tracking his gaze to a sky suspended between day and night. The faint outline of a crescent moon was visible high above. The world below was wreathed in shadow. It was impossible to make out the fortress grounds.

I tore my gaze from the view and fixed it on Hrath. "You got a minute?"

His gaze was intense as it locked with mine. "You could have been killed," he said bluntly.

"Great, I'm glad we could get straight to the point."

He exhaled through his nose. "I would not have left

you if I thought doing so would put you in more danger. I believed it to be the only way to save you at the time."

It sounded like *he* was apologizing to *me*. "I know that. I'm sorry I couldn't keep my promise."

He exhaled again and his dark eyes bloomed with warmth. "I understand that you do not know our ways. You may not understand that a vow is an oral contract that must not be broken. I accept this. Therefore, on this occasion, I will accept your apology."

The knot I hadn't known was in my chest eased. "Thanks. I'm glad we smoothed that over, but we still don't know who put us in that position. Who wanted to hurt Artimus?" I gnawed on my bottom lip. "Speaking of which, do you know where Artimus is?"

Hrath pressed his lips together. "Yes, he's attempting to get an audience with the princes. He wishes to arrange a time for the spawn to petition them in private before the ball tomorrow."

"You think it's safe for him to be alone? I mean, someone tried to kill him."

"The culprit would be a fool to attack the seneschal within the fortress walls. His plan failed. He will no doubt recoup and try again at a later date."

Nice. So the spawn weren't the only ones with a target on our backs. And why did that make me trust Artimus even more? "I think I was too harsh on him. He wouldn't put us in danger without a good reason."

"Agreed," Hrath said. "But I fear the danger has not passed."

"What do you mean?"

Veena, Gus, and Mallini drifted over to join us, but Tristeene remained seated across the room.

Hrath's gaze flicked to her before returning to me. "There is something amiss here. It is the day before the ball and yet the fortress is as silent as a tomb, the staff subdued...frightened almost." He shook his head. "When I arrived earlier to get help there was no one at the guard's entrance. I was forced to wait and finally entered through an upper window without resistance from any wards. I was eventually able to locate a guard and alert the Erinyes patrol of the issue, but this is not the order of things. The fortress should not be so undefended and unmanned. We must all be on our guard."

A shiver crawled up my spine and settled at the base of my skull.

"Whatever happens, we'll face it together," Veena said, reaching for my hand.

I believed it, because together we could beat anything. Still, the sooner we got the meeting with the princes out of the way the better, because my gut told me getting involved with whatever shit was going down here at the fortress was a bad idea.

"Let's hope Artimus got us that meeting."

CHAPTER FORTY-FOUR

Keelan's room was a copy of mine except for the seat beneath the large arched window letting in the night.

He was in bed, propped up by several pillows, tendrils of dark hair clinging to his pale cheeks. His bare chest was taped up with gauze and bandages, and the covers were drawn up to his waist.

He looked like a stone statue, unyielding and peaceful. Was he asleep? I took a step back. I'd come back later rather than disturb him.

He cracked open his puffy eyes and locked me in place with a look.

"Hey." I smiled.

"You're insane," he said gruffly.

I shrugged a shoulder and approached the bed. "I've been called worse."

His gaze was somber, almost chastising. "You could have died."

I was tempted to roll my eyes, to make light of it, but I couldn't bring myself to do that. To pretend what had happened hadn't been a fucking big deal.

We'd almost died. "I know, but so could you."

He closed his eyes for a moment. "I'd accepted my fate as soon as that thing tore into me."

My stomach tightened as an image of him propped up against the tree while the monster ate him filled my head. "Yeah? Well, I'm not as accepting."

He exhaled through his nose, exasperated. "I want to berate you, but I can't help but be grateful that you came for me."

I parked my ass by his hip. "I don't need or want your gratitude, Keelan. We're family, and family sticks together."

His throat bobbed. "Yes. They do." The corner of his mouth lifted. "You are not Minorax and yet you have the heart of one." His gaze softened. "Thank you, sister."

My throat pinched. "Anytime, brother."

He wrapped his fingers around mine.

I blinked back stupid tears. "Hey, you're not getting soft on me, are you?"

He chuckled, then groaned in pain.

"Shit, sorry."

His mouth turned down. "It's fine. But I have been

thinking... What will we do if the princes refuse to burn the contract?"

Ice pricked at my veins. It was a possibility I hadn't allowed myself to dwell on because that outcome wasn't something I wanted to think about.

"There is no guarantee we will get what we want," Keelan said. "No matter what united front we present."

"I know. But we have to try. We have to try with everything we have."

Refusing to participate in the trials would kill us all, because our blood through Satan's blood was bound by the contract to participate in the trials. The only way out lay with the princes, so if we failed to convince them, then all but one of us would die.

Keelan sucked in a sharp breath.

"Keelan?"

"I believe the tincture the healer gave me for the pain may be wearing off."

"I'll go find her and get you some more."

He didn't protest as I left the room. The others had retired to their bedchambers and Hrath wasn't in his room. I hurried to the main doors, expecting to find Minorax guards, but the hallway was empty. Strange. I'd planned on asking one of them to go fetch the healer. I had no idea where she might be.

But with no Minorax and no Hrath, it was up to me to get Keelan the meds he needed.

"Nyx?" Mallini called from behind me. "Where are you going?"

"To look for the healer."

She frowned. "You shouldn't go alone. I'll come with you."

I wasn't going to protest. The silence of this place gave me the creeps. "Thanks." We left the quarters and cut through the hallway and down the nearest corridor. "There's got to be someone we can ask."

"You'd think so, considering there's a ball tomorrow," Mallini said. "But the place was dead when we got here."

Yeah, Hrath had mentioned he'd struggled to find someone to speak to when he'd gotten here. "It's almost as if people are hiding."

"Or there *are* no people," Mallini said.

As if to prove her wrong, voices drifted down the corridor. I slowed my pace instinctively, straining to hear what they were saying, but they were speaking in demon tongue. I looked to Mallini, who stood with her head cocked, listening.

I gave her a questioning look and she shook her head slightly, frowning as she concentrated.

Then the language switched to mortal tongue.

"I do not see why we must speak this way," a female said.

"It is required for the ball. The prince's orders," another female voice replied.

The first speaker said something in demon tongue.

"Stop. You know what will happen if you disobey. Train your brain to speak this. The prince demands it."

"But why?"

"I do not presume to know, and you should not question lest you end up like the others."

She replied in rapid demon tongue and the sound of a slap cut her off, followed by soft sobbing and reluctant soothing sounds.

The voices drifted away.

I turned to Mallini. "What was that about? I didn't catch all of it."

"They were talking about the prince. Something about him being...dangerous."

"What do you mean?"

She blinked, frowning. "They said he'd already killed too many and that there was no way out."

Huh? "What the fuck?"

"I have no idea, but they sounded scared."

Knowledge was power. "So let's find out why." I hurried after the two females.

Mallini followed. "Nyx, this might be a bad idea."

"We need to find that healer and they could help."

"Good point."

We rounded the corner, and I spotted a figure carrying a basket up ahead.

"Hey!" I broke into a jog toward her.

She froze and turned to stare at me, her body tensing in fight-or-flight response.

Mallini called out something in demon tongue and she relaxed a little.

She looked zuni but she had tiny horns like an imp,

and her skin had an ochre tinge like Gus's. She also looked young, her dark-lashed amber eyes wide with wariness as her gaze flicked between us.

"What can I do for you." She enunciated the words carefully and ended on a wince as if she wasn't quite sure she'd gotten it right.

"We're looking for a healer," Mallini said. "Erantha?"

Her eyes flew wide. "You are the Satan spawn."

I guess news of our arrival had spread. "That's right."

She caught her bottom lip between her teeth and glanced over her shoulder.

"What is it?" Mallini prompted softly. "You look frightened. We'd like to help."

The zuni shook her head slightly, muttering something in demon tongue then wincing again. "Sorry. I forget."

Mallini soothed her in the demon language, shooting a quick glance my way. I nodded, letting her know it was okay to continue in that language if it helped to get the information we needed.

They spoke softly for a couple of minutes, Mallini's nods encouraging her to keep speaking. The zuni rattled off stuff I couldn't understand, but the tension in Mallini's jaw told me it couldn't be good.

My scalp prickled and the sensation of being watched tightened my nape. I glanced over my shoulder, down the empty corridor. A cold breeze brushed the tendrils of hair that had fallen free of my ponytail and the conviction we were being watched intensified. But there was no one there, and nowhere for anyone to hide.

I shook it off and turned back to Mallini and the maid.

The maid finally fell silent, and Mallini patted her shoulder and said something else.

The maid nodded, then broke away and headed round the corner.

"Well?" I waited for Mallini to fill me in.

She jerked her head back the way we'd come, then started off down the corridor.

I fell into step beside her.

"Looks like ever since Prince Merihem's favored mistress was murdered he's gotten a little execution happy," she said. "Apparently Merihem fell sick and blames himself for not being there to protect her."

"Wait...fallen get sick?"

"Not often, rarely really, and never in the mortal realms, but they are not invulnerable to the demon realm."

"So, his mistress was killed while he was sick?"

"Yes. They say his right-hand man Dhuma killed her. That he was in love with her and she spurned him so in a fit of rage he killed her."

Dhuma...that name rang a bell. Why did it ring a bell? And then it hit me. Sev had mentioned that name. He'd been the general in the daimon queen's army. He'd also been her mate.

"Dhuma is a daimon," Mallini continued.

Of course he was.

"I'm not sure what the story is there, but I've heard rumors from Dhuma saved Merihem's life to Dhuma is Merihem's prisoner. I don't know."

There was a lot they didn't know about the true history, and it was time to fill them all in. I'd gather them as soon as I got back to the quarters and tell them what Ignatius had told me.

"The maid said the prince has mood swings," Mallini continued. "And when he falls into a bad mood, creatures die. Apparently, he's had five guards and six fortress staff executed in the past month and several more imprisoned. Everyone is terrified for their lives, but they can't leave because they're bound in servitude to him, so the majority are hiding out in the south keep, the staff residences. They only leave to do the jobs they need to and go straight back."

"That would explain why no one was here when Hrath arrived."

"Exactly. She seems to think we might be able to help—you know, as potential Satans."

"Wait, why does she need us? What about the other princes? The conclave is happening. They're here. If there's something wrong with Merihem, they'll step in, right?"

"It doesn't work that way. This is Merihem's

domain. His fortress. His realm. Levistus and Ramiel have no authority here. Although she said that Prince Ramiel has been a frequent visitor, attempting to steer Merihem away from his black moods."

"So the princes know he's going nuts?"

"It would seem so."

"Then they need to take away his power."

"I don't think they can. From what I remember, there are ancient binding contracts that give the princes power and autonomy over their realms and their citizens. The right to protect them. Satan is the only authority who can petition a change. The ancient contracts cannot be altered without Satan."

"Because Satan is a neutral party..." It was making more sense why someone would want the Satan seat in their power. "But there is no Satan yet, so in the meantime, he just gets to kill people?"

She sighed. "It would seem so."

Anger flared inside me. "That's fucking bullshit." I exhaled sharply. "You know what, I hate fucking contracts."

"The princes won't rock the boat by challenging Merihem. Not overtly anyway. Besides, knocking off a few zuni and imps means nothing to a fallen, not in the grand scheme of things."

An awful thought filled my mind. "What about a bunch of Satan spawn?"

"What?"

"We came here sure we'd be safe. That the princes

wouldn't want to hurt the only creatures who could fill Satan's seat, but that's assuming they're thinking with logic and reason."

"Which Merihem isn't..."

"No. In fact, if Satan is the only being who has the potential to take away Merihem's power, then—"

"We might all be in terrible danger."

CHAPTER FORTY-FIVE

ARTIMUS

It's been hours; surely the conclave will break soon. This isn't my first conclave. I've come to several, accompanying Satan as his aide, never permitted into the meeting room but on hand during breaks to discuss issues and advise.

My chest feels hollow as I sit in this plush waiting room as memories of the last time we were here fill my mind.

He'd been standing by the window, his huge frame blocking the sunlight, dark hair so much like Nyx's gleaming where the rays touched it.

I'd been young then, excited for this opportunity, starry-eyed around the other princes and eager to please but they'd shunned me. Looked down on me.

We'd been about to sit down to eat, but before I

could take my place beside Satan, Ramiel had spoken. "Fetch some more wine and more bread." He hadn't even looked at me, just gestured for me to be off.

I'd faltered, unsure.

"Are you deaf?" he'd snapped.

"No, he is not," Satan had said, his expression stony granite. "And he isn't here to serve you."

Ramiel rolled his eyes. "I'm sure you can share your *help*, Beelzebub."

My cheeks had burned with shame then, but Satan's next words had filled my chest with pride.

"He's not the help. He's my advisor and my adopted son."

That was the first time he'd claimed me as such. With that one sentence he'd elevated me, but now he was gone.

Still, his legacy lives.

It lives in all the spawn, but mostly in Nyx. More than anyone can ever know. I've vowed to him that I'll protect her and I've almost failed because of my weakness. My fear.

It can't happen again.

I'd agreed to bring the spawn with me, and I need to ensure their petition is heard and granted.

The double doors to the meeting room open and Prince Levistus and Ramiel come out. I've forgotten how large the original fallen are. Over seven feet tall, powerful males with wings that span twelve feet and eyes like flame. I've forgotten, and seeing them brings an ache to the pit of my belly because they remind me desperately of my adopted father. It's been just over a month...How can I have forgotten his presence already?

I swallow the lump that forms in my throat and stand tall as Ramiel's gaze falls on me.

His brows flick up slightly. "Ah, Satan's representative. What was your name..."

He knows my name, but he likes to make others feel small. "Artimus."

"Yes, yes. You're early. Petitions are the day after tomorrow."

"I'm aware. I wished to speak to you before then."

"Feel free to speak," Levistus says.

The golden-haired fallen takes a seat at the table set for two...two? Where is Merihem's place?

"Well?" Ramiel demands.

"I wish to address all three princes."

Ramiel and Levistus exchange an indecipherable look.

"Merihem is indisposed," Ramiel says. "You may speak to us. We will pass on the message."

Something is wrong here, but I'm in no position to argue. "I have Satan spawn with me, and they wish to make a private petition to you."

Levistus's eyes widen in surprise. "You brought the spawn here?"

Ramiel's mouth tightens. "On whose authority did you bring them here?"

The sense of wrongness grows. "I wasn't aware I required permission."

Ramiel's eyes flash, jaw tightening. "You ignorant fool, you have no idea—"

"Enough," Levistus intervenes. He looks to me. "You must take the spawn back to Morningstar immediately."

"Why?"

"Do not question me, boy."

My insides quiver but I stand tall. "They won't leave without an audience and an opportunity to put forth their petition."

"They do not have a choice," Ramiel snaps. "I'll arrange for a conji to open a portal back to Morningstar for you within the hour. Be prepared."

"A portal like the one we took here. The one that left us in the old forest."

Levistus pales.

Ramiel curses.

The door on the other side of the room flies open and Merihem saunters in. His shirt is untucked, his caramel hair in disarray, and there's a goblet clutched in his hand.

His eyes sparkle eerily as they sweep over Ramiel and Levistus to land on me. He makes an "o" with his mouth. "Artimus? Oh my, how you've grown."

I incline my head. "Prince Merihem."

He waves a hand in dismissal. "Call me Meri."

What the fuck? I glance at Levistus and he shakes his head a little in warning.

"How have you been?" Merihem flops into the nearest seat and throws his boots up onto the table. Wine sloshes out of the goblet and onto the table but he doesn't seem to notice.

He's a handsome male, slender, tall, and lithe in comparison to the other two muscular males. I remember him as being quick to smile. Warm and empathetic, totally at odds with the male he chose as duke for the Court of Shadows. But this male is too relaxed, too...euphoric.

"Are you looking forward to the ball?" Merihem swigs from the goblet.

I'm suddenly certain I shouldn't be here. That I shouldn't have brought the spawn here because something is very wrong with this fallen.

"I came to pay my respects." I smile warmly. "But I won't be staying for the ball."

Ramiel's shoulders relax as he realizes I've finally gotten the message that the spawn and I need to get the fuck out of here.

"Oh?" Merihem pouts. "But I was so looking forward to meeting the spawn." He gives me a knowing, wicked smile, and my stomach turns.

He knows about the spawn. It's too late to leave.

"They don't belong here," Levistus says. "They should not have come." He stands. "I'll be sending them back to Morningstar where they belong."

Merihem's expression goes cold. "You will do no such thing. This is my realm. My rules. I say they stay. They stay and feast and..." His lips curve. "Present their petition for our consideration." He takes a slow sip from his goblet. "It is the least we can do for the Satan-to-be."

There's no denying the tension and threat in the air, and I know with certainty that bringing Nyx and the others here was a big mistake.

Chapter Forty-Six

NYX

"I can't believe it." Gus stared at me, wide-eyed. "The lies..."

"Yep." I sat back in my seat. "But it makes sense."

"It does," Tristeene said.

"I bet my mother knew." Mallini's tone was bitter. "She knows everything."

I'd filled them in on what Ignatius had told me about the abyss being a metropolis and about the djinn world. About how they'd lived alongside the daimons just like the fallen had until Lucifer had fucked with the pit.

"Propaganda," Veena said. "Appearances. It's all that matters here."

"Does Keelan know?" Gus asked.

"Yeah. I filled him in once we got back from the Court of Flame." He was asleep now. The healer had come and dosed him up, leaving enough tincture for the next dose.

Veena sat up suddenly and looked toward the entrance.

"What is it?" Tristeene asked.

She frowned and shook her head. "Nothing...I just...I thought I saw something."

We all looked toward the door. There was nothing of note to see but my scalp crawled.

Veena shuddered and curled against me. I put my arm around her. I'd felt that weird sensation of being watched earlier too... The warm breath on my neck...

"Maybe this place is haunted," Mallini said.

The door opened, making us all jump. Hrath entered, followed by a harassed-looking Artimus. The seneschal's waistcoat was open, top buttons of his shirt undone, sleeves rolled up, hair mussed like he'd been raking his fingers through it. His sapphire eyes were dark, the corners of his mouth tight.

I tensed. "What happened?"

"I'm not entirely sure." He strode over to the window and stood with his back to us. "But I believe bringing you all here was a bad idea. I believe you may be in danger."

"Agreed," Hrath said. "I spent the last few hours speaking to the staff in the south side of the fortress. Prince Merihem is not...well."

Looked like we'd come to the same conclusions. "Yeah, we heard. We spoke to a maid earlier."

"And it's too late to leave," Artimus said. "Merihem knows you're here and he demands you attend the ball and present your petition." His jaw flexed. "Princes Ramiel and Levistus tried to warn me…"

"Do you think the carriage diversion was Merihem?" Veena asked.

"I don't know. It makes no sense."

"If Merihem is going crazy, then only Satan has the power to force him to step down, right?" Mallini said.

Artimus went pale.

I gave him a mirthless smile. "Kill us all, stop Satan being picked."

"And lose the power in the seat," Artimus said. "Why would he risk that?"

"Maybe he doesn't care," Gus said. "Insanity doesn't thrive on logic and reason."

"Insanity is not so premeditated either," Hrath said. "I believe we must be wary and not too quick to draw conclusions."

He was right. "Agreed. So what do you suggest?"

"That we play the game. We attend the ball, and you present your petition. Remember there will be two other princes present. Both of whom will want to protect the potential Satan. Both who will be willing to provide an escape route." He lifted his chin. "I will speak to Levistus and ensure we have a portal back to Morningstar as soon as the petition has been heard.

That way we satisfy Merihem's demand that you attend the event and our need to be safely away from this place."

"Sounds good to me," Mallini said.

"Get some rest," Artimus said wearily. "I have a suspicion we'll need our wits about us tomorrow."

He broke away from us and disappeared down one of the corridors leading to whichever room he'd picked.

Hrath walked over to the main door and studied it for a long beat before raising his hand and running it along the frame.

"What are you doing?" Gus asked.

"Setting an alarm system. If anyone enters through this door, I will know." He looked at me. "You will be safe."

"Can I sleep in your room?" Veena asked me.

"Sure you can."

"Maybe we should all sleep in here. Together." Tristeene's nonchalant shrug belied the unease in her eyes.

I returned the shrug. "Sure, sounds like a plan."

Everyone hurried off to get changed for bed and bring duvets and pillows into the main room. I stood and stretched, about to do the same, but Hrath blocked my path.

"Ignatius has charged me with protecting you," he said. "You must know that if the worst occurs, I will put your life above your siblings."

I gave him a wry smile. "I can't control what you do, Hrath, but you should know, if you try to stop me from protecting my family, if you try and take me away from them, you'll have a fight on your hands."

I turned and walked away but not before I caught the flare in his eyes. Pride? Hope?

No. It was respect.

Chapter Forty-Seven

The soft snores of my siblings filled the moonlit room. We'd pulled the cushions off the sofas and brought mattresses in from the bedroom, so the floor was now one huge mattress. Hrath had retired to his room an hour ago and exhaustion had pulled everyone into sleep soon after. Tristeene had stayed awake a little longer and we'd chatted for a while, but she'd drifted off too now.

Veena was tucked between us, her cheek pillowed on her folded hands. She looked so sweet and vulnerable. Even though she was technically an adult, she was still child-like, needing comfort and protection.

In this world, they were all young and inexperienced.

Tristeene was the most mature with all she'd had to endure growing up. There was wisdom and the echo of pain in her eyes. It had flared in the carriage when Hrath had rejected her.

I still hadn't spoken to her about that, and it felt like the time to do so had passed. I rolled onto my side and closed my eyes, willing sleep to come.

Long minutes ticked by, and I was still wide awake.

Fuck this.

I carefully climbed off the makeshift bed and crossed the room to the corridor Artimus had vanished down a couple of hours ago.

There were several rooms, doors open, empty and dark. I stopped at the closed door with light spilling out from the crack beneath it and knocked.

Artimus pulled the door open a moment later, his dark brows pinched, expression troubled, but my gaze had already slipped down to his chest, skimming over the bare expanse of creamy skin stretched over powerful muscle and sinew. He was pale compared to the fallen and the efreet, compared to most of the creatures in Morningstar.

What would he feel like?

"Nyx?" He stepped back and I entered the room.

"I couldn't sleep."

"Me neither." He snagged a shirt from the back of a chair and slipped it on but didn't do up the buttons. "You want to talk?"

I wanted to run, hit something, or fuck. Exertion to tire me out.

Talking would have to do. "Sure." I sat in the chair and crossed my legs. "Let's talk."

He sat on the end of his bed. "What do you want to talk about, Nyx?"

"Why didn't you feed when we asked?"

"I knew you weren't going to let that go."

"I need to know, Arty. I need to know so that I can forgive you for what happened to Keelan."

"Maybe your forgiveness doesn't matter to me."

I just stared at him levelly until he sighed.

"I don't feed fully, ever. I can't. Not without risking losing control, and with you all in the carriage, in a confined space, it was too much of a risk. I thought I had enough time. That I could hold the allure. I was wrong."

"You were afraid of losing control over your demon."

His head whipped up and then his lips curved in a bitter smile. "I see that rumors are still rife. What have you heard?"

I relayed what Zinichi and Tristeene had told me. "But I've learned not to listen to rumor. I prefer to get the story from the source."

He pressed his palms to the bed and tucked in his chin. "There are some stories that are too painful to speak of, but you're right. You and Keelan could have died because of me. You deserve to know why. You deserve to know why so you can be sure that it will never happen again." He met my gaze. "That you can trust me to protect you."

"I get a lot of that. I don't need it. In fact, I'd give it up in a heartbeat for some truth. The truth will help me decide if I can trust you, if I can let my guard down, but for some reason, the truth is sorely lacking in Morningstar."

His chuckle was raw and abrasive. "You have no idea."

I waited for him to continue, noting the way his fingers curled into the duvet, the tension rippling up his forearms. Whatever he was about to tell me wasn't going to be easy.

"The first time I fed fully after reaching incubus maturity I killed ten females."

I stared at him, speechless for long seconds. "Go on."

"My bloodline, the Bsar bloodline, is...different. The males are required to feed intensely during their transition from boy to man. It lasts two to three days. Satan knew this. He found ten females willing to feed me blood and sexual energy. But when the hunger hit, I lost control. My demon side took over, and when I surfaced the women were dead. Drained, throats ripped out." He swallowed and licked his lips. "But it wasn't over. The hunger wasn't done with me. Feeding in a frenzy had awoken something. They had to lock me away for months. Months of alternating between lucidity and insanity. Months in which I starved myself rather than risk losing control. But starving myself made the hunger and the demon stronger. It took months to find a balance, to wrangle my demon into submission and control it. I learned to feed sparingly, to always be teetering on the edge of hunger and never to fully satisfy myself. It's the only way to be sure I won't lose control like that again."

His reticence in the carriage made sense now. He'd made a judgment call that had gone wrong. "I'm sorry for what you went through."

He looked up in surprise.

"I get it now. But do you? How much do you really know about your bloodline?"

He frowned. "I know my father was close to Satan."

"What else?"

"I'm not sure where you're going with this?"

"I'm not going anywhere. I'm trying to find out what you know about who you are and where you came from, not just what you were told. Because I'm beginning to think that there are blinkers on a lot of eyes in this place. That history has been manipulated to hide the true reason behind your Chaos War."

His eyes narrowed. "What have you learned?"

Could I tell him? Yes. My gut told me now was the time. That he could be trusted. That he deserved to know the reality of the world he came from. That his kind, abyssbloods, weren't something dirty like the fallen liked them to believe.

I told him what Ignatius had revealed to me.

He sat in silence for long, aching minutes and then he let out a harsh bark of laughter. "Satan knew…"

"Yeah, he knew."

His throat bobbed. "But he didn't tell me. I can understand that. He probably had some kind of agreement with the fallen not to reveal the truth, but he would have told me if something about my bloodline made us dangerous."

"Would he though?" I tilted my head. "I get that you cared for him, that he raised you as a son, but what did he do for you? How much did you get out of the deal and how much did he? I mean, he got a sidekick, molded and shaped into what he needed."

His jaw ticked. "You didn't know him. He had a good heart. A noble heart."

"He left contracts that enforce murdering his offspring. Yeah, he sounds like a fucking peach."

We faced off in an eye lock, each confident in their worldview. I dropped my gaze first because I hadn't come here to argue, to make him feel like shit, or take away the only parent he'd ever known. I knew what that felt like. I wasn't about to inflict it on someone else. Let him have his happy mind palace where he and Satan held hands and skipped through a field of sunflowers. Whatever. I didn't care.

What I did care about was keeping my siblings safe, and I needed him in top form to help me do that.

"You should speak to Ignatius about your bloodline. He might know more. I mean, maybe the answer to the reason you're struggling to control your demon side is hidden in the Bsar history."

"Maybe," he conceded.

A wave of weariness washed over me, telling me it was time to turn in. I stood slowly. "Tell me we're going to make it out of this fortress alive."

He stood and approached, standing a mere foot away so he towered over me. "I can promise you that I'll do everything in my power to keep you and your siblings safe."

The fact that he'd included the others in his vow made my cool heart warm even more to him. I tipped my chin up and studied his beautiful face made of planes and angles where the shadows caressed it.

"Why are you sleeping with her?" My question came out as a whisper, like the prompt to a secret.

His throat bobbed. "To keep you safe." He reached up and ran a finger down my cheek, ending at my jaw. "To make sure I know what she knows, what she plans. To make sure she doesn't do anything that could hurt you." My pulse leapt as he grazed my bottom lip with his thumb. "But when I'm with her, inside her... fucking her, all I think about is you."

My stomach flipped hard, and my breath caught and twisted in my throat. "She lied to you and almost made us miss this trip. I don't think your cock magic is working on her."

His gaze dropped to my mouth. "I think you might be right."

My heart beat faster, the pulse at the base of my throat thrumming erratically.

His hand slid down my throat, fingers sliding to curl around my nape and squeezing slightly so that my head tipped back. He brought his mouth close, breath feathering across my lips. "Erinea doesn't like to lose. She doesn't like being dropped by her lovers."

I'd had my no-kiss rule shattered by Sin, then Ignatius, and I'd broken it for Sev, and now my lips ached to taste Artimus. My body vibrated with the need to press against his.

I wanted him.

But I wasn't going there, not until he got rid of that bitch Erinea.

I brought my head closer so my lips almost brushed his and whispered, "When you decide you no longer need to stay on her good side, then let me know." I slipped free of him and headed for the door.

I had a crazy prince to deal with tomorrow, and I had no doubt I'd need my wits about me to do it.

Chapter Forty-Eight

I'd never been so bored and on tenterhooks at the same time. The ball would begin at sunset, but until then, Hrath and Artimus insisted on keeping us cloistered in the quarters to keep us safe.

Keelan was still healing, asleep in his room with a fresh poultice on his abdomen. He wouldn't be attending the ball.

There were enough rooms and corridors to wander through, but after an hour I'd explored them all, and there was only so much sitting around I could take, so when Hrath returned from his morning excursion, stone-faced and agitated, and suggested we play a game to pass the time, I was in.

He produced a pack of cards and we settled around the table. Artimus joined us, sleeves rolled up, shirt buttons undone. Again. I was getting way too much skin on show from him for my liking. Or maybe it was just to my liking and that was the problem, and the look in his eye, that slight smirk on his lips as he settled himself directly fucking opposite me, told me the bastard was perfectly aware of said effect he was having.

I didn't get flustered by a man's naked body. Not usually, but I think the whole forbidden fruit thing when it came to Arty was getting to me.

I wanted that juicy, delicious fruit.

But I'd set the boundaries. Drawn the lines, and I had to stick to them. Plus, there was Sev to think of. He'd wheedled his way into my heart, and although we hadn't discussed what our relationship was, the boundaries, the whole *are we exclusive* thing, I owed it to him to talk it through before I...before I what? Took another lover?

Damn. I was totally into that idea.

"Nyx?" Gus nudged me, drawing me out of my thoughts to find that everyone was staring at me. Waiting.

For what? I had no clue. I wasn't gonna bluff my way out of this. "Sorry, I spaced out. What?"

"Oh?" Artimus smirked and sat back in his seat, folding his bare forearms so that they were on display. Again. "What were you thinking about?"

I narrowed my eyes threateningly.

"Would you like me to go over the rules again?" Hrath asked with infinite patience.

"That would be great, thank you, Hrath." I shot him a warm smile.

He went over the rules. A simple bluffing game where the cards were distributed between us all and we had to get rid of them by placing them face down in pairs, trios, or groups of four, then state what cards we were getting rid of. I'd played it before in the taverns back home. It was called all sorts of names, depending on the circle it was played in—liar, bullshit, cheat, to name a few of the tamer ones.

"I get it." I jerked my chin to the deck. "Deal them out."

Hrath dealt and everyone sorted their cards. Veena struggled with all her cards, her hands too small to hold them, and ended up placing them in piles in front of her.

"I'll go first," Artimus said.

The game began, first two rounds no one contested and then the calls of liar began. It didn't take long to realize that Mallini and Veena were bad at bluffing. Gus seemed to be the one calling everyone out and won the first game easily. We played again and again, getting rowdier and rowdier until we were calling each other out just for the sake of it, until Tristeene had way too many cards in her hand and my stomach hurt from laughing.

For a couple of hours I forgot where we were or why we were here. I forgot the stakes. I forgot the danger and simply enjoyed the company of my siblings and friends.

But time flies when you're having fun, and before we knew it, there was a knock on the door.

Hrath answered and let in several zuni carrying piles of clothes. I recognized one as the maid we'd spoken to earlier, but the warning in her eyes stopped me from greeting her.

Mallini kept silent too.

It was obvious she didn't want the other maids knowing she'd spoken to us.

"Offerings from Prince Merihem," one of the maids said. "We are here to help the female spawn dress. Guards will arrive in an hour to escort you to the ball."

Tristeene picked up one of the items—a flowing tunic top with a gauzy overlay studded with tiny gems. There were leggings to match and soft-soled slippers.

The guys had fitted tunics, silk shirts, and fitted pants.

Tristeene passed out the clothes and we exchanged outfits until we had stuff we thought would fit.

A maid drifted to my side and smiled shyly at me. "May I help you?"

"Sure."

The other three maids latched on to Mallini, Veena, and Tristeene. We split and wandered to our rooms to change and get our hair done.

I pulled the clothes on quickly and sat at the

dresser as the zuni brushed out my hair. She worked silently, glancing up at my reflection from time to time with a shy smile.

I caught her gaze in the mirror. "Have you worked here long?"

She blinked sharply, then nodded. "I was born here."

"Your mortal tongue is very good."

"Thank you, my mother was strict about my learning it well. She hoped..."

"What?"

"Nothing."

Yeah, that didn't work for me because now I needed to know. "You can tell me. What's spoken in this room stays in this room."

She paused in her braiding and met my gaze. "My mother hoped I would find my way to working for Satan one day in Morningstar."

"You have fallen blood?"

She smiled wryly. "Many of us do. The fallen sowed their seed well."

There was no bitterness in her tone. She was stating a fact. "There are lots of Nephalem?"

"Most demon bloodlines have a little fallen in them now. Abyssbloods too. Pure demon blood is rare, but there are a handful of bloodlines that refuse to procreate with the fallen."

"Oh?" I was intrigued. "Who are they?"

"House Mairva is the main one in Libidine. There are some in the other realms and then there is the house of Istmee, but no one knows where they are."

"What do you mean no one knows?"

"They vanished centuries ago. Some believe that they live among us, hiding in plain sight, others believe that they succeeded in opening a portal to a new realm."

"Why would they need to do that?"

A shiver ran up my arms, gooseflesh chasing in its wake. The maid stilled, her eyes going wide in the mirror.

"What is it?"

She shook her head quickly and smiled. "You have beautiful hair. I think braids and then we can put it up."

I wanted to press, but the tension in her neck and shoulders warned me not to. She worked in silence for several minutes, twisting and pinning my hair and leaving a section loose to fall over my shoulder and accentuate my slender neck, giving me a graceful look.

My skin prickled and I looked down as the gooseflesh smoothed out. What the heck?

The maid exhaled as if she'd been holding her breath.

"What's your name?"

"Neema."

"Neema, what the hell just happened?"

"I'm not sure I should speak of it."

I turned in my seat so I could look her in the eye. "I beg to differ. Tell me what I just felt wasn't in my head."

"It was not. It was real and I have felt it before many times over the past few months. A presence."

"A ghost?"

"I do not know but others have felt it too. It listens and watches. People disappear or are taken to be punished. People who may have said things they should not."

An invisible spy, then...Intriguing. "Thank you, Neema."

I stood and adjusted the flowy tunic that fastened over my boobs and left my lower abdomen bare. The ensemble was feminine but practical too.

"You look beautiful," Neema said.

"Thanks to you."

Her cheeks pinkened. "No, the beauty was there, I simply helped to make it shine."

I fingered a tendril of hair that lay against my cheek, softening my features. It was deceptive and I loved it.

There was a knock on my door. "Guards are here," Mallini called.

I took a deep breath. "Show time."

I joined the others in the main room and let out a low whistle at the sight of my siblings all trussed up and glittery.

Tristeene's hair was in a French braid woven with

stars. Veena's hair was pinned in a high ponytail that was then braided and woven with tiny gems. Mallini's plumes gleamed as if they'd been brushed and polished. Gus's ochre skin stood out against the sparkling material of his tunic, his hair slicked to one side. Hrath stood by the door, dressed in the clothes he'd arrived in, or something similar, it was hard to tell. Artimus was missing.

I raised a questioning brow in Hrath's direction, and he glanced at Keelan's door. Artimus emerged a moment later, closing the door softly behind him.

He straightened and turned to us, and I lost my breath for a moment, because I'd forgotten how devastatingly slick he could look in his formal attire— midnight blue tonight. A color that made his sapphire eyes pop and a cut that hugged his frame in ways that accentuated his toned body. That waistcoat and pants must have been tailor-made for him.

He met my gaze, and a spark ignited in my chest. He raked me over, a slow, leisurely sweep that was almost primal in nature.

"You'll do," he said.

Fucker.

"Will Keelan be safe here on his own?" Veena asked.

"There's a Minorax guard with him," Artimus said. "An old friend of Briatzu. Keelan will be watched over while we are gone."

There was a knock at the main door.

"Our escorts are getting impatient," Hrath said.

"Then let's go." Artimus led the way to the doors.

We followed him like good little sheep.

We were about to go to a ball, so why did it feel like we were headed to an execution?

Chapter Forty-Nine

We climbed flights of stairs made of dark stone that glittered as if embedded with moonlight, and strolled down corridors with dark marble floors and walls made of gray stone hung with tapestries of fantastical patterns and gorgeous vistas. The music of wind and string instruments drifted toward us, designed to provide a backdrop to the hum and buzz of conversation.

The guards led us through a vaulted doorway and onto a semi-circular platform that looked down on a massive ballroom held up by pillars and swirling with color. So much fucking color that it made my eyes hurt. Red and orange, cerulean and turquoise, gold and silver.

Demons, devils, and abyssbloods danced or stood talking in clusters or people-watching as servers dressed in…what the fuck? Were they wearing the same outfits as us?

I looked to Artimus. "Do you see that?"

His jaw flexed. "I do."

"He's dressed us like the staff."

"It's a message," Hrath said.

Anger flared in my chest. "He's telling us we're beneath him."

"I don't like this," Tristeene said. "It feels off."

No one seemed to have noticed our presence, probably exactly what Merihem had wanted. Dress the spawn like staff and make them feel small and invisible.

The sensation of being watched prickled across my back. I turned my head to find a male watching me from across the room. He stood apart from the others, goblet in hand, his chin tipped up. His dark hair was tousled, falling across his forehead and giving him a boyish look, but there was nothing boyish about those whiskey eyes. They were hard, ancient, cutting…knowing.

I leaned toward Hrath. "Who is that?"

Hrath followed my gaze. "Prince Ramiel." He shifted closer to me. "He's coming this way."

And he was. He was winding his way toward us, people stepping back to let him through.

This was one of the original fallen.

My breath came shorter and faster the closer he

got. Finally he was standing in front of us, his gaze fixed on me, probing, intense. There was something familiar about his face too, the arch of his brows, the flat, high cheekbones and the sharp edge of his jaw, but I couldn't put my finger on what. His mouth was thin but wide. I imagined it could look cruel if he wanted it to, but there was something enticing about the shape of those lips, the way the corners lifted ever so slightly as if on the verge of a smile.

And he was still staring at me.

Artimus stepped closer, his silk shirt brushing against my bare arm.

"Ramiel," he greeted the fallen.

Ramiel blinked sharply and looked across at Artimus, then back down at me. "I apologize. For a moment there...You reminded me of someone."

"She is Satan spawn," Artimus said smoothly. "And she has his eyes."

Ramiel focused on my eyes, his gaze softening. "Yes...Yes, that she does." He looked down at my tunic and his brows pinched. "I assume Merihem sent you that attire?"

"He did," Artimus said. "Where is the prince? If we could step into a private room and have an audience with you all, then—"

The sound of a gong, an actual fucking gong, vibrated the air, cutting off Artimus. The room fell silent and still as a set of doors across from us swung open.

A male entered. Long, rich caramel hair threaded with gold and in disarray. He wore pants, but his shirt was open, and he had no shoes on.

Everyone parted to let him through.

Wait a fucking second, could that be—

"Merihem," Ramiel groaned. "Excuse me." He hurried across the platform and down the steps, beelining toward the prince.

But Prince Merihem wasn't alone. A huge male trailed in after him, hands bound before him, head bowed. He was easily over seven feet tall. Larger than the fallen in stature. His feet were also bare, his clothes dirty and in tatters, and a silver collar around his neck was attached to a chain that Merihem was holding.

He was leading this male into the room like a dog. A beaten, abused dog.

I grit my teeth.

"Dhuma..." Hrath said softly. "So it's true..."

"You know him?"

"Yes...from a long time ago."

"They say he killed Merihem's mistress."

"I do not believe that. Dhuma would never kill an innocent."

A soft buzz skittered across the crowd below as they made way for Ramiel's imposing form. He was almost to Merihem now.

But another male beat him to it. This one was huge like Ramiel but smaller than Dhuma. I couldn't see his face properly, just the wavy fall of his golden hair that was pinned back in a half pony.

"Levistus," Hrath said. "They will get him under control."

"I doubt it," Artimus muttered.

He was right. Merihem shrugged them off with a cackle that was high-pitched and eerie.

My scalp tightened at the sound, my gut clenching. Something was so off about it, something about the prince himself, and when he raised his head to look right at us, a sick feeling bloomed inside me.

Tristeene sucked in a sharp breath and Veena whimpered.

"It's okay." Gus put his arm around her. "It's okay."

Merihem's gaze zeroed in on me and that sick feeling intensified, forcing me to swallow back bile. He smiled, slow, deliberate, and wicked.

"Well, hello there, uninvited guests." The room fell silent as all eyes turned to us. "Yes, yes, look at them. Satan spawn, come to petition the princes. To petition *me*."

Ramiel leaned in and said something to Merihem, but the prince shrugged him off again. "This is my realm. My rules. And I know what they want. I know what they came here to ask for. But I feel that we should *all* hear it."

Artimus took a step forward. "Prince Merihem, the spawn would like a private audience."

His lip curled. "They will get what I give them!"

Oh, God. He was fucking nuts.

Levistus placed a hand on Merihem's shoulder, leaning in to whisper something.

Merihem shook his head. "Now. Here. You will petition, and we will decide."

Ramiel and Levistus exchanged glances over Merihem's head and then Ramiel spoke to us. "Who speaks for you?"

"That would be you, Nyx," Artimus said.

I took a deep breath, lifted my chin, and walked forward. "I, Nyx of no family name, speak for the Satan spawn." My voice carried throughout the room, strong and almost regal. There was movement behind the three princes as Dhuma lifted his head and looked straight at me. His eyes, dark pools of sorrow, widened slightly. His chest heaved, and his mouth parted as he stared and stared.

I flicked my gaze back to the threat, to the crazy prince who was grinning manically at me.

"State your petition, child." He waved a hand to rush me along.

I'd spent ages running the words over and over in my mind, and they flowed from my lips smoothly now. "The Satan spawn petition the princes to abolish the first and final contracts of the ascension trials."

Silence followed my words for a long beat, then Merihem burst into laughter. "You wish to keep your competition alive?"

I raised my chin. "I wish to keep my family alive."

Ramiel's head whipped up, his gaze latching on to me. I forced my attention to stay on Merihem's laughing face.

"Family?" Merihem taunted. "They're your family now? How long have you known them?"

"Long enough. We don't deserve to die simply because of the blood that runs through our veins. We don't deserve to die because of a contract that was forged without our consent. We are not pawns in a game."

His eyes narrowed.

"The contracts were created after much deliberation," Levistus said. "To protect the seat and the power within it. To protect Satan."

I met his gaze. "We don't need a contract to protect the new Satan. We have each other. We will protect whoever wins the seat."

My siblings stepped beside me, a united front.

Levistus pressed his lips together, shooting Ramiel a questioning glance, but Merihem spoke before either of them could.

"A united front? Because you know them so well, right?"

A prickle of unease teased my nape. "Yes. I know them."

He smirked and canted his head. "Are you willing to bet your lives on it?"

Where was he going with this? I shot a sharp

glance toward Artimus, who shook his head slightly in warning.

"What are you doing?" Ramiel asked Merihem, impatience tainting his tone.

"Laying out the stakes, brother," Merihem sneered. "If they want us to abolish the petitions, then they need to prove their united front. *Prove* this familial connection."

"What did you have in mind," Levistus asked warily.

"A game. A simple little game, and if they win, we'll give them what they want."

Yeah, there was a catch. Always a catch. "And if we lose?"

"You die. All of you including your maimed Minorax sibling. All except..." He scanned us. "That one." He pointed at Veena, who let out a squeak. "She'll live. And with all of you dead, there'll be no need for any more trials."

"No," Veena said. "We won't do it."

Ramiel turned away from us, speaking urgently to Merihem and Levistus.

Merihem shoved him aside. "Answer me now. Play the game and claim your win or leave with the contracts intact."

"You do not get to decide for us," Levistus snapped. "Merihem, this must be a joint decision."

"You don't wish to abolish the contracts?" Merihem asked.

Levistus's mouth tightened. "I did not say that. The fact that the spawn have come all this way, together..." He glanced up at us, pressing his lips together, his gaze almost nostalgic. "I believe the contracts may not be necessary, that we can alter them, forge one to protect the new Satan. A contract that does not require unnecessary death."

The knot in my chest eased.

"And you agree with this?" Merihem asked Ramiel.

Ramiel nodded. "I do."

Merihem shrugged. "And so do I."

I sagged, but my relief was premature because his next words had tension radiating through me once again.

"But this is my realm, and I want a game first. A game to prove their connection. Only then will I agree to the changes in contract." He tipped his head up and smiled at us. "They can't give you what you want without me."

Fuck.

"Nyx..." Mallini's voice trembled. "I don't like this."

Neither did I. "We don't have a choice. Are you with me?" I looked to my siblings, needing them to agree, needing them on board.

"We are," they said in unison.

Tristeene slipped her hand into mine. "We can do this."

Her grip was firm and secure, giving me strength.

I met Merihem's challenge with a resolute nod. "We accept your terms."

Was it my imagination or did flames gleam in his eyes? He blinked and they were gone. "Good. And you, the *mouth* of the group," he sneered, "will be the one tested."

I smiled, cold and unaffected. "Bring it."

Chapter Fifty

Challenge accepted, everything moved fast. A Minorax guard approached Veena and steered her to the edge of the platform.

She went but not before shooting a glare toward Merihem.

Artimus and Hrath were asked to step aside, and I caught the disconcertion on their faces as they obliged.

It was just me and my siblings on the platform now, the focus of everyone's attention.

"Nyx, you will step down," Merihem said.

I made to move forward but Tristeene tugged me back and wrapped her arms around me. Mallini joined us, then Gus too, hugging us around the waist.

"Get off me," Veena snarled, and the next moment she was with us, drawn into the huddle by Gus.

I breathed them in, allowing their strength to course through me. "I'll be okay. We'll be okay."

"I know." Tristeene stepped back. "We know."

I broke away from them and climbed down to the main floor. The crowd parted, making a path to the princes.

I didn't look left or right. I didn't want to see their faces—the doubt, the fear, the concern. I'd seen enough from the podium to know that they didn't agree with Merihem's test.

The princes loomed closer until I was standing in their shadow. Merihem was the threat here, but for some reason my attention was drawn to the behemoth chained to Merihem and stationed to one side.

His head was no longer bowed. His eyes no longer filled with shadows of sorrow. He looked alert, poised, as if he was preparing for something. My attention dropped to his hands, curling and uncurling into fists at his side.

"Hello, spawn, are you with me?" Merihem taunted. "Ah, you like my pet? He is so pretty, is he not?"

Pretty was the last word I'd use to describe the daimon. Fierce was more apt.

"He was a bad boy, and now I have to punish him, don't I, Dhuma?"

The daimon's nostrils flared and he spoke, but not to Merihem, to me. Words that made no sense, but words that I knew instinctively weren't demon tongue.

"Shut up!" Merihem said. "You know the rules. You speak mortal tongue or demon tongue. Not your filthy archaic daimonword. There will be no secrets in my realm!" he screeched, hands balling into fists, veins in his neck popping.

What the fuck was his problem?

Dhuma's attention went to me. He said something else, his tone almost desperate.

I shook my head. "I'm sorry, I—"

Merihem yanked on the chain and white lightning circled Dhuma's throat. He let out a bellow of pain, eyes rolling back in his head.

Merihem cackled. "I love that sound."

"Stop it!" I rushed forward on instinct, intent on grabbing Merihem's hand, but Ramiel blocked me by throwing out his arm to create an unyielding muscular barrier. I pushed against it, my anger directed at the crazy prince. "What the fuck is wrong with you?"

Merihem stilled and his head slowly turned toward me. "What did you say?" His tone was lethal soft, and a shiver of fear shot up my spine.

"Allow me," Ramiel said.

He looked down his nose at me, his expression impervious even though his eyes were filled with conflict. "Speak to my brother that way again and I will rip out your tongue."

Merihem grinned. "Thank you, brother." He clapped his hands, his mood changing instantly. "This will be so much fun!" Ramiel let out a slow breath that I might have missed if I hadn't been so close to him.

"And now we begin." He waved a hand toward the platform where Tristeene, Gus, and Mallini stood.

I caught sight of a robed figure looming up behind them. His hood was up, casting his face into darkness.

"What are you doing?" I took a step back to the platform. "Who is tha—"

My siblings vanished and so did the figure.

I stared at the empty space where they'd just stood, heart pounding against my ribs in an effort to escape. I rounded on the princes. "Where are they? What did you do to them?"

"Merihem," Ramiel snapped. "Enough with the theatrics. Get on with the test. Now."

The command in his tone made me flinch, but Merihem seemed unperturbed. "Spoilsport." He sighed. "Your siblings are fine...For now. But they won't be for long. Find them before the sands run out, or lose."

"What do you mean?"

"They're hidden, but as you know them so well, as you are *family*, you should recognize them easily, right?" His eyes sparked with wicked glee.

"I don't understand."

"You will."

I felt a presence at my back, a hand on my shoulder, then the room melted away.

CHAPTER FIFTY-ONE

I materialized alone in a room filled with clutter. Like piles of items, stuff just chucked about. It looked like a storage room filled with paintings and ornaments, rolled-up carpets, and all sorts of bric-a-brac. A thick book with an ornate cover was propped on one shelf beside a pile of silken fabric and a set of silver plates. There was no order to this chaos that I could find.

Everything was piled onto wooden shelves that lined the room, taking up all the wall space.

"What the hell?" I walked into the center of the room—the only uncluttered part as far as I could tell. There were no doors or windows, just an overhead light and way too many shadowy corners. "What is this? What do you want me to do?" The robed figure stepped out of the gloom to my left, making me jump. "Motherfucker!"

"How rude." Merihem's voice echoed around me, coming from everywhere and nowhere.

The robed figure drew an hourglass from the folds of his robe and held it in his knobbly fingers.

The sands...Was this the time Merihem was talking about?

"Your siblings are in this room," Merihem said. "Hidden amongst my collection, and as you know them so well, you have as long as it takes for the hourglass to empty to find them."

He wasn't making sense to me. "What do you mean? There isn't anyone here but me and your...minion."

"Minion... I love it." He laughed with delight but sobered quickly, his voice dropping to something almost menacing. "Oh, they're with you all right. Just not in the form that you remember."

Realization dawned, horrific and impossible. "You turned them into *objects*?"

More laughter. "Isn't it genius? All you need to do to release them is touch an item and say your sibling's name. If you guess correctly, the item will vanish, and your sibling will be returned to the ballroom. If you're wrong...well..."

I didn't need him to clarify. "I get it."

"Wait." Ramiel's voice filled the chamber. A lifeline, maybe? I hoped so. "A benevolent prince would give some concession. A grace. I suggest three strikes. Three opportunities to be wrong."

"Agreed," Levistus said.

"Two strikes," Merihem huffed. "Two chances to be wrong. After that, once the time is up or you guess incorrectly, you lose."

He fell silent. Were they watching me? Could Artimus see me somehow?

The robed figure stepped forward and held out the hourglass. I peered into the dark recesses of his hood, desperate to see his face, and sucked in a breath when I caught sight of two glowing golden eyes.

My scalp crawled, nausea gripping me, and possibility bloomed in my mind. But there was no time to dwell on it, to pull it forth and examine it, because he flipped the hourglass and vanished, leaving the object floating mid-air, leaving it leaking sand much too quickly.

How much time did I have? My gut told me not nearly enough.

THE SAND WAS DRAINING, and so far, I hadn't come across any item that felt right. I was working on instinct, *feeling* for items, seeing if I'd be drawn to something. So far nothing. I picked up a paperweight, set it down, then fingered an ornate candlestick with rubies embedded in it.

No, that wasn't right.

Think, Nyx, think.

What did I know about my siblings? Gus first. Okay, so he was an imp. Smart, no... super smart. A wealth of knowledge, really. A bloody walking encyclopedia of...wait... I turned and scanned the room, searching for the huge tome I'd spotted when I'd materialized in the room earlier.

There!

I hurried toward it. The book was bound in leather with an ornate gold foil pattern that looked like...wings.

Tiny wings.

Gus's wings!

Please let me be right. I placed my hands on the book, took a deep breath, and said, "Gustus of House Solar." For a moment, nothing happened. My heart sank.

But then my hands smacked the wooden shelf with a soft, satisfying thud. The book was gone.

"Yes!"

"I wouldn't get so excited, Nyx," Merihem drawled. "Your time is running out."

I glanced at the hourglass. The sand ran faster. "What the hell? What did you do? That's cheating."

"Tick tock."

Bastard. Okay, think. Tristeene was a succubus. Gorgeous and graceful. I moved back to the candlesticks. Those were gorgeous and graceful, but so were several statuettes. Shit. What else? She was kind, empathetic, and charming.

Charming...

That was her gift. The ability to charm others. I moved across the shelves, scanning them for anything that might relate to charm, and spotted a bracelet hung with tiny charms.

It had to be.

I clutched it tight. "Tristeene of House Moray." I waited. Long seconds passed. Nothing happened. Fuck.

"Strike one," Merihem said.

The sands seemed to quicken through the hourglass. My head whirled and panic tightened my chest. I couldn't lose this. I couldn't fuck it up. We'd worked so hard, come so far, fought to be here, to be together.

Losing wasn't an option.

Focus.

I closed my eyes and took several breaths to center myself, and when I opened them, I saw it.

An item I'd passed several times.

A flute.

The snake from our first trial came to mind. Tristeene had charmed it. Snake charmers used flutes to charm snakes. Could it be? I picked it up.

Please be right. Okay...I could do this. It had to be right. "Tristeene of House Moray."

The flute vanished instantly. "Yes!" I let out a whoop and fist-pumped the air. "Take that, bitch!"

Two down, one to go, and I had one strike left. Merihem was silent. No taunts now. He knew he was about to lose. Problem was, Mallini was the sibling I knew the least, the one who'd held back the most. I scanned the room, hoping for inspiration. She was fast and strong. A warrior. Great with blades. Could she be a weapon?

I crossed the room to a set of daggers. They all had ornate silver hilts and serrated blades. I mean, Mallini could be pretty jagged and prickly when she wanted to be. I picked one up and turned it over, but it didn't feel right. I set it down, skimming the items on the shelf above. My gaze snagged on a painting propped up at the back of the shelf.

A bird in flight, kinda tilted to one side to avoid the arrows aiming for it.

A bird...Mallini had plumes and she was dodging arrows. It had to be. I grabbed the painting off the wall, confidence swelling in my chest as I said her name. "Mallini of House Furorem."

My words echoed around the room and the painting clung to my fingers, stubborn and solid.

Not Mallini.

My heart sank and my stomach dipped.

I was wrong.

"You're out of strikes, Nyx, and almost out of time."

I dropped the painting and ran back to the

hourglass. Oh shit, there was barely any sand left in it. I was fucked.

No. I had to find her. I had to!

I jogged back across the room to the first set of shelves. I'd missed something. I must have. I shuffled the paperweights about, noting a pendant and a quill. The feather?

No. It had to be more than that.

"One minute left…" he sing-songed.

My pulse raced, adrenaline flooding me, and my gaze zeroed in on one of the paperweights, focusing on the pattern. A yin and yang. Except on this one the yin was cracked and faded.

Broken.

"Ten seconds…" There was glee in the bastard's tone.

I grabbed the paperweight and held it up. Fuck it. If I was wrong, at least I'd go out trying. "Mallini of House Furorem."

The air cracked. The world tipped and my body slammed onto marble.

I was back in the ballroom. Triumph left me breathless. I'd done it.

I pulled myself up and stared at the platform, at my siblings, safe and sound. Tristeene had her hand to her mouth, tears in her eyes. Gus was grinning. Mallini smirked, head held high, and Veena beamed, her face alight with joy.

Artimus lifted his chin proudly and Hrath gave me

a nod of approval when our gazes caught.

I'd done it.

I'd won.

I turned to the princes, ready to claim my prize.

Merihem's expression was one of twisted, dark rage. "No," he snarled. "I want another test."

He sounded like a petulant child.

"Enough!" Ramiel said. "We had a deal, and we *will* honor it. We will—"

A roar battered my senses and fire lanced through me. I looked down at the hilt of the dagger sticking out of my chest, then across at Merihem, who was standing by the princes, staring at me in stunned horror.

Not him.

He hadn't done this.

No, the killer was beside me, shielding me with his shadow.

I looked up into Dhuma's granite-hewn face. Confusion, shock, and pain clouded my mind.

Why? The word was a whisper that didn't make it past my lips.

The world began to fade on a never-ending cacophony of screams as the daimon cupped my cheeks and spoke words that were now clear to me.

"It is time to be reborn. Find the power to return and—"

Lightning crackled, lighting up my vision, then darkness swallowed me.

· · ·

Nyx's journey continues in *Demon Gate.*

OTHER BOOKS BY DEBBIE CASSIDY

The Gatekeeper Chronicles (Gatekeeper World)

Marked by Sin

Hunted by Sin

Claimed by Sin

The Witch Blood Chronicles (Gatekeeper World)

(Spin-off to the Gatekeeper Chronicles)

Binding Magick

Defying Magick

Embracing Magick

Unleashing Magick

The Fearless Destiny Series

Beyond Everlight

Into Evernight

Under Twilight

The Chronicles of Midnight (Chronicles World)

Protector of Midnight

Champion of Midnight

Secrets of Midnight

Shades of Midnight

Savior of Midnight

Chronicles of Arcana (Chronicles World)

City of Demons

City of the Lost

City of Everdark

City of War

Chronicles of Deadworld (Chronicles World)

Deadworld

Dead City

Dead Sea

Dead End

For the Blood

For the Blood

For the Power

For the Reign

For the Hunt (novella)

Heart of Darkness

Captive of Darkness

Bane of Winter

Fate's Destiny

The Nightwatch Academy (Nightwatch World)

Shadow Caster

Shadow Weaver

Shadow Warrior

Shadow Master

The Nightwatch Series (Nightwatch World)

Ghost of a Chance

Give up the Ghost

Ghost at the Feast

Lay the Ghost

Deadside Reapers Series (Deadside World)

Reaper Unexpected

Reaper Uninvited

Reaper Untamed

Reaper Unveiled

Reaper Undone

Reaper Unhinged

Reaper Unleashed

The Thirteenth Sign (Deadside World)

Witch Unexpected

Witch Undecided

Witch Untold

Witch Unbound

Wolves of Hawthorne Cove (Accords World)

A Shifter's Sin

A Shifter's Trial

A Shifter's Heart

A Shifter's Curse

A Shifter's Choice

Demons of Morningstar (Accords World)

Demon Throne

The Iron Fae Series

Taste My Wrath

Feel My Power

Dragon Guard Series

Dragon Trial

Dragon Rising

Dragon Ashes

Eldritch Blues (New Blood World)

Aberrant Monsters

Insidious Monsters

The Monsters Among Us

When Monsters Lie

Survivor's Heart (Planet Athion World)

Novellas

Rogue

Rebel

Survivor

Standalone Novellas

Blood Blade

ABOUT THE AUTHOR

Debbie Cassidy lives in England, Bedfordshire, with her three kids and very supportive husband. Coffee and chocolate biscuits are her writing fuels of choice, and she is still working on getting that perfect tower of solitude built in her back garden. Obsessed with building new worlds and reading about them, she spends her spare time daydreaming and conversing with the characters in her head – in a totally non-psychotic way of course. She writes Urban Fantasy Romance, Paranormal Reverse Harem Romance and Sci Fi Romance. Stay in touch with Debbie Cassidy by joining her Facebook reader group Debbie Cassidy's Fantasy Realms. Check out her website, debbiecassidyauthor.com. Find her on Bookbub, Goodreads, or follow her on Amazon.

www.ingramcontent.com/pod-product-compliance
Lightning Source LLC
Chambersburg PA
CBHW021756190726
48290CB00005B/1288